BROTHERS' TEARS

BROTHERS' TEARS

J.M. Gregson

This first world edition published 2013
in Great Britain and in the USA by
SEVERN HOUSE PUBLISHERS LTD of
19 Cedar Road, Sutton, Surrey, England, SM2 5DA.
Trade paperback edition first published
in Great Britain and the USA 2013 by
SEVERN HOUSE PUBLISHERS LTD

British Library Cataloguing in Publication Data

Gregson, J. M.
    Brothers' tears. – (A Percy Peach mystery ; 17)
    1. Peach, Percy (Fictitious character)–Fiction. 2. Blake,
    Lucy (Fictitious character)–Fiction. 3. Murder–
    Investigation–Fiction. 4. Police–England–Lancashire–
    Fiction. 5. Detective and mystery stories.
    I. Title II. Series
    823.9'14-dc23

ISBN-13: 978-0-7278-8274-5 (cased)
ISBN-13: 978-1-84751-480-6 (trade paper)

All Severn House titles are printed on acid-free paper.

Severn House Publishers support the Forest Stewardship Council [FSC], the
leading international forest certification organisation. All our titles that are printed
on Greenpeace-approved FSC-certified paper carry the FSC logo.

Typeset by Palimpsest Book Production Ltd.,
Falkirk, Stirlingshire, Scotland.
Printed and bound in Great Britain by
MPG Books Ltd., Bodmin, Cornwall.

A brother's tears have wet them o'er and o'er;
And so my brother, hail, and farewell evermore!

Catullus

To Kathy Hogan, long-time friend and
fellow sufferer from life's ills and ironies.

ONE

Jim O'Connor was enjoying himself. He hadn't eaten much tonight, not compared with what he'd shifted back in his rugby days. He'd had a couple of glasses of burgundy with his sirloin, but his head was perfectly clear. He didn't want to get drunk, because he wanted to enjoy the evening. That meant having all your senses alert and missing nothing of what was going on around you. He had a speech to make, too, but he was trying not to think too much about that.

He could see everything in the room from his position at the centre of the top table. He wasn't talking very much, because he was in a reflective mood. Some people probably said he was self-satisfied, but he didn't have to consider what other people might say nowadays. And you were allowed to savour what you'd achieved. Surely that was permissible on an occasion like this. He'd come a long way from the Irish village where he'd started. It was surely only right to pause once in a while and consider what he'd achieved.

The rugby had been the start of it. There was no doubting that. Forty-three times he'd played for Ireland, twice he'd toured with the British Lions. It had opened doors to him; those were the years when he'd met important people, when he'd appreciated just what might be possible for himself in the future. He was only forty-six now and he'd played until he was thirty-one. Yet the rugby years seemed to belong to a different life and a different man.

Sarah was looking good tonight. She'd been right to go for the deep crimson dress, when he'd wanted her to settle for a brighter red. It set off the long, lustrous black hair she still gathered into a ponytail behind her slender neck. Not too many women in their forties could get away with a ponytail, she'd told him. Well, it set off the bare shoulders above her dress perfectly. She might have a few laughter lines around her eyes now, but it was appropriate for her. That was a point of agreement between them: he didn't like mutton dressed as lamb and Sarah had no use for Botox.

She glanced up at him, almost as though she knew that he was thinking about her. 'You all right, Jim?'

'Sure I am. More than all right.' The brain is an unpredictable and sometimes an inconvenient instrument. For some reason, his words flashed him back now to his first real girlfriend in Dublin, who had called him Seamus and thought the sun shone out of him. For a moment, he wanted the innocence of those days, wanted again to be that young man who knew little of the world but still had it all before him.

Moira had been the good Catholic girl his dead mother would have wanted for him, and for a little while he had thought she was perfect. She'd said she didn't want to sleep with him, not until they were certain it was serious. He'd had her though, with her back up against the wall behind the dance hall, thrusting at her urgently, ignoring her pleas to be gentle with her. It had been just narrowly on the right side of rape, he thought. But Moira would never have accused him of that; she would have thought it was her fault for leading him on. The convent had taught girls things like that, in the old days.

Jim O'Connor wondered where Moira was now. He hoped she was happy and well. He had a sudden wish to find her, to give her money, to let her have some small part of what he'd achieved, for old times' sake. But you couldn't turn the clock back. He was indulging himself even to think of those times. He hadn't thought of Moira for years – well, months, anyway. Better to kill off such thoughts than indulge them. Each man kills the thing he loves. It had been a fellow Irishman who said that. He hadn't thought of him for years, either.

He wondered why he had wandered into this melancholic mood, when he'd been happily congratulating himself upon his achievements only a moment earlier. He glanced over his shoulder at the toastmaster, resplendent in his bright red jacket – or ridiculous, according to your taste. Ridiculous, Jim decided. A toastmaster had no function until he announced the speakers, but how could he blend discreetly into the background, wearing clothes like that? The man moved forward, as if he had taken O'Connor's glance as an invitation to speak. 'Do you want the speeches before or after the coffee, Mr O'Connor?

'Before. They won't be very long. I'll see to that.'

He stood up, moved round the table until he stood behind his daughter as the waiters prepared to serve the desserts. 'It's *bombe surprise* for sweet, Clare. At least, that's one of the options. I put it in for you.'

He wondered why he needed to say that, then realised that it was just an excuse to talk to her, because she had arrived late and they had scarcely spoken at the beginning of the evening. Clare looked up at him, then laid down her knife and fork together on her plate. 'There was no need for that, Dad. It's your evening, not mine.'

'Of course there was no need. I wanted to do it, that's all.'

He was aware of the young man she'd brought from university beside her, looking down at his plate with a small, supercilious smile. He had spots still on his forehead; his wrists were thin as they poked out from jacket sleeves which were too short for him. He'd have been no use on the rugby field, this scrawny specimen. Jim wondered whether they'd slept together yet. He tried not to think of his daughter's lithe young limbs wrapped around this fellow. It didn't seem long since he'd watched her unwrapping her birthday presents as a seven-year-old.

'You want me after we've finished here tonight, boss?'

O'Connor started at the voice in his ear. It was Steve Tracey, of course. Jim glanced past him, saw the chair he had pushed back from the table behind him. He had moved softly, as big men often do, and Jim hadn't heard him rise. Now he wanted to reject him, as if his presence and his question cast a shadow over the innocent celebration this was supposed to be. But that wasn't fair on a loyal servant. Tracey had been with him almost from the start, rising from simple heavy to the director of the small group of hard men who enforced 'security'.

Jim forced a smile, kept his voice neutral. 'I shan't need you or anyone else to look after me tonight, Steve. This is a social occasion, not a business dinner. We're among friends.'

'If you're sure, boss.' Steve Tracey looked round at the

noisy, laughing tables as if searching for some hidden menace. He could see none. He looked back at O'Connor uncertainly for a moment, then nodded and moved back to his chair. Within a moment, he was laughing loudly with the rest of the table around him, working hard to be anonymous. The boss didn't like his security to be obvious.

Jim O'Connor went back to his seat and fingered the card in his pocket which carried the notes for his speech. He pulled it out and looked at it; surely it couldn't be a sign of weakness to show you wanted to be well prepared to speak. Public speaking wasn't something he was good at – he was going to say as much in his first sentence. Then he'd make that reference to James I knighting a loin of beef here and making it sirloin. They'd all know the story, but he'd explain that's why they'd had sirloin tonight and then slide in the joke he'd prepared.

He thought of that funny old poofter James I, passing through here to London and his coronation as the first Stuart king of England. And then his daft son had caused a civil war and brought Butcher Cromwell and his fierce Ironside army to Ireland. Three and a half centuries later, 'The curse o' Crummell on ye!' had still been one of the fiercest oaths in his village – he hadn't known what it meant, when he was a boy. There went that brain again, diverting him from the present, when he was trying to concentrate on his speech.

They were serving the desserts now. He took a spoonful of his *bombe surprise* and raised it with a smile towards his daughter a few yards away. She didn't see him; he was left waving the spoon awkwardly in front of his face and feeling ridiculous. He put the ice cream and meringue hastily into his mouth and looked again at his notes. He was going to welcome them all here, explain that it was twenty years since he had come to the Lancashire town of Brunton and founded his business. He'd picture himself to them as the naïve young man he had certainly not been, so as to imply how far he'd come since then. He'd emphasize how good Brunton had been to him, then say modestly how he hoped that what he had brought to the town had also been good for Brunton.

There would be calls of 'hear hear!' and applause then. But

he'd hold his hands up modestly and sit down a few seconds later, when he'd told them all to enjoy themselves in this wonderful place. He didn't need to announce his other speaker, because the toastmaster would do that.

Jim O'Connor finished his dessert, took a final look at his watch, then tapped his glass with the fork he hadn't used. 'Ladies and gentlemen, there will be a comfort break of no more than ten minutes. Please be back in your seats by then for coffee and *petit fours*. Oh, and the odd speech. I promise you they'll be very short!' There was a little laughter, then a shifting back of chairs, a swift and grateful exit by the men who had been drinking beer earlier in the evening. The noise level rose as people took the opportunity to move round the room and chat to people on other tables.

The toastmaster leaned over the man who'd paid for his services, as for everything else in the evening, and said resentfully, 'I could have made that announcement for you, sir.'

'Spur of the moment!' said Jim, waving an arm vaguely towards the noisy room, as if the gesture could explain things. 'You'll get your fee, never fear.'

The man bristled at this coarse reference to money. He shuffled back to his position, standing upright against the wall and staring unseeingly ahead, looking like a small, ageing and rather ridiculous version of a soldier on guard outside Buckingham Palace. O'Connor was already regretting his impulse. The comfort break had been a mistake. He had merely postponed his ordeal, when he could have had it over and done with. He was suddenly desperate to relax. He was getting things out of proportion, a thing he never did in his business life. Sarah was in earnest conversation with the man next to her. Jim whispered in her ear, 'I'm just slipping out for a breath of air,' and was gone before she could reply.

The night air was cool and welcoming. He stood for a moment at the top of the steps beneath the house's high, rounded entrance, looking down the long, very straight drive to the lights of the gatehouse which were all he could discern in the darkness. The family who owned this place had been here since the Norman Conquest, they said. Almost a thousand years. But things had changed – and had changed fastest of

all in the last century. They needed to open the place to visitors now. They were glad of people like him to hire the
banqueting hall and bring in the money. They were glad to
entertain people who would never have been allowed past the
gatehouse at one time.

The world belonged to people like him now. To Irish peas-
ants who might once have come to the estate as casual workers
in the haymaking season. Move over, Sir Cuthbert or Sir Jasper
or whoever you were. Make way for Jim O'Connor and his
raft of ways of making a quick buck. This is the twenty-first
century, mate. And that stuff about the past was a romantic
notion: he'd never been an Irish peasant. He'd had a good
education and he'd used that and his rugby to get himself
started.

Jim turned and wandered back through the house, taking
care not to catch the eye of any of his guests he might meet.
He didn't want to talk now. And least of all did he want to
hear the sycophantic small talk which the people he'd
invited here might think compulsory if they met their host.
He tried the handle of another door, a tall, wide affair, probably oak, he thought. To his surprise, it turned easily and he
slipped out into some sort of garden. There was fallen cherry
blossom at his feet, thick, pink, almost luminous as his eyes
grew used to the pale light from the stars in the clear night
sky. He moved around the building, glancing up beyond the
high stone wall beside him. There was a wrought-iron gate,
not quite closed and latched. He pushed it and walked through
to the open area beyond it.

He recognised where he was now. This was the edge of the
car park. He could see the rows of neatly parked vehicles,
their roofs shining almost white where they caught the light
from the crescent moon which was visible in this more open
area. Even as he thought how still it was on this early May
night, the slightest of breezes swept through the car park,
ruffling the dark outlines of the trees away to his right, sighing
a little in the tops of their canopies as it passed through them.
It was cool and unthreatening out here. Jim O'Connor breathed
deeply of the clear, clean air, knowing that soon he would be
back in that warm and crowded room and facing the ordeal

of his speech. He glanced down to check the time on his wrist before he turned back towards the house and duty.

It was his last conscious action. But he felt the steel of the pistol against his temple, heard the sudden roar of the weapon as the swift and final violence of the bullet ended his life.

TWO

'You heard the news this morning?'

It was a small hotel, allowing a friendly relationship between owner and client, and the proprietor was eager to drop his little bombshell and then talk about it. Murder was better than politics for a conversation – better than most things, better even than sport. You could get into trouble with politics: it was surprising what strong views some people had, whatever the evidence you cited. Sport was pretty safe, but even there you had to be careful; people had their favourite teams and they could be very blinkered. Even worse, the guests could sometimes be totally uninterested in sport. And then you were left at the end of the diving board, without anything to do except tumble into the pool and look silly.

But a good juicy murder was pretty safe. Everyone enjoyed talking about death; everyone enjoyed wondering what the world was coming to. They thought the crime was terrible, but they usually wanted all the details of it with their breakfasts. The older ones often wanted to bring back hanging; he'd got used to that. And he had his reaction ready: you shook your head gravely and retreated into the illusions of how much safer a now long-departed world had been.

These two were young. The woman was quite a looker, with that striking red-brown hair and those bright blue eyes which seemed to be taking in everything and smiling at it, not to mention that healthily curving body beneath. When you wore your white chef's hat and asked whether they'd enjoyed the food, people thought you didn't notice how they looked, but you did. He wondered for a few seconds how that little bald-headed bloke with the moustache had got himself a girl like that, but he'd long since ceased to give much time to such speculation. You saw all sorts of couples here, some married, some not. These two were married, he was sure of that. They were easy with each other; they had the air of amused tolerance which he saw only in long-term couples.

They must surely have heard his question, but they gave no sign of it, seeming to be immersed in their choice of cereals from the wide range provided at the side table. The proprietor repeated a little less certainly, 'I expect you've heard the news this morning, Mr Peach?'

The man's near-black eyes turned sudden and full upon him. 'No, we haven't. And we don't want to. No offence, Mr Johnson, but it's part of the holiday for us to get away from what's happening in the world. No newspapers, no radio, no television. That's been a rest in itself, these last four days.'

'Fair enough.' The owner nodded four times, which was at least two too many. 'Very understandable. Very sensible, I'm sure. I can see the point of that.' He went back into his kitchen, leaving the pair to breakfast in peace. They were the first ones down this morning. The others would want to talk about this killing when they came, might even broach it with him, if they'd been listening to the radios in their rooms. Took all sorts to make up a world – that was one of the clichés he loved to swap with his clients in the peculiar world of hotel-speak. He could still picture those dark eyes in that round, unrevealing face. The man had been perfectly polite, but he'd decided in that instant that he wouldn't want Mr Peach as an enemy.

The couple he'd left behind were deliberately friendly towards him when he served the breakfasts they'd ordered, as if they wished to emphasize that there was nothing personal in their rejection of his conversational sallies. The man must be ten years older than the girl, he thought – when you were approaching sixty and had grandchildren, all women under thirty were girls to you. She had bacon and egg and tomato. The man had the full English, which he despatched with amazing speed and obvious relish. He told the chef it was good bacon and sausage and cooked just right. It seemed he wished to compensate for his earlier brisk rejection of the news.

They disappeared from the dining room as the first of his other guests entered it, as if they wished to preserve themselves from any further discussion of events in the vulgar world around them. Detective Chief Inspector 'Percy' Peach and Detective Sergeant Lucy Peach had signed into the hotel as plain Mr and Mrs Peach. In a few minutes, they would pay their bill and sign out again. Peach would put something complimentary in the visitors' book, but they would remain Mr and Mrs Peach as they departed. There was nothing unusual in that. Police officers prefer to conceal their calling; they consider it politic to do so in our civilized twenty-first century. Most of the men and women who serve in uniform prefer to don the garb of their trade only at work; they leave it behind in the locker room when they finish the working day, shedding their work along with their clothing.

Percy and Lucy were members of the CID, of that elite police section which operates throughout the day in plain clothes, attempting as far as possible to blend into the world around it. But they still preferred to keep the nature of their work secret, unless they were asked directly about it by innocent strangers, when both of them found it difficult to lie. As Lucy brushed her teeth vigorously in their bathroom, Percy said, 'Our last day. Best make it a good 'un.'

'If you'd let me listen to the weather forecast, we'd know better what to do now.'

Percy eyed the small patch of blue sky he could see through their window, watched a white cloud race quickly across it. He said with all the confidence he could muster, 'Bright. Breezy. Possibility of an occasional shower. Keep waterproofs handy in the rucksacks.' He sought something which would add the edge of reality to his forecast. 'Probably not warm enough for outdoor nooky.'

'Thank you, Mr Weatherman. That's quite enough of that.' She emerged from the bathroom in jeans and anorak. 'Ready for action when you are.' She caught an instant reaction in those dark eyes as he reached out lustful arms. '*Walking* action please, Casa-bloody-nova!'

Three hours later, they were two thousand feet up on the slopes of Crinkle Crags, looking back at Red Tarn and the track they had climbed. No rain yet, but a brisk breeze around their ears as the sun climbed higher. Percy breathed deeply of the cool, clean air and accepted a square of chocolate as they paused to rest before the steep climb up to the crags above them. 'All this bracing air, all this spring sunshine, all this magnificent scenery, and the finest backside in Britain moving two yards ahead of me!' he murmured euphorically.

'Don't you ever think of anything else?' said Lucy, shifting a little on the rock to accommodate the backside in question.

'Not if I can help it,' said Percy happily. 'You said we had to forget all about work and your bum helps me to do that more than most things. It's good to have such ambrosia perpetually on tap, now that we're married. It's like having your own real ale on draught, only better!' He lay back with his head flat against the sloping fellside, chewing happily on the stalk of coarse moorland grass he had plucked.

Lucy felt that she should make a feminist protest about male assumptions of ownership, but she couldn't quite isolate the right phrase to attack. It was much better to be appreciated than ignored, her mother always reminded her. Mrs Blake was an enthusiastic and consistent admirer of Percy, when she might have been expected to reject him as a divorced man ten years older than her daughter. The elderly widow of seventy and the bouncy little detective of thirty-nine got on as no one could have predicted and it was a formidable alliance. The starting point had been Percy's twinkle-footed prowess as a Lancashire League batsman; Agnes Blake had been a devoted cricket fan since her girlhood.

Lucy contented herself in the end with saying firmly, 'A mature man like you should be able to control your lust after almost a year of marriage. You can lead over the next bit. You'll need to keep your attention off my contours and firmly on Wainwright.'

Percy consulted the famous guidebook ostentatiously. 'Piece of cake, for a fit youngster like you, he says. Old men like me have to watch their step on the second Crinkle.' It was over fifty years since the grand old man of Lakeland had published this book. He was long dead now, but still overwhelmingly the best guide to walking in the mountains. Percy felt that using the guide he had first handled as a boy, with its detailed drawings and helpful, humorous text, was a kind of homage to the man who had so loved these heights.

They worked their way up the long, zigzag climb to the first Crinkle, then along the mile of magnificent scrambling, with its series of dramatic views to either side and the gradually emerging view of Bowfell to the north. The wind was strong here, at nearly three thousand feet, so that sometimes you used hands as well as feet to keep your balance. But they had anoraks zipped high and woollen bobble hats, so that the stiff breeze only made the experience of the finest ridge walk in Britain more exhilarating.

The Easter holiday for schools was well over now, and they met only a few fellow enthusiasts in this wild place, most of them traversing the ridge in the opposite direction. They were completely alone when they reached the end of the ridge and stood looking down into Great Langdale. Percy put his arms round Lucy, with their bodies braced against the wind. They didn't need words as he held her for a long thirty seconds. In this high, remote place, where you felt nearer to whatever gods you did or did not believe in, the moment felt like another step forward in their relationship.

Then they retraced their steps along the ridge and began the descent. As they left the last of Crinkle Crags, the cloud dropped like a damp grey blanket around them and there was a sudden fierce shower. It seemed that nature wished to remind them that this could be a dangerous as well as an invigorating place. They were soon out of the cloud as they descended, and their clothes dried quickly in the steady breeze. They made rapid, easy progress back towards the car they had parked on Wrynose Pass.

They grabbed a meal in Ambleside, where Percy bought Cumberland sausage as a culinary reminder of their first days in Lakeland together. Silence dropped in over tired limbs as they drove the car to the M6 and so south to Brunton and to work. They were passing Lancaster when Lucy said sleepily,

'Alfred Wainwright came from Brunton, you know. He worked in local government there. Then he discovered the Lakes.'

'As we have done all over again, together,' said Percy dreamily. It was an uncharacteristically sentimental vein for him. As if to correct himself, he added a moment later, 'The best backside in Britain will be even more muscular and rounded, after all that effort.'

'Keep your brain alert and your eyes firmly on the road, please.'

When they reached Percy's ageing semi-detached house in the old cotton town, they made mugs of tea, unpacked swiftly and prepared to tumble into bed and into sleep. 'That bathroom's as cold as ever. I'm going to do something about it before next winter!' said Lucy as she emerged in her nightdress and leapt breathlessly beneath the duvet.

There was no reply from Percy. He'd been checking the messages left on his phone. The last of them was from the detective sergeant who was his bagman, now that the rules of the police service prevented him from working with his wife. He listened carefully, then pressed the repeat button. DS Northcott's deep, dark brown voice said urgently, 'We've got a murder, Guv. High profile, at Claughton Towers. Tommy Bloody Tucker's been out to it. He's making a right balls-up. We need you, Guv.'

THREE

'A murder, Peach.' A prominent local businessman killed in sensational circumstances. And you weren't there.' Superintendent Thomas Bulstrode Tucker made it into an accusation.

'No, sir. Do you think the killer chose his moment? Waited until I was safely off the premises?'

'This is no time for frivolity, Peach. Murder is a very serious business.'

This was also no time for Percy to meditate on his senior's

penchant for the blindin' bleedin' obvious. 'I understand you attended the scene of crime yourself, sir. Used surprise tactics.'

'Surprise tactics?' Tucker assumed the baffled-goldfish expression which always gave Percy a dubious pleasure.

'Working at the crime face, sir. You usually prefer to cogitate in your office here and provide us with your overview of the situation.' Or sit on your idle arse in this ivory tower and produce fuck-all, if you take the alternative and majority view.

'If I cannot attend the scenes of crimes as often as I once did, that is one of the crosses I have to bear, Peach. Much as I should prefer to adopt the hands-on approach, none of us can be in two places at once.'

'No, sir. Not even you can manage that.' Peach smiled bleakly, as if he had discovered some form of consolation.

The man he had long ago named Tommy Bloody Tucker stared at him suspiciously over the tops of his rimless glasses. He said again, 'You weren't here, Peach.'

'No, sir. I was enjoying two days of my precious leave, sir. Attaching it to the weekend to give us a blessed four days in a quiet hotel in Coniston and some walking in the high hills, sir.'

'Yes. Well, as I say—'

'Scafell Pike on Monday, sir. Crinkle Crags yesterday. Before returning refreshed to the fray, as you suggested.'

'Me? I don't think I—'

'And in the evenings, sir, good food and drink, and then connubial bliss. I find there's nothing like a damned good—'

'Yes. There's no need for any more detail, thank you.'

'No, I'm sure there isn't, sir. I've no doubt you know all about connubial bliss, sir. Enough said.' Peach stared at the ceiling, as if he could see there an evocation of his chief in congress with his formidable wife Barbara, whose Wagnerian proportions had led Percy to christen her Brunnhilde Barbara. He shook himself violently, ridding himself of the vision with difficulty. 'But enough of pleasure, sir. Are you near to an arrest?'

Tucker's jaw dropped further at this outrageous suggestion. 'No, Peach, I am not. And even to suggest that an arrest should be possible at this stage shows how little you appreciate the complexities of this case. You should be out there beginning your belated enquiries, not wasting my time with accounts of your squalid activities in Cumbria.'

'I'm sorry, sir. I understood that you had asked to see me or I should not be here. I have already visited the scene of the crime this morning. I was expecting you to brief me on the current progress of your investigation.'

'*Your* investigation, Chief Inspector Peach. I have held the breach in your most inconvenient absence. I am now formally handing over the responsibility for this case to you. I shall maintain my overview and conduct whatever media briefings are appropriate. You will be the person with responsibility for the conduct of this enquiry. Is that clear?'

'Crystal clear, sir. I seem to remember you reminding me last year that the first thirty-six hours on a case are always the most crucial. What can you report to me from this period?'

'Me? Well, I . . .'

'DS Northcott tells me you let people leave the scene of this death almost immediately. Is that correct?' Peach's black eyebrows arched impossibly high beneath the shining bald pate.

'There were important people at this gathering, Peach. It was already ten o'clock when I got there. They were anxious to get away to their homes. I could foresee that they were going to become fractious.'

'I see, sir. I knew you would have a good reason for letting obvious suspects leave so quickly.'

'There were no obvious suspects, Peach. This was a killing in a car park, with the banqueting hall in chaos during a break before the speeches.'

'Yes, sir. You didn't think it politic to keep behind even the occupants of the top table where the victim had been sitting for a few brief questions before they left?'

'No I didn't, Peach. These are influential people. They can do the police image a lot of damage in this town, unless we handle this case sensitively.'

'Yes, sir. Sensitively, you say. I'm not sure sensitivity is my forte, sir. You wouldn't consider reversing your decision and retaining the case in your own capable hands, sir?'

'No, I wouldn't. Get out of here and get on with it!'

'Very well, sir. What have you done to date?'

'Me? Well, I put house-to-house enquiries into immediate action, yesterday morning.'

'I see. I wouldn't have thought house-to-house would be the most productive line of investigation, with a crime committed amongst sixty-two people at a dinner at Claughton Towers. But that just shows how stereotyped my thinking is, I suppose. That's where a chief superintendent's superior intellect and imagination tells. Have you conducted any interviews, sir?'

'No. I thought I'd leave that for you, Peach. You know that I don't like to tread on people's toes.'

'Yes, sir. Your use of the first thirty-six hours after the crime has been quite subtle, sir. Low-key. Whoever did this must be baffled by your tactics.'

'I've put you in the picture. I think you should be on your way now, Peach.'

'I agree, sir. We don't want the scents to get cold, do we?'

Chief Superintendent Tucker stood looking out over Brunton from the window of his penthouse office after his DCI had left. He'd had this problem for years now: he'd like to put that insolent man Peach in his place, but he needed the results the man provided to bolster his position as Head of the Brunton CID section. He sighed, sat down behind his desk and shut his eyes. Two more years and he'd be rid of all this and retired on a fat pension – provided they didn't find him out before then.

Two floors below him, Peach brightened. He'd spotted his old friend Jack Chadwick writing his report in the CID section.

The two had been colleagues once as detective sergeants, before Chadwick had been shot and wounded in a bungled bank robbery. His wounds had brought him much sympathy and an aborted career. He'd continued as a uniformed sergeant for several years, carving out a reputation for himself as a scene of crime officer. He was a civilian now, but still doing the same job, still the best man to conduct a thorough investigation of a crime scene that Peach had ever known.

His face brightened a little when he saw Percy. 'Thank God you're back. I never thought you'd hear me say that. Don't let it go to your head.'

'You had Tommy Bloody Tucker to contend with.'

'The man's a wanker. I used to think you exaggerated. He's every bit as bad as you said.'

'It's best not to let him get under your feet.'

'I didn't. I told him to piss off – well, as good as. I'm a civilian now. I don't have to put up with wankers like T B Tucker.'

'So what did you find for us?'

'Precious little. We've bagged all sorts of interesting little items, but the car park at Claughton Towers is a public place. Most of them were probably there before this happened. We've got five different fag-ends, but it's the first outdoor spot people come to when they slip out for a smoke. I doubt whether any of them belongs to your killer. Two of them have got lipstick on.'

Peach noted without comment the assumption that their killer would be a man. It was no more than a statistical assumption. Over ninety per cent of killings where a firearm was involved were by men. But until they knew otherwise, he wouldn't rule a woman out. The use of a pistol meant that no physical strength had been required. This big man O'Connor could feasibly have been shot by a woman, or even a child, though it seemed there'd been very few of those around.

Percy looked at the polythene bags on the other side of the little alcove. There was what looked like a hair grip, a couple of fragments of soil which might just have come from the sole of someone's shoe but probably hadn't, a ballpen which could be fingerprinted if it had anything to do with this crime. No used condoms, which were often collected from more remote spots, thank God. 'What do you know of the victim?'

Chadwick smiled grimly. 'Less than you, I'm sure. Successful businessman. Popular figure, as you'd expect an ex-international sportsman to be. Also a dodgy bugger, according to the police grapevine.'

Peach grinned. 'You keep in touch, then. We've been watching him. So has the Drug Squad.'

'You won't need to watch the poor sod any more. Someone had it in for him.'

'Or someone paid to have him killed.'

'Contract killer?' Jack Chadwick pursed his lips. 'Entirely possible. A single bullet through the temple. No wasted ammunition. No extra noise. Mind you, even an amateur would have realised he was dead after one shot. This was a Smith & Wesson. You don't need two slugs with those. Not when you hold the pistol against a man's head.'

'The bloke who lives in the entrance lodge didn't see any vehicle drive out. Not until much later, when everyone left.'

'I wouldn't rely too much on that. Johnny Wilson lives in the lodge; he was always a dozy bugger.'

An ex-copper whom they both knew. Many ex-officers took on low-level security jobs when they left the service. Peach grinned ruefully. 'One of the doziest. And he wasn't even on duty at the time.'

Chadwick said thoughtfully, 'If I'd been hired to kill O'Connor, I don't think I'd have brought a car on to the site. There are plenty of quiet spots around the edge of the property where you could leave a car and enter on foot, if you were up to no good. Vehicles give people away.'

'Thanks, Jack. You're making this very easy. I gather it was well into the next day before Tommy Bloody Tucker got you out there.'

Chadwick joined with enthusiasm into the condemnation of inefficiency from above. 'He hasn't a bloody clue, that man. Tucker let the lot of them go without questions, I'm told. He makes you look like a genius, Percy.'

'Geniuses need help, Jack. Or should that be genii? What can you give me?'

Chadwick shook his head gloomily. 'Bugger all, probably. We've got the slug, so forensics will match it to the weapon if you ever find it – which I don't believe you ever will. We've got prints from the door-jamb and the handle, but some of them are sure to be O'Connor's and I'd lay five to one that none of them is chummy's. A man like O'Connor is going to have lots of enemies; you'll have lots of candidates for your killer.'

Chadwick left on that thought, with a smile which evinced considerable satisfaction.

It was happening, at last. It seemed a long time since Jim O'Connor had been so brutally removed from her. Sarah had been expecting to speak to the police ever since then; she knew enough about these things to know that they always spoke with the wife first. She would be the leading suspect, until they knew otherwise. That chief superintendent hadn't seemed to know what to do. She'd been surprised when he'd allowed them all to go home, even more surprised when the next day had dragged past without any request to see her.

Jim had died on Monday night. It was midday on Wednesday when the police finally came to see her. The senior CID man who came seemed anxious to make up for lost time. Perhaps because she had watched too many TV series, she had somehow expected a grave, experienced man nearing the end of this service. This man wasn't particularly young, but he was a bouncing rubber ball of energy who seemed to have to force himself to sit still and speak to her quietly. The tall black man he introduced as Detective Sergeant Northcott looked as hard as nails, but he stood very still until she asked him to sit, a calming presence compared with his chief.

Detective Chief Inspector Peach apologised for disturbing her at a time like this, but assured her it was essential. He said she must surely know about Mr O'Connor's enemies and would thus be a vital source of information for them.

Sarah O'Connor felt an immediate need to distance herself from the death. 'I'm sure he had business enemies. I know very little about his business dealings. We both preferred it that way.'

'Did you, indeed? That's a pity, from our point of view. But I'm sure you're as anxious as we are to find out who fired that bullet.' Peach made it almost a question, as if there were some doubt about her feelings. He looked at her evenly, studying her closely, despite his initial apology for intruding upon her grief. He saw a striking woman in a high-necked, dark blue dress, with glossy black hair in a ponytail style which made her look younger than her years. She was forty-four and her husband had been forty-six; it was a first marriage for both of them and they had been married for nineteen years. Northcott had provided him with this basic information as soon as he returned from his leave.

Peach left his words hanging in the air, knowing that nervous people felt a compulsion to break silences and sometimes offered things they had meant to conceal. Mrs O'Connor eventually said acerbically, 'Of course I want you to find who killed Jim. We'd been married for almost twenty years, for God's sake. My daughter's devastated by this.'

'Understandably so. But you seem to have complete self-control. An admirable quality, in these circumstances.' Peach was nervous himself, conscious of the late start on what might be a difficult crime. It made him willing to push a widow harder than he would normally have done, once he had noted her composure.

'Are you trying to be offensive, DCI Peach?'

He noted that she had remembered his rank, which a woman desolated by woe would not normally have done. 'I'm sorry if you find my attitude offensive. I wish to accelerate an investigation which has so far moved sluggishly. What sort of man was your husband, Mrs O'Connor?'

This was not at all what she had expected. The man was direct and abrupt, where she had anticipated sympathy. 'Jim was a good husband. He was kind and considerate. He was an even better father.'

'In what way better?'

How sharp the man was! 'We have only one child. I suppose what I'm saying is that he was an indulgent father. I had to stop him spoiling Clare at times.'

'But he didn't try to spoil you?'

'He was a good husband to me. Don't try to make out that he wasn't.'

'I'm not trying to make out anything, Mrs O'Connor. I'm trying to establish the truth. Your husband has been brutally murdered. He isn't here to tell us who might have done it, or even whom we might suspect and thus investigate. We have to find out as much about him as we can, if we are to discover who killed him. You are the most obvious source of information for us.'

She had been matching aggression with aggression, determined not to be browbeaten by this stocky, combative opponent. She looked at him now with her head a little on one side, like a boxer eyeing an opponent from his stool between rounds. Then she made a deliberate effort to relax. 'All right, I see that. We're on the same side. Ask away.'

'Thank you. You say you know little about the enemies Mr O'Connor made during his business dealings. Can you give us that little?'

She thought hard, anxious to give them something, anxious to support her contention that they were on the same side. Then she shook her head glumly. 'Perhaps I should have said I knew nothing rather than very little. I can give you the name of a man who can tell you more. Steve Tracey. He was at the dinner on Monday night. He should have been protecting Jim.'

Clyde Northcott made a note of the name before he spoke for the first time. 'You think this man Tracey should have protected the victim. What was his job title, Mrs O'Connor?'

'You'd have to ask him that. I know he'd been with Jim a long time and that Jim trusted him. He must have done – he didn't promote people he didn't trust.'

Northcott looked at her steadily. His face was as dark and as hard as ebony. Sarah had a sudden, disconcerting realisation that this was a man you wanted with you and not against you. He now said, 'There were business associates at the dinner on Monday night. Were there also business rivals?'

'I don't know. I don't think so. Why would rivals be there?'

Peach came back at her whilst she was watching Northcott and his notebook. 'That might have been our next question for you, Mrs O'Connor. That's the normal process, you see. We ask the questions and you provide the answers.'

But he was smiling now, as if he had accepted her assertion that they were on the same side. She said, 'I'm sorry, but I can't help here. Jim compiled the guest list for Monday night, not me.'

'Thank you. That in itself is the kind of information we need from you. Perhaps Mr Tracey will be able to help us there, when we speak to him. The people who were at Claughton

Towers on Monday night have gone their separate ways, but our team will need to speak to most of them, in due course. The one indisputable fact from which we start is the shooting of a defenceless man at that function. We're not ruling out the thought that someone might have come in from outside, not yet. But there is at the very least a strong possibility that the killer is a name on the guest list for Monday night.'

'I suppose so. I was too stunned to think it through, but I suppose I shall have to face that.'

'The majority of the people there were family and friends. Or people he thought were his friends. Your thoughts will be treated as confidential. Can you think of anyone who sat at those tables who might conceivably have done this?'

The pale face looked shocked by the question. She shook her head gently from side to side, as if she wished to reject the notion but could not. 'No. It was a total shock to me at the time. It still is.'

'I understand that he was killed during an informal break in the proceedings. What he called a comfort break. Where were you at the time of his death?'

'I don't know, do I? No one knows exactly when he died.'

'True. Perhaps you should have been a detective, Mrs O'Connor.' Peach gave her a tiny smile, as if acknowledging a worthy opponent.

'I think I went to the ladies' cloakroom, found it very crowded, and decided not to wait for a cubicle. I was certainly back at the table when someone came and told me . . . told me what had happened.' When neither of them said anything in reaction to this, she added nervously, 'Perhaps you'd like to know that I've never fired a pistol in my life.'

They left her then, with instructions to get in touch with them immediately if any useful thoughts about this death and the people who had been close to it came to her. She sat for a long time after they had gone, wondering what they had made of her. She hadn't been as calm as she'd intended to be: that man Peach had ruffled her at the outset. But she'd held her own after that.

She didn't think they'd gone away having learned anything she hadn't intended them to know.

FOUR

Y ou would never have thought he was a policeman, still
less one who carried the rank of sergeant.

But that was exactly as he meant it to be. The most
dangerous of all roles in the police service of the twenty-first
century is operating undercover. It is in many respects the
equivalent of being a spy in wartime. Spies provide vital
information, but their whole trade is based upon deceit. If they
are caught the Geneva Convention does not apply and their
country makes no attempt to save them. More often than not,
it does not acknowledge their existence. They disappear
without trace, liquidated by the enemy they were trying to
deceive.

The rules, in so far as rules are acknowledged at all, are
very much the same for police officers working undercover.
The vast majority operate in the perilous field of illicit drugs
and report to the Drug Squad. They swim in dangerous waters.
The small fish with whom they swim to gain information are
erratic and unreliable, being in most cases drug-users themselves. The bigger fish they are trying to identify are wary and
vicious. The infiltrator in the world of drugs will be eliminated
as swiftly and as finally as a wartime spy, if he is discovered.
And there will be no chance of bringing his executioners to
justice. He will disappear without trace. It is unusual for the
body of a liquidated victim ever to be discovered.

Even though the struggle for gender equality was fought
and won many years ago in the police service, there are still
only a tiny number of female officers working undercover and
they scarcely touch the world of drugs. The men who work
here are strange creatures. Their bravery is unquestioned. But
bravery wraps itself in a variety of different personalities, many
of them twisted away from the normal by their previous experience of life. Few undercover men are married, though many
have broken relationships behind them. Indeed, not many of

them are successful in maintaining serious and enduring relationships of any kind. Most of them are loners, though anyone with experience of undercover men will recognise that there are many sorts of loners.

Jason Crook had never been married. He had never in fact been quite certain of his sexual orientation, though he had chosen to keep that hidden in the notoriously macho world of the police canteen. He was not sure how he had ever become a policeman at all; he put it down to a craving to live dangerously, which he now recognised in himself as he had not done earlier in his life. He was twenty-four, though the work he had done in the last year made him feel much older than that.

He certainly looked much older. His hair had thinned early; he had chosen to accentuate that by letting it grow long and unkempt. He occasionally clipped it himself, but he never visited a barber. His complexion was poor, with spots dotting his forehead and his chin. His eyes were pale blue; he kept them for the most part lifeless and unrevealing above pallid cheeks. It was a long time since he had seen much sunlight.

No one in the squat suspected him. He was just another user to them. They survived from day to day, even from hour to hour, as they awaited their next fix and schemed how to get it. You didn't pay much attention to your neighbours in the squat. Your whole life centred around yourself and your needs. The others were vaguely accepted as companions, but not friends. Entitled to a roof over their heads, as you were. If they became rivals for the next fix, you treated them as enemies and took whatever steps you needed to take. There was no loyalty here which could survive addiction. The people Crook lived with were dangerous and unpredictable.

Jason knew all of this and lived with it. He was a user himself, now. The police rules said that you mustn't do anything against the law as you gathered information, but that was impossible. He wasn't an addict, though he pretended to be and aped the behaviour of those around him who were. But you needed to be a user, if you were to convince the dangerous men who supplied, the ones you were here to find out about. He took a little horse by mouth. And he injected himself with

water: he had marks on his arm which he hoped signified he
was a regular heroin injector to those he allowed to catch a
glimpse of them.

He tried not to move when he'd had the horse. You were
in danger when you were high; you felt that dangerous
overconfidence which led you to take chances. It was now
the middle of the day in the squat. It was the only one of
a terrace of derelict houses awaiting demolition which still
had a door and most of its windows. In the world outside,
there was patchy sun and no immediate prospect of rain.
Yet all but two of the squatters were in the house. Fresh air
and life in the open had no appeal for them. They were
addicts, with nowhere to go between fixes.

When the five men and three women who lived here went
out at all, it was usually in the evenings. Darkness seemed a
natural environment for them, but that was not the only reason.
All eight of them were small-time dealers. Their supplies were
tightly controlled and they made little profit – the rich pickings
of this sinister four-billion-pound industry went to men much
higher up the chain than they were. The wretched denizens of
the squat dealt merely to support their habit; they were allo-
cated and sold just enough to provide the drugs they needed
for themselves.

Jason Crook emerged cautiously at the rear of the house
and stood blinking for a moment against the brightness of the
light. His head switched from right to left, like that of a rodent
checking that it was unobserved. Then he set off to fulfil his
assignment, passing through streets where few vehicles
ventured and litter accumulated steadily in the gutters. His
battered trainers were serviceable still; he moved with the
rapid, shuffling gait of someone older than he was. His head
was low and his eyes flicked rapidly to right and left as he
went, to make sure he was not being followed.

He had chosen the meeting place himself. The van had been
there for five days now, at the end of a street where the houses
had already been felled and the bulldozer had levelled the site
ready for the builders. It had probably been dumped there by
joyriders, or an owner whom it had finally failed. The one
wheel with a newish tyre had already disappeared from it, so

that the van slumped crazily sideways. But Crook had already checked that the driver's door opened.

His contact was waiting for him as he'd demanded. The man sat low in the passenger seat on the nearside, his face almost invisible beneath the cap pulled forward over his eyes. He was almost as unkempt as Crook, but his dirt was less ingrained. He was adopting a disguise, whereas the man who had come from the squat had been living his part for months.

The officer who sat in the passenger seat glanced at Crook as he slipped into place and shut the driver's door. 'You've done a good job on yourself. You look like a junkie.'

Jason didn't reply, didn't even smile. This man who had spoken didn't feel like a colleague any more. Those wretched creatures in the squat weren't colleagues, but he felt nearer to them than to this being from the real world. This was one of the hazards of working undercover. The people who volunteered for the work were almost by definition unbalanced. Some of them took on the lifestyle of the user so thoroughly that they became genuine addicts rather than undercover agents. They disappeared into the anonymous underclass which peopled the lower reaches of the drug world and were lost permanently to the police. The officer who was slumped anonymously in the driver seat of this stinking vehicle wondered if Crook was in danger of this.

As if he read that thought, Jason said while still gazing straight ahead at the filthy windscreen, 'I got the name of one of the big men for you. This man's taking control of the dealers round here. He's taking over Strangeways.'

The big jail in Manchester was a hotbed of drug use, as are most of the major prisons in the brave new world of Britain. Controlling the supply of drugs and the network of dealers involved was lucrative in itself. It was also far more important among the barons of this sinister trade for its prestige value. The man who supplied Strangeways controlled much else as well. The men and women who worked for him as well as his rivals recognised that.

The inspector beside Crook said, 'Give us the name. We'll see if it tallies with the information we're getting from other—'

'O'Connor. James O'Connor.' Jason wasn't interested in the

man's garbage about other sources: he knew what he knew. 'He's taken over from Read. He's planning to get bigger still.'

'Right.' The man in the passenger seat nodded. Jason Crook was out of the vehicle immediately, departing down the street with the same rapid shuffle with which he had arrived. The Drug Squad inspector watched him to the end of the road, waited another two minutes. That poor sod couldn't know that O'Connor was dead, couldn't know that the information he'd risked his life for was almost valueless now. Crook was sunk so deep into his role in the squat that he probably hadn't read a newspaper or heard a radio for weeks.

James O'Connor wouldn't be extending his empire any further. But the fact that he'd been spreading his wings in dangerous skies had brought some big criminal names into the possibilities for his murderer.

Dominic O'Connor was slimmer and shorter than his brother. More flying winger than flanker, a rugby man might have said. DCI Peach was not a rugby man. Soccer was his winter game; he'd supported Brunton Rovers through thick and thin – and there'd been plenty of thin lately.

He studied his man unhurriedly, after he'd introduced himself and Clyde Northcott. Nervous, he reckoned, trying to look as if he wasn't on edge but not succeeding. He liked that: people who were nervous gave more of themselves away. But you couldn't read too much into it. Bereavement affected people in all sorts of ways and it was possible that this man had never been questioned by police before. That would make him different from his dead brother; James had had many exchanges with the police, but had been always been too wily to end up in court. He had even been helpful to them at times, when it suited his own agenda.

'You never worked with your brother, Mr O'Connor?'

'No. I'm six years younger than him. That meant we were never particularly close. We had different talents and different interests. He was already the great rugby player back in Ireland when I was still a schoolboy.'

'I see. But James made a successful business career. He was quickly in charge of his own business and it rapidly diversified.' Peach paused for a second on the word, allowing it an ironic ring, studying the man's reaction. 'You didn't feel inclined to join him and make it a family business? Or perhaps James didn't want you working with him?'

'I could have had work with Jim if I'd wanted it. I decided I didn't.'

The younger man had almost no trace of an Irish accent, whereas the dead man had seemed almost to cultivate it, both in his rugby days and in his later business dealings. 'And why did you decide that?'

O'Connor looked for a moment as if he would refuse to answer. Then he folded his arms and said deliberately, 'I suppose I decided I wanted to make my own way in life. It was easy enough for me to do that. My Dad had made money by the time I was ten or eleven. I wasn't educated in Ireland, like Jim. I was sent to Stonyhurst College in England as a boarder. I grew up with the Jesuits.'

He jutted his chin a little, as if challenging Peach now to follow this up. Instead the DCI said quietly, 'You've made it clear that you hadn't much in common with James. It sounds almost as if you didn't like him.'

This time his man did react. O'Connor said irritably, 'This isn't relevant. You're supposed to be finding out who killed Jim, not running a lonely hearts column. You appear pretty baffled, so far.'

Peach was not at all put out. He gave Dominic O'Connor one of the more enigmatic of his vast range of smiles. 'When I was a young copper, my first inspector said to me, "If you can't find a solution, always come back to the family". You'd be surprised how often he's been right over the years. I can assure you that the sort of relationship you enjoyed with your brother is extremely relevant to this enquiry.'

'You mean that if I wasn't close to Jim I become a suspect.'

'I mean that your complete frankness would not only be appreciated but would be much the best policy for you. Any attempt at deception in a murder enquiry would be ill-advised; it would excite suspicion. That much will be obvious to an intelligent man with a Jesuit education.' This time Peach's smile had a hint of impish enjoyment.

Dominic O'Connor ran a hand swiftly through his rather untidy fair hair. His brown eyes glittered, but he spoke evenly enough. 'Jim and I were never close. I could have worked with him – for him – but I had other options. He thought I was a Puritan, I thought he was too much of a Cavalier.'

'You mean he took short cuts in his business affairs.'

'I wouldn't have put it like that. But yes, he was a little too free and easy for my tastes. He made rapid progress, but to my mind he was a chancer. We had different temperaments, I suppose. But he could laugh at me and what he called my caution. He expanded quickly. As you say, he diversified.' This time it was Dominic O'Connor who gave the word a slight ironic emphasis.

'You're an accountant, I believe.'

'I'm a financial manager in a smallish firm. But the basis of that is accountancy, yes.'

'But you don't believe in cutting corners.'

'I believe in operating within the law. I may not have moved as far or as fast as Jim, but I'm successful in my own way.'

'I imagine these different attitudes must have led to a lot of tension between the two of you.'

'You shouldn't imagine, DCI Peach. You should confine yourself to facts. And the fact of this matter is that Jim and I got on perfectly well with each other. We'd agreed to go our separate ways and we didn't spend much time in each other's houses. But our wives got on perfectly well – probably better than Jim and I did. We've met up mainly on family occasions, over the last few years, but we got on quite adequately with each other.'

'"Quite adequately". That is a strange phrase for brothers.'

'But well chosen, I think. It implies a lack of passion. You need passion to kill a man the way my brother was killed.'

'Or a good reason.'

'All right, or a good reason. As I had neither of these, you can conclude that I did not kill my brother.'

'So who did, Mr O'Connor?'

'Surely that's for you to discover. With the vast range of resources available to the police service.'

'And the full and intelligent cooperation of those civilians in a position to help us. That's why I'm asking you who you think killed your brother.'

'I've no idea. I've given it plenty of thought, but I'm no nearer to an answer than I was when it happened on Monday night. And before you say that I must have some ideas, I would remind you that we've spent some time establishing that I was no longer in close touch with either Jim or his associates.'

Peach gave the tiniest nod to Northcott. The detective sergeant cleared his throat and said formally, 'Where were you at the time of this death, Mr O'Connor?'

Dominic looked at the dark, unrevealing features as if he suspected a trap. 'As I understand it, no one knows the precise moment of death. When the interval was announced, I left my chair and moved across the room to speak with my niece, my sister's daughter. Even you may well conclude that was an innocent mission, since Alison is thirteen.'

Clyde Northcott made a note and remained impassive. 'And did you then return to your seat?'

Dominic O'Connor regarded him steadily for a moment, his brown eyes alert, assessing. Then he said sardonically, 'Not immediately, no. I moved around, chatted to one or two people I knew. Then I went to the Gents' and did the same thing in there. I also had a pee.'

'How long were you missing from the main banqueting hall?'

'You mean did I have the opportunity to creep outside and commit fratricide, don't you? That's the word for it, you know, in case coppers don't have a Jesuit education.' In his wish to score a meaningless point, he'd almost said 'black coppers'. That showed how carefully you needed to watch your words, that did, he told himself.

Northcott said calmly, 'It's a question our team will be asking of everyone who was present on Monday night. Unless we make an arrest before the process is completed, of course. Do you own a firearm, Mr O'Connor?'

'No. I don't need one in the sort of work I do.'

'But you imply that your brother did. Did he carry a pistol?'

'I don't know. I think he might have done. I think I would have done, if I'd moved among the people he associated with and the rivals he dealt with.' For a moment, his distaste for the dead man flared about Dominic's lips. It was instantly dismissed.

Peach stood up. 'In the meantime, we'd like you to go on thinking, Mr O'Connor. You're a shrewd and intelligent man. You also know a lot of the people who were at that function better than any detective. If you have any thoughts, please ring this number: whatever you say will of course be treated in the strictest confidence.'

They'd arranged to meet and this is where it had to be. Steve Tracey didn't like it, but he wasn't in a position to call the shots.

The big Toyota saloon drew up alongside the murdered man's head of security on the top of the multi-storey car park. He'd specified the spot himself. The woman on the other end of the line had gone away to consult, then returned to the phone and agreed to it. They'd determined on the multi-storey, but he'd said it must be on the top floor. Somehow, he felt more public up here; with the open air around him and the sky above him, he must surely be safer. Now he wondered whether that was so.

The window beside the driver slid slowly down. 'Hop into the back, Mr Tracey,' the face said with false cheerfulness.

'No way. You get out and we talk here.'

The big face beamed like that of a man with four aces in his hand. 'You don't have a choice, Steve.' He grinned sideways at the invisible muscle beside him, then repeated, 'Hop into the back, Mr Tracey.'

Steve opened the door, slid his bulk swiftly over the leather of the rear seat. One down already. But with his employer dead, he didn't see how he could call the shots.

'Boss wants to see you. You could be a fortunate man.'

They were the only words spoken in fourteen miles. They drove fast, over the moors on the A666 to Bolton, through the town and into the urban sprawl where it merged into greater Manchester. Tracey didn't know this area and he was correspondingly more nervous. If they beat him up and pitched him out here, he wouldn't know where to turn for help. If they shot him, there were plenty of places beneath water or concrete where they could dump his corpse so that it would never be seen again. Strange roads and strange buildings brought the sort of wild fears which you did not feel on your own patch.

He said nothing. They wouldn't answer his questions and he wasn't going to attempt any other sort of talk with men like this. They were alien, yet strangely like himself. They were acting under orders and they had no interest in him, unless he prevented those orders being carried out. He knew one of these men and that told him a lot. He thought he knew who they worked for. He wondered whether it was one of the two close-shaven, squat men he could see in front of him who had shot his boss. And then he wondered as he moved off his own patch and on to theirs whether they were going to shoot him.

It was a hut on a building site where they finally stopped. A strange, deserted, sinister place. Silent when it should have been noisy, quiet and motionless when it should have been busy with activity. The gorilla got out of the driving seat and looked at Tracey curiously. Strangely, his thickset shape and unintelligent features gave Steve reason to hope. This was low-level security, the kind of loyal, unquestioning thug he would have used himself for enforcement work, for scaring small people into a resentful obedience. If they'd been licensed to kill him or even rough him up, they'd have done it in a dark alley somewhere, not brought him here.

The man motioned towards the door of the hut, but he remained outside as Tracey entered and shut it carefully behind him. The man behind the desk inside the shed was as alert and watchful as he was, but he had affected the trappings of respectability. He was probably from Jamaica, in Steve's view. He wore a three-piece suit, with a thin gold watch-chain stretched across his bulging chest. He clasped his well-manicured hands in front of him, as if anxious to show off his perfect nails to the man instructed to sit on the other side of the desk. Steve wondered if he would complete the parody by lighting a cigar, but he merely sat back and looked at the new arrival with a smile, relishing the situation.

He was a strange figure in a strange environment. Apart

from his colour, he was a caricature of a nineteenth-century industrial baron in this dingy twenty-first-century setting. There was a chart on the wall with what seemed to be a plan of foundations for the buildings to be erected here. It had words scribbled across it which were illegible from where Steve Tracey sat. Lumps of drying mud from people's boots littered the floor; a week-old tabloid newspaper lay in the corner of the shed. There was something ludicrous about the overdressed central figure which gave Tracey a sudden, unexpected spurt of confidence.

It wasn't the big boss, as those idiots outside had said it would be. It was *their* boss, the man in charge of security for some organisation. A big concern, by the look of it. A well-organised business: this was a suitably anonymous place for a meet, whatever the dress affectations of the man conducting it. Tracey sat motionless and waited; he wasn't going to let the man with the watch-chain know that he was nervous.

The man sat back, steepled his fingers, continued his impersonation of a different kind of executive. 'Well, Mr Tracey. So your boss is dead. And your job was to protect him. Didn't do a very good job there, did you?'

'I offered to stay with him on Monday night. He said it wasn't necessary.'

'You didn't kill him yourself, did you, Steve?'

'Of course I didn't! He'd be alive now if he'd allowed me to stay with him when he went outside Claughton Towers on Monday night.'

Watch-chain smiled. 'I wouldn't be too sure of that. You might have been dead meat yourself, Steve, instead of enjoying this conversation. You don't mind me calling you Steve, do you?'

'You can call me what you like. You're in the box seat. You and your gorillas outside.'

'Box seat. Yes, I suppose that's so.' He smiled contentedly, his teeth looking very large and very white in this ill-lit place. 'But I have good news for you, Steve. I have been empowered to offer you employment. Generous thinking, that, after you failed in your last assignment. But then I work for a generous man.'

'Lennon.' Steve had been thinking furiously, trying to work out who could be behind his virtual kidnap.

Watch-chain looked a little surprised, even for a moment discomfited. 'Best not to speculate at this stage, Steve. But I suppose you have a right to know who'll be paying your wages. So yes, Mr Lennon. He's prepared to take you on. He's taking over most of your organisation following the unfortunate demise of James O'Connor. And he wants as smooth a transition as possible. So he's prepared to take on you and whichever two of your staff you recommend. You'd be deputy to me, of course.' He ran his hand lightly over the front of his waistcoat, fingering the watch-chain as if it offered him reassurance. 'But you'd be second in line in our security department. It's a very generous offer, if you ask me.'

Steve wanted to say that he didn't ask him, that he'd had quite enough of this patronising nonsense. But this fellow was making a generous offer on behalf of his employer, offering a job to a rival in the same trade of violence. He was going to have to work with the Jamaican. If the man was vain enough to indulge in silly charades like this, he might even take over from him, in due course.

Tracey took a deep breath and stood up. There was no possibility of refusal. He knew too much about the empire of James O'Connor for that. If he opted out of work for the new ownership, he might well be eliminated. He thrust out his hand and said, 'I accept, subject to proper remuneration. I'm sure I can rely on Mr Lennon for that.'

The man in the waistcoat winced again at Tracey's mention of that name. He had planned to reveal it himself at this stage to this man who would operate in his shadow. But he stood up and thrust his hand forward. 'Peter Coleman. Here's to a long and successful working relationship.'

Middle management making a new appointment. Steve completed the bizarre playlet by shaking the big hand firmly, then closing his left hand over the right as the two big men came together. He wondered how many victims these hands had dispatched in the last ten years.

FIVE

There had been a mill here once. It had been built in bright-red brick, with a square tower at one end, like that of a great church. A chimney had risen high at the other, dwarfing everything else around. The long terraces of low houses had been built in meaner brick, but they had been homes to many hundreds of people. The streets here had once reverberated with the sound of clogs clattering to work, hastening to beat the morning whistle at the factory gates, to shut their wearers in with the greater clatter of the steam-driven machines within the smooth brick walls.

All that was long gone. Percy Peach didn't remember it, but he'd seen pictures and been instructed in his primary school on the proud industrial heritage of the area. Manchester had been not only the workshop of the world but also Cottonopolis, and Brunton had been one of the great cotton-spinning towns. Now all was changed, changed utterly. That expression came back to Percy from some point in his chequered school career.

The area was now part of an industrial estate. There were bright new buildings with big windows. Volkswagens and Audis and Toyotas dominated the car parks, as if to remind people that the world had moved on. The headquarters of O'Connor Industries was a surprisingly small building near the entrance to the estate. It had ample parking and a much more impressive entrance than any of the utilitarian buildings which predominated here. Dark red wooden doors opened between a pair of high granite pillars, a style determinedly out of fashion with more muted modern styles.

Jan Derkson rose automatically to greet them, as she had greeted so many hundreds of visitors here before. She said, 'We can go through into Mr O'Connor's room if you like. We won't be disturbed there.'

'Then let's go there. We certainly don't want to be disturbed,' said the bald-headed man in the trim grey suit. 'I'm DCI Peach and this is Detective Sergeant Northcott.'

It didn't feel right to Jan to be taking this room over. She realised now that she had always adopted a deferential air when she brought in the boss's visitors. Now she forced herself to take charge, inviting the very tall black man to sit in one of the two luxurious armchairs, seating herself carefully on the edge of the matching but smaller armchair alongside him. She invited Peach to take the swivel chair behind the big desk, but he declined and came and sat in the armchair which matched Northcott's and was directly opposite to her.

He smiled briefly and she felt him assessing her, with his head tilted fractionally to one side. It wasn't the sort of sexual review to which she had accustomed herself and learned to deal with over the years, but rather a cool estimation of her usefulness, of how much she might be able and willing to give them in the way of information. She found it disconcerting. It felt as if she was being interviewed without warning for a job, as she had not been for many years now.

She was relieved when Peach eventually smiled and spoke. 'We have great hopes of you, Ms Derkson. As James O'Connor's personal assistant, you can probably tell us more about him than anyone we have seen so far.'

'I doubt that. I understand that you have already seen his widow.'

'And how do you know that, Ms Derkson?'

'I'm Mrs Derkson and I have no objection to your calling me that. I would prefer it, in fact. And I had occasion to be in touch with Mrs O'Connor yesterday, about a business decision. I imagine there will be many other such occasions in the weeks to come.'

Her voice faltered a fraction on that last thought, but then she was instantly her business self again. Her watchful, intelligent grey eyes were exactly the colour of her straight skirt. The paleness of her cheeks was accentuated by the whiteness of the perfectly laundered blouse beneath them. The heels on her black shoes were precisely the right height to combine elegance with efficient movement. Yet Peach noted that she was clearly uneasy. Perhaps she was unused to sitting in an armchair in this room, where she had deposited so many people who had come here to see her employer. Or perhaps some deeper malaise was troubling her.

The DCI spoke slowly and soberly, as if respecting the place where they sat. 'You know more about James O'Connor's business dealings than anyone else we are going to speak to. You were also on the top table, the host's table, at Claughton Towers on Monday night. That implies that you were regarded as a friend as well as a trusted employee. We need both information and opinions from you, Mrs Derkson.'

'And you are welcome to both, in so far as it is in my powers to offer them. I shall be as open as I can be, but I fear you will be disappointed. James O'Connor was rather a private man, in his business dealings as well as in his family life. I made appointments for him, typed whatever letters he thought appropriate. I fear I know less of the various businesses which have their headquarters here than you would like me to.'

'Your employer played things close to his chest?'

They caught the tiniest smile on the wide mouth. 'That is one way of putting it, yes. He committed as little as possible to paper. He once told me that you could be more flexible that way. People couldn't quote back at you from what you'd written in different circumstances months earlier.'

'Do you know that he was under police investigation?'

She frowned. But she took plenty of time over her reply and took care not to let any annoyance show. 'No, I didn't know that. I'm surprised to hear it.'

'How surprised?'

She crossed her legs, made a deliberate attempt to appear more relaxed than she had seemed hitherto. 'Mr O'Connor was a good employer to me. He never treated me any way but fairly. I wouldn't trust some of the people I've seen in here at times, but it wasn't my business to pronounce upon them. When I think about it, I can accept your view that my employer "played it close to his chest". I know quite a lot about some of his work and nothing at all about large chunks of it.'

'It is those sections which interest us, for obvious reasons. We need every scrap of information you can give us. We're not Fraud Squad or Drug Squad; we're interested only in solving a murder case.'

'You've already taken away my files and my computer. I fear you won't find much of interest.'

'In that case, what you are able to tell us now will be even more important. We know that he was heavily involved in casinos and betting shops. These are lucrative enterprises in their own right; they are also often used as means of laundering money brought in by illegal trafficking.'

'Drugs?'

'Principally drugs, yes. We have learned since James O'Connor died that he was moving to take over a large portion of the illegal drugs market in north-west England. It is a lucrative trade as well as a highly dangerous one. When people move into new areas, powerful interests are affected. He chose to make enemies of some very nasty people. People who may have decided it was time to be rid of him.'

'You shock me. I have to accept what you say, but I had no idea that Mr O'Connor was involved in anything like this.'

Despite what she said, she didn't look very shocked. The death had plainly upset her, but Peach was pretty sure that she had at least suspected the nature of James O'Connor's interests. Jan Derkson was far too intelligent not to have wondered exactly where all this money was coming from. She was measuring this interview, trying to find how much they knew, how much she could safely conceal. He said abruptly, 'You know more than you're telling us. If you obstruct our enquiries, we shall take whatever action is appropriate.'

This time she was shaken. His sudden loss of patience and change of tack disturbed her, despite her attempt to remain calm. 'I'm sorry that you feel I'm being obstructive. I'll answer whatever questions you care to put to me as honestly as I can.'

The snag with that was that he didn't feel he knew enough yet to ask the penetrating questions he needed. He'd never felt so little in touch with an investigation he was supposed to be directing. There was a huge field of suspects and Tommy Bloody Tucker had cocked up the vital first stage of the enquiry. He looked hard at the white-faced, watchful woman in front of him. 'Did you compile the invitation list for Monday night's function?'

'I suppose I did, under Mr O'Connor's direction. The family guest list was pretty obvious from previous occasions; I merely duplicated that, with one or two small changes. My employer gave me the names of the business people he wanted to see there.'

'I'm in your hands here, Mrs Derkson. My team is doing routine checks on everyone who attended on Monday night. I want to see the most significant ones myself. Business rivals of the host perhaps. Anyone outside the family whom you were surprised to see included on your list.'

He wondered if she would insist on going into the outer office to retrieve the full list of those to whom she'd sent letters of invitation. It would have given her time to think, to decide just what information she was prepared to volunteer. But she obviously had that information already in her mind; the difficulty for him was going to be in deciding exactly how frank she was being. Her fingers flicked briefly to her lips, but otherwise she was quite still. Percy wondered if she was a former smoker who had given up the awful habit, as he had. She eventually said very distinctly, 'There were two people I was surprised to include on the list, because I knew they'd been rivals of his in the fairly recent past.'

'Did you query their inclusion?'

She allowed herself a wry smile, which showed what an attractive woman she would be in a different context. 'You didn't query things with James O'Connor. He knew his own mind. If those names were on the list, they were there for a purpose.'

'But you don't know what that purpose was?'

She pursed her lips, looked down at her right foot in concentration. 'I don't know. I can speculate. My guess would be that they were former rivals whom he no longer felt were threats to him. I don't know, but I suspect he'd taken over enterprises which were once theirs. I think perhaps their presence on Monday night was intended as a conciliatory gesture. But I should stress again that I don't know that; I'm merely trying to be as helpful as I can, as you encouraged me to be.'

'I appreciate that. And we'd better have these names.'

'Joseph Lane and Linda Coleman.'

Clyde Northcott made a careful note of the names, but neither of the CID men gave her any clue as to whether they recognised either of them. Instead, the tall black man said, 'Do you remember which table these people sat at, Mrs Derkson?'

'They were both on table two, but they weren't sitting together. I was sitting within a few yards of both of them.'

'Do you know where they were during the break which Mr O'Connor called in the proceedings?'

'No. I don't know where they were when their host was shot down.' She waited for a reaction to this sharpness, but received none. 'I expect you'd like to know where I was, too. I can tell you that.'

'If you would, please.'

'I stood up and walked around the room. I found I was quite glad to stretch my legs a little and talk to one or two people I knew. I didn't leave the main banqueting hall. So there's one person you can rule out of your murder calculations.'

Clyde made a note, nodding without comment. It certainly didn't rule her out, not yet. They'd need corroboration from some other source, and if she'd spoken to different people as she claimed, it was probable that no one person would be able to confirm that she'd remained in the banqueting hall throughout the break.

Peach said very quietly, 'The PA is a key figure in any businessman's life. We expect the wife to be able to tell us most about domestic arrangements and complications. The PA tells us about a man's working life, which occupies as much or more of his time than his home life. Who do you think shot down James O'Connor on Monday night?'

She had uncrossed her legs whilst he spoke, as if an informal pose was inappropriate for the discussion of these grave matters. She sat not with arms folded but with a hand palm down on each thigh. 'I don't know. I don't know much about his family life: he preferred to keep that totally separate from his work. Any successful businessman makes enemies. I know it's a long step from enmity to murder, but my feeling is that it was one of those business enemies who had him killed.'

Peach nodded slowly, as if accepting the logic of this. The black eyebrows rose a little beneath the bald pate. 'Had him killed?'

'You know far more about this than I do. I believe the use of professional killers is not unknown.'

'"Not unknown".' Peach savoured the negative for a moment, as if relishing her ladylike way of phrasing something unpleasant. 'Contract killers, we call them. And you're right: the use of such people is fairly common in the more dubious circles in which James O'Connor chose to move.'

She winced a little at the involvement of her employer in this murky world, but she wasn't stung into a defence of Jim O'Connor, as he'd hoped. They left her with the usual request that she should go on thinking about the matter. Peach said in the car as they drove away, 'She told us what she'd planned to tell us. No less and no more. How much more the efficient Mrs Derkson knows remains to be seen.'

Peach felt suddenly tired as he neared the shabby semi-detached house which had been his home for the last eight years. He worked fourteen-hour days without complaint when he was cracking a case, but the feeling that he was getting nowhere despite many hours of interviewing and poring over files always exhausted him. Frustration was always much more wearing than progress.

He had his eyes down and his brain deep in thought as he manoeuvred the car between others parked on the suburban street. He was so preoccupied that he almost missed the old Fiesta parked just far enough from the gates to give him easy access to his drive. His mother-in-law was here. Most coppers would have been depressed by that conclusion to a taxing day. Percy had never been most coppers, and his eyes now brightened at the prospect of a little time with Agnes Blake.

The seventy-year-old turned with a smile as he entered the kitchen. 'I'll be on my way in a few minutes, Percy. I was just showing our Lucy how to make a good curry. She's far too ignorant in the kitchen to make a good wife, but I'm working on it.'

'He didn't marry me for my cooking, Mum!' said her daughter daringly.

'Wash your mouth out, our Lucy! You weren't taught to talk dirty in my house.'

'Nor in mine, Mrs B!' said Percy promptly. 'I don't know where she picks these ideas up. Police canteen, I expect. I'm often shocked myself, the things I overhear in there. Sometimes I think it's no place for a wife of mine.'

'Go on with yer!' said Agnes delightedly. She came from the old Lancashire school, where it was all right for men to be racy but quite unladylike for women to join in with them. In her youth in the long-vanished mill, the women had been bawdy enough among themselves at meal breaks, but chaste and demure in the presence of men. But her son-in-law understood all of this – indeed it sometimes seemed to her that he understood all of her world. She loved it when they tuned in to each other and embarrassed the daughter she loved.

Percy said firmly, 'And you can't possibly leave this curry now. You'll need to stay and give your verdict upon it. I'm just an amateur in these things.'

Though Agnes made her protestations that she did not want to disturb them after a working day, she was clearly delighted to stay and even more delighted that it was Percy who insisted upon it. The curry more than passed muster. Although Mrs Blake insisted that Lucy had conducted every stage of its preparation, Percy maintained that he detected the expert supervisory touch of the older woman in the delicate aromas and subtle flavours of the finished product.

Agnes Blake giggled like an adolescent as Percy laid on the praise with his shameless trowel and insisted that they finished the lot. Lucy indulged him and took her teasing in good part, because she was so delighted to see her widowed mother enjoying herself here rather than disappearing dutifully to her empty cottage. Then she stood up and announced, 'You two don't need me. You're like two excited kids when you get together. I'll get the dessert. Ice cream and blueberries all right for you daft pair?'

Percy growled appreciatively as her rear end disappeared into the kitchen. 'It might be true, you know, that I didn't marry her for her cooking. And when she pours herself into tight trousers like that, I'm putty in her hands. It's worse than her mucky language, Mrs B. I'm only a weak-willed man; we're no match for clever creatures like you.'

Agnes tried and failed to look disapproving. 'No sign of any grandchildren, yet, though. I'm not getting any younger, Percy. I want to see my grandson playing cricket for East Lancs, like his dad.'

'You mustn't put pressure on the lad. He might turn out to be a golfer.'

'A GOLFER!' Agnes Blake's contempt brayed out in capital letters, which caused her daughter to giggle in the kitchen. One of the best things about her mum was that she always rose to the bait. 'He'll not be a golfer, if I'm still around to stop it. With Bill's genes and yours, he'll be a CRICKETER!' Her husband had been a consistently successful opening bowler in the Northern League, whilst Percy had until two years previously been a nimble-footed batsman in the Lancashire League. 'You retired far too early, you know, Percy. You could still do it if you'd a mind to. I was only saying yesterday to—'

'There's no guarantee it would be a boy, you know,' said Percy hastily. He didn't want Agnes to get on to her hobby-horse of how he should still be playing cricket for East Lancs.

'No guarantee it will be anything, the way you two keep putting it off,' said Agnes gloomily.

'Better get on with your sweet quickly. I've already brewed the tea,' said her daughter breezily, returning to the room with an energy which showed that she had been listening to the conversation.

'She has a career to make, you see, Mrs B,' said Percy, his dejection echoing that of his mother-in-law. 'I'm not getting any younger myself, but these girls want it both ways nowadays.' He considered the bawdy possibilities of the phrase, but decided not to exploit them. 'At the rate we're going, I'll be crippling about with a stick before any lad we produce is playing cricket.'

'It's true, our Lucy,' said Agnes eagerly. 'Your man's older than you are and I'm seventy now. Don't you think you're being a bit selfish, love? You've got our needs to consider as well as yours, you know.'

But Agnes Blake's forte wasn't being pathetic, and underneath her insistence on a new generation she was torn; she wanted her bright daughter to have the career which had never been possible for her. Percy assured her that they would discuss the matter seriously and she was content to leave it at that.

Percy took her out to the old Fiesta, saw her safely into the driving seat and watched her drive to the end of the road and turn out of sight towards Longridge and home. He stood for a moment looking at the stars on this warm, clear spring night, then turned and went thoughtfully back indoors.

Lucy was watching him more carefully than he knew. 'Thanks for being nice to Mum.'

'It's no effort. She's the mum I always wanted. I'd have had you with whatever baggage you brought, but Agnes is a bonus.' He turned the water on at the sink, waited for it to run warm. 'I think she might have a point, you know.'

Lucy was silent for such a long time that he eventually turned and looked at her. 'You'll need to give that washing-up your full attention,' she said sternly. 'The curry stains the bowl unless you're thorough at the end.'

It was Percy's turn to be uncharacteristically silent. He stacked three plates carefully into the drainer before he said very quietly, 'She's not getting any younger and neither am I.'

'And nor am I. You both talk as if I'm a slip of a girl, but I'll be thirty soon.'

'You're saying we should try for a baby?'

'I'm saying we should give it some thought.'

Twenty minutes later, Percy Peach, who had the capacity to be undressed and between the sheets faster than seemed humanly possible, lay on his back and watched his wife disrobing with low growls of approval. 'You're making me self-conscious,' said Lucy.

'I'm giving it some thought,' he said. He watched her remove her pants and growled again.

'I've warmed my hands for this,' he said when she joined him.

'That's nice!' she said presently. And then, 'I only said we should give it some thought.'

'I'm thinking hard. Very hard. And I shall need lots of practice.'

SIX

'You're a difficult man to get hold of, Mr Tracey. That's why we had to come into your home.'

'I don't have an office. I don't need one. I have a watching brief in different areas. I operate in many of the businesses owned by Mr O'Connor.'

'Yes. You batter people wherever you are directed to do it. I can see you don't need an office for that.'

Steve Tracey started almost out of his chair at this, so that Clyde Northcott took a pace towards him from where he had been standing by the door of the shabby lounge. DCI Peach seemed amused by this reaction. 'I should watch your step if I were you, Tracey. DS Northcott has a history of violence, but I try to keep him in check. If you assaulted a police officer and gave him legitimate grounds for violence, there's no knowing what he might do. And I'd have no grounds to restrain him, you see, under those circumstances.'

Tracey forced himself back into the armchair, gripping the wooden ends of its arms fiercely in his fists to make his body rigid and prevent any other movement. 'You can't go round making allegations like that, Peach. Not nowadays.'

'So sue me. You'd have to prove I was slandering you to get any redress, and both of us know you can't do that. Just as both of us know that you'd never dream of going to court. People like you don't like courts.' Peach let his full contempt curl over this seemingly innocent statement.

'And people like you don't believe a word we say.'

Peach seemed to find this amusing again. He didn't trouble to deny it. Instead he asked, 'So make me believe you. Tell me what you really did in the James O'Connor organisation.'

Tracey noted the past tense but said defiantly, 'I am in charge of security. I make sure that things which are confidential remain so. It is important that certain facts and certain plans remain secret until we choose to reveal them. I make sure everyone knows that and that rival organisations don't get information they shouldn't have.'

He was obviously repeating a well-rehearsed script. Peach wondered aloud where the words had come from. 'Jim O'Connor handed you that stuff, did he? I shouldn't think the palookas you use to enforce things would understand a word of it.'

'I don't know what the hell you think you're—'

'Good word, that. Palookas. Straight out of black-and-white Hollywood gangster films. Which is where you and your muscle belong, Tracey. You're as out of date as that.'

The big man with the cropped hair stayed in his seat with difficulty, his knuckles whitening on the wooden ends of the arms. 'You wouldn't say that if you . . .'

He stopped dead just short of a threat, realising where he was being led, wondering what he could do to get out of this. Peach gave him a smile which combined amusement with derision. 'Did you shoot your boss, Tracey?'

'No. Course I bloody didn't.' He stared sullenly ahead of him, willing himself not to be riled by this bouncing ball of a chief inspector. 'Why the hell would I want to do that?'

'Because some other tycoon paid you handsomely to do it? Because this other villain's now guaranteed you employment at a higher price? Violence is always there to be bought by the highest bidder, isn't it?'

'Get stuffed, Peach!'

'So why didn't you protect O'Connor, Steve? That was your job, surely? Can't do your reputation any good, when the man you're supposed to be protecting is shot down in cold blood, with you in attendance. Sheer bloody incompetence, I'd say. Wouldn't you, DS Northcott?'

'I would indeed, sir. Make it very difficult for Mr Tracey to secure other employment, I'd say, a cock-up like that would.'

Tracey was in before he could stop himself. 'That's where you're wrong, black boy! You've no bloody idea about these things. You should stick to what you fucking know!'

There was a silence in the room, with the only audible sound that of Tracey's heavy breathing. He'd given himself away.

He'd forgotten how temper could betray you with the filth. An elementary mistake, for one with his experience.

Peach savoured the moment, letting a grin which became impossibly wide steal slowly over his expressive features. Finally he glanced at Northcott. 'So he's got himself other employment already. The biggest rat has deserted the sinking O'Connor ship with record speed. But then he probably couldn't believe he'd been offered a new job, after his evident incompetence in the previous one. Or was this by prior arrangement, Tracey? If you didn't shoot O'Connor yourself, did you leave him deliberately exposed because you'd already sold out to an even bigger rogue?'

The big man with the close-cropped hair glared at him, then said sullenly, 'Get stuffed, Peach!' But this was no more than muted, ritual defiance. He had sold himself by his temper; he wasn't going to say more than he needed to from now on, but he'd done the damage.

Peach was determined to make the most of the gift he had been offered. 'Who's taken you on, Tracey? You and a couple of your palookas, I should think.' He savoured the obsolete word again, pronouncing each syllable resoundingly. 'My money's on Lennon. Wouldn't you say so, DS Northcott?'

'From information received, I'd be almost certain of it, sir.' Clyde brought his uncompromising face closer to Steve Tracey's and gave his adversary a grin which held much aggression and nil humour.

Tracey, still reeling from his earlier mistake, was now shaken by the accuracy of their information. 'Get stuffed, black man! It's my business who I work for, not yours, pig!'

Peach regarded him balefully. Men like these, who dealt out violence to order, without even the passion of rage or resentment which drove domestic disputes, were the lowest as well as one of the most dangerous forms of life for him. 'Not true, that. You've no right to privacy, when your business is beating up people. Or killing them, when the need arises. Did you kill O'Connor? Was that part of the deal with Lennon?'

'No!' There was panic in Tracey's insistence. He had realised now how bad it looked for him. He hadn't thought they'd have known anything about his new employment with Lennon. It must look as if he'd defected immediately after O'Connor's death, or more probably by prior arrangement. If these startlingly well-informed pair of filth thought that, they probably thought he'd killed the man as part of the deal. 'I served James O'Connor well – did everything he asked me to.'

'I'll bet you did.' Peach looked at him as though he was something he'd scraped off his shoe. 'As long as it suited you. Until someone else offered you more. Until one of your employer's rivals bought you and your palookas.'

Steve wished the man wouldn't keep throwing in that strange word. He was fighting for his life here, with the pig flinging in daft words whilst he tried to think straight. He said between jaws which were suddenly stiff, 'I didn't shoot O'Connor.'

'Then who did, Tracey? You seem like our prime suspect to me, and I'm happy to have it that way.' Percy gave the man a smile which emphasized that pleasure.

'I don't know.'

'You'll need to do better than that, won't you? From your point of view, I mean, not mine. I'm happy to let suspicion gather around you.'

Peach wasn't, of course. They'd need significant sightings to pin this on Tracey. The Crown Prosecution Service wouldn't look at it until they were given solid evidence to mount a case. But men on the other side of the law didn't always appreciate that: they thought coppers could rig a case against anyone they chose to frame. Peach had no real reason to think this man had killed O'Connor, but he would exploit his fear as he would exploit any other emotion to help to elicit facts. 'You claim you didn't kill this man you were handsomely paid to defend. So who the hell did?'

'I don't know.' Tracey thrashed his brain in search of words to frame some defence, then shook his head dumbly.

'Because even scum like you would have to admit that it doesn't look good for you. You've just been offered new and lucrative employment with the man who is planning to take over O'Connor's dubious empire. Immediately after your previous employer has been gunned down in cold blood. Now why would an efficient sod like Lennon take on someone who has just failed to protect the man who previously paid his wages? Answer: because he was rewarding an assignment which had been efficiently completed.'

'He wasn't. I didn't fire that bullet.'

'Looks like an open and shut case to me, DS Northcott. Wouldn't you say so?'

'I would indeed, sir. An open and shut case.' Clyde Northcott repeated the cliché appreciatively, as if he had just encountered it for the first time. 'I should think the Chief Constable will be delighted to have this cleared up so quickly.'

'I didn't do this,' Tracey repeated, dogged but hopeless. 'I want a brief.'

Percy beamed delightedly. 'Most sensible thing we've heard from you this morning, Mr Tracey. But you're not under caution. Not yet. On paper, you're a good citizen helping the police with their enquiries.' He shook his head and smiled a little at the absurdity of that. Then his voice was suddenly as hard as steel. 'So if you didn't kill him, Tracey, who the hell did?'

'I don't know. I'd tell you if I did.'

'Would you, indeed? Let me put this another way, then. Why didn't you protect the man who paid you to do just that?'

Steve Tracey wanted to say that the protection of his employer had been only an incidental part of his brief; that his job had been principally to frighten others and to bring them to heel by violence if they did not comply. But beating people into submission was hardly a job description he could pursue with the filth. He took a deep, hopeless breath. This wasn't going to sound good. More importantly, it wasn't even going to sound believable, not to these men who wanted to put him away for a long stretch. But he couldn't see how to dress it up as anything stronger. 'I asked James O'Connor if he wanted protection only minutes before he was shot. He announced a comfort break before the speeches which hadn't been scheduled in the programme and I offered to stay with him through it. He said he didn't need me.'

He did his best to make it sound like a dereliction of duty on O'Connor's part, thought Peach. And it was true that his departure from the official programme was the sort of change security men never liked. In this case, indeed, you could say it had been a fatal change. 'But what happened showed that he did need you – assuming that we accept for the moment your claim that you were still on his side. So who killed him? You must see now that if it wasn't you, it's very much in your interests to reveal who did this. You don't need a brief to tell you that.'

Indeed he didn't. Steve desperately wanted them to believe him, but he knew that in their place he'd be every bit as sceptical as they were. He stared straight ahead of him. 'I don't know. My money would be on a hit man employed by one of his enemies.'

'Evidence?'

'The way in which he died. The papers say he was shot in the head. I haven't anything else.' Still he gazed straight ahead. To look into the round, unbelieving face of his tormentor would shake his own belief in the words he was mouthing.

Peach let those words hang for a moment, as if he wished to emphasize how inadequate they were. Then he said, 'Where were you during this interval?'

'I was in the reception area at the front of the building. I spoke to two of my men who had been on the lowest table, at the end of the banqueting hall, where they could see everything that was going on. I wanted to know if they'd seen anything suspicious.'

'I'm sure you did.' Peach let his cynicism hammer each monosyllable hard. 'And no doubt they hadn't.'

'No. And I had to tell them that Mr O'Connor felt he didn't need protection that evening. If he hadn't said that, maybe he'd be alive now.'

'Maybe. And maybe you wouldn't. Assuming, that is, that you're telling the truth. Very big assumption, that is. Make a note that this man was absent from the banqueting hall at the moment when James O'Connor was killed, please, DS Northcott.'

Clyde nodded. 'Already done, sir.' He shifted his chair even nearer to Tracey's. 'What weapon do you carry, Mr Tracey?'

Steve started a little as the point of attack changed from the white and smiling round face of Peach to the stern black features of his bagman. He wanted to say he wasn't armed, but that would be ridiculous in someone paid to do the things he did. 'A Smith & Wesson .357.'

Northcott didn't comment, but allowed himself a rare grin as he wrote the details down. Tracey said defensively, 'There are a lot of them about.'

Peach was back in immediately. 'There are indeed, Mr Tracey. Especially in criminal circles. And a lot of them are used as murder weapons, as in this case. Don't leave the area without telling us exactly where you're intending to flee to, will you?'

And as suddenly as they had arrived, they were gone, leaving Steve Tracey feeling more limp than he had ever felt in his adult life.

It was a bleak May day in north-east Lancashire. No rain threatened, but the sky was the colour of pewter and a light but cutting wind blew from the east.

Detective Chief Inspector Peach's temper had not been improved by his morning interview with Steve Tracey, who was the kind of villain he found most frustrating: violent and destructive but also elusive. He couldn't see any easy or swift solution to the Jim O'Connor murder. The toad in the hole in the canteen was undercooked and indigestible. When he returned to his office, his gloom was completed by a summons to consult with the head of the Brunton CID section, Chief Superintendent Thomas Bulstrode Tucker.

'Are you near to an arrest, Peach?' was Tucker's greeting.

'Your statement to the media said that enquiries were proceeding satisfactorily, sir.' Percy decided to sit down in front of the chief's large and noticeably empty desk.

'Stalling exercise, as you well know, Peach. The official bullshit for "We haven't got anywhere yet, but we're trying".'

'Yes, sir. Fair summary. Surprisingly percipient of you, sir.'

Tucker couldn't remember anyone calling him percipient before, but he supposed it was a compliment. 'Don't try to bullshit me, Peach! I handed this investigation over to you with a brisk start made and house-to-house enquiries already under way. I want to know what progress you've made.'

'A brisk start? I see, sir. Well, I'm afraid the house-to-house

has produced nothing. There aren't too many houses around
Claughton Towers and their occupants tend to be safely indoors
during the hours of darkness.'

Tommy Bloody Tucker ignored this, as he ignored most
things which made unpleasant hearing. 'You have a huge team
on this, Peach. I expect results. Jim O'Connor was a well-
known and popular figure because of his rugby past. He was
also a successful local businessman. This is a high-profile case.
I'm having to hold radio and television at bay, as well as the
press. I need something to feed to them.'

'You could tell them that O'Connor was under investigation
by the Inland Revenue for tax evasion and by the Drug Squad
for supplying and selling illegal substances, sir.'

'I can't go saying things like that about a murder victim. It
wouldn't be good PR. You don't understand the importance
of our image among the public, Peach.'

'No, sir. I'm more concerned with putting villains behind
bars, sir.'

'Don't take that line with me, Peach. It won't work.'

Percy reflected that putting away criminals was hardly a
controversial line, save in the strange world of Tommy Bloody
Tucker. 'The wife wasn't able to provide us with anything
useful, sir. It's my view that Sarah O'Connor isn't grief-stricken
by this death, but I could be wrong.'

'Ah! You may have stumbled upon something vital here,
Peach. A woman could have done this, you know. It takes no
great strength to pull the trigger on a pistol.'

'Yes, sir. That thought had occurred to me. I think DS
Northcott is aware of it, also.'

'Bear it in mind, that's all. You can't trust women, you
know.'

'Yes, sir. I've become aware of that, during my twenty years
of service. However, not many of them possess Smith &
Wesson revolvers which can blow a man's head to bits.
Nevertheless, it seems there were several such weapons around
O'Connor and his henchmen. It wouldn't have been too difficult
for his wife to get her hands on one, if she had a mind to
murder her man. So far, we have no evidence that she had.'

'The press are beginning to moan about our failure to protect the public. You know the kind of stuff – anarchy is stalking our streets unchecked, that sort of thing.'

'I do sir, yes.' For a tiny moment, these two very different men were united in the face of an unfeeling media. Then Peach said, 'O'Connor employed his own muscle. It didn't protect him very well, did it?'

'His own muscle?' Tucker did his goldfish impression, but on this occasion it merely irritated Percy.

'I interviewed a man called Steve Tracey this morning, sir. He's been in charge of Jim O'Connor's security for the last four years.'

'Security?'

'It's the current euphemism for enforcers, sir. Tracey and his men beat up people who tried to obstruct O'Connor's activities.'

'That's illegal, Peach.'

'Your grasp of technicalities is as accurate as ever, sir. The problem is that we can never get witnesses to speak up in court, sir. There have been some bad beatings, but the victims aren't prepared to stand in the witness box and point out the people who put them in hospital.'

'This man Tracey sounds like a dangerous man, Peach. You should regard him as a serious candidate for this crime.'

'Thank you, sir. Your overview of the crime scene in our area is as useful as it ever was.'

Tucker looked at him suspiciously over his rimless glasses. 'There were a lot of people at that dinner, Peach.'

'Sixty-two, sir. No doubt you considered that, before you decided to dismiss them to their homes on Monday night.'

Tucker decided to ignore this; he had long ago developed a deaf ear to turn towards unpleasant facts. 'There must be other possibilities as well as the two you've mentioned. I learned long ago that one mustn't jump to conclusions when engaged on a murder investigation.'

'Another penetrating finding for your juniors, sir. We haven't ruled out the idea that this may still be a domestic.'

Tucker stroked his chin judiciously. It was a gesture he'd worked on over the last couple of years. He felt it gave him gravitas when speaking to television presenters. 'That seems unlikely to me, Peach. But I suppose you know your own business best.'

'Very gracious of you, sir, I'm sure. The victim has a younger brother – six years younger. His name is Dominic O'Connor and he didn't approve of the victim's lifestyle. He called his brother a "chancer", which he undoubtedly was. That and much more. I think Dominic had a much clearer idea of James's businesses and the way he ran them than he cares to admit. That doesn't mean he had anything to do with his death, of course.'

'Indeed it doesn't. Dominic O'Connor is also a successful local businessman. He could do us a lot of damage if we offend him.'

'Even if he should turn out to be a serious criminal, sir?'

'No, of course not. But you'd better be damned sure he's broken the law before you move against him, or you'll have me to deal with.' Tucker jutted the chin which he had lately stroked in what he had decided from ancient photographs was his Churchillian mode.

'Very well, sir. Just for the record, I have no reason to think at this point that Dominic O'Connor is anything other than the most upright of citizens.'

Peach thought as he descended the stairs from Tommy Bloody Tucker's penthouse office that life dealt the cards in a very random fashion. Simply because of the insufferable T.B. Tucker, he would now be delighted if he could dig some dirt on the unsuspecting Dominic O'Connor.

SEVEN

You wore plain clothes when you joined the exalted ranks of the CID. It was supposed to make you less conspicuous. In some cases the idea didn't work. One of these cases was Detective Sergeant Clyde Northcott.

When you were a lean six feet three inches and very black, people tended to remember you, whatever you wore. Most of the time Clyde didn't mind that. His formidable physical presence made him feared. Clyde had grown used to that and secretly rather enjoyed it. He'd learned to survive in a harsh world before he became a policeman and it pleased him that people were nervous about what he might do to them. The police rules were strict and Clyde observed them. But people didn't always know that, did they? There was nothing wrong with a little bluff, if it produced the right results. The fact that DCI Peach referred to his sidekick as a 'hard bastard' whenever the opportunity arose also pleased Clyde, who played up to the image whenever he felt it useful to him.

But you couldn't be at once a hard bastard and unnoticeable, as the job sometimes demanded you should be. When Clyde Northcott spotted something which interested him on that Thursday evening, he slid swiftly behind the wheel of his car. You weren't as obvious in a car, especially when it was a routine silver Ford Focus. You might need to slide the driver's seat as far back as it would go, but six and a quarter feet of muscle and bone was still less noticeable in a vehicle than on the street.

Clyde hesitated about what to do next, because he'd had a hard and boring day which hadn't produced anything significant. Days like that were always the worst; he didn't notice the time passing or count the hours he was putting in when there was progress. But when you spent long hours getting nowhere, you always ended up fatigued as well as frustrated. He wondered for a moment whether he should follow the woman or not, then decided with a sigh that he would need to postpone his takeaway and his tin of lager.

He was trained to observe. He saw things which other people would have missed without any conscious effort. In truth, that was not all police training. He had been a drug dealer, even a suspect in a murder case, before Percy Peach had rescued him, persuaded him to become a copper, and then recruited him into CID a couple of years later. Northcott had learned early in life to watch his back and keep his eyes and ears open. It was a quality very useful to him, even now that he had joined the right side of the law.

The woman might be going somewhere entirely innocent

– statistically she probably was. But he'd been lucky to spot her as she turned onto the main road at the T-junction and he was pretty sure she hadn't seen him. He hesitated for but a moment, then eased the Focus out into the traffic, two cars behind the blue BMW, and kept it in view as they moved out of Brunton and into the countryside.

This might be a wild goose chase, but it would be interesting to see where the widow of James O'Connor was heading.

She was alone in the sports car and he was confident she hadn't spotted him. She drove north, out along the A59, accelerating as the traffic thinned, so that at one stage he was afraid of losing her. But he saw her indicating a left turn and followed her at a safe distance as she eased the sleek blue car on to a much narrower lane. Clyde knew this road; he'd roared over it many times on the Yamaha 350 motorcycle which was his preferred mode of transport. The lane climbed upwards over the flank of Pendle Hill, the height which rose towards two thousand feet and dominated the softer country of the Ribble Valley beneath it.

It was past nine o'clock now and the cars all had their lights on. Clyde kept a discreet distance behind the BMW, watching the red of its rear lights appearing and disappearing as it climbed the hill ahead of him. He thought he knew where it was heading. There was a pub on the side of the hill, busy at weekends but dependent on people who drove out on summer evenings for much trade beyond that. It was still spring and still quite cool up here by this time of night. Clyde guessed correctly that the pub would not have much custom tonight, despite the handwritten notice advertising food at the bar. As Sarah O'Connor turned the blue BMW into the car park, there were only two other cars parked there. Clyde waited until she had hurried into the pub before he eased the Focus gently into the car park. He chose the opposite end of the parking area and reversed the Ford in so as to be ready for a swift exit.

The other two vehicles were a battered Ford Transit van and a green Honda Civic. Clyde wondered whether Sarah O'Connor was meeting the driver of one of these or someone yet to arrive. He would wait ten minutes and then decide whether to venture into the hostelry. He couldn't hope to preserve his anonymity if he did that.

It was very quiet on the hillside as the sky darkened above him. Because of the silence, he heard the car when it was still a long way away. He watched its headlights appearing and disappearing as it wound its way along the lane and climbed closer, felt a thrill of anticipation as it indicated and then swung swiftly into the car park and drew up next to the blue BMW Z4. Clyde slid down in his seat, but the man who emerged from the red Jaguar did not even glance towards him in the semi-darkness.

Dominic O'Connor strode swiftly into the pub and his meeting with his brother's widow.

Northcott reported his Thursday-night journey to Peach as they rode out on the following morning to their next interview in this sprawling case. 'Interesting,' said Percy. 'You're sure neither of them saw you?'

'Absolutely sure. I decided there wasn't much point in hanging around in the pub car park, so I don't know how long they were in there. It could have been a completely innocent social meeting, of course.'

'And Tommy Bloody Tucker could win the final of *Mastermind*. Meetings like that are suspicious until proved otherwise, to cynical fuzz like us. You showed initiative surprising in a man recruited to be a hard bastard.'

'I've told you before: I'm not just a pretty face.'

Peach appeared to think this even more amusing than Clyde had expected. But there was no time for further discussion. They were outside the high electronic gates of the house they were visiting. Much to Percy's disgust, they had to announce themselves into the speaker in the tall brick gatepost. The gates swung silently open thirty seconds later.

It was a modern house, but a large one and set in extensive grounds. Between two and three million pounds, Peach estimated; you got a feeling for prices when you moved around the area. The maid led them into a huge lounge, where the woman who waited for them was as well-groomed as the lawns and gardens around her house. She was a phenomenon which was still rare in north-east Lancashire: a rich and powerful woman who had made her money almost entirely by her own efforts. It was even rarer to find a woman who reputedly had used criminal activities to underpin her success.

Linda Coleman seated them on the sofa opposite her armchair, with the light directly into their faces. Then she ordered that coffee should be served, without asking them whether they wanted it. Mrs Coleman had the air of a woman who was used to being obeyed; no doubt that was exactly the impression she wished to convey. She said, 'I shall give you all the help I can in the matter of James O'Connor's death. It will be very little.'

She was a woman at ease with herself and her surroundings. Her dark green dress was in a smooth fabric which neither of the men could identify. 'Expensive' was as accurate as Clyde Northcott could get. He wondered how much she had paid to get soft leather shoes which exactly matched the shade of her dress. They knew from research before they came here that the face beneath the golden, short-cut hair was forty-four years old, otherwise they would have assessed it as younger. The clear blue eyes looked these two contrasting men up and down as they sat awkwardly on the deep-seated sofa. Those cold eyes announced that she was in charge here and that they would do well to remember that.

Peach was not a man who took kindly to such subordination. He said without preamble, 'Why do you think you were invited to Monday night's celebration at Claughton Towers, Mrs Coleman?'

'That is surely a question you should ask of the man who invited me. As he is no longer here to answer it, perhaps his PA or his wife could provide your answer.'

'But I am asking you. It is surely a question you must have asked yourself when you received the invitation.'

She stared at him for a moment before deciding to answer the question after all. 'We were business rivals who had become business partners. Jim was recognising that by asking me to sit with the people who'd been working for him for years.' The answer came clearly and without hesitation, as if she had dispensed with the idea of deceit.

'James O'Connor had taken over some of your enterprises.'

'If you care to put it like that, yes. I prefer to regard it as a profitable merging of mutual interests. I'd hardly have been placed on the table immediately below his if Jim hadn't regarded me as an important player.'

Peach gave her a sour smile. 'An important player in what particular game, Mrs Coleman?'

'Retail interests, principally. I own a town-centre woollens shop, one of the few independent traders left outside the big chains. We also have a men's outfitters, which supplies most of the school uniforms in the town.'

'And makes surprising profits.'

'We do all right.'

'Profits which are out of all proportion to the turnover in these shops.'

'I didn't realise you claimed to be an expert in retail merchandising. The modern police service must be amazingly tolerant, if you are encouraged to develop such interests.'

'Did James O'Connor also take over the prostitution rings for which these shops are a front?'

She looked at him steadily. It seemed she had expected what he had planned to drop as a bombshell. 'Highly imaginative. But also rather dangerous for you, Detective Chief Inspector Peach. I'm sure my lawyers would be interested to hear you repeat these views in a more formal context.'

Peach's smile contrived to express distaste rather than amusement. 'Lawyers, eh? A single legal expert not enough for you, when all that is involved is two or three dull and successful shops?' His fierce revulsion burst out suddenly against the wall of her calmness. 'All the lawyers in England won't help you, when we finally expose the rape and prostitution of minors which has been happening in this town.'

Both he and his unlikely looking adversary in the armchair knew what he referred to. Young white girls in the area, many of them still children and most of them from care homes, were being lured into prostitution by Asian men, who selected them carefully and set up rings they could control. The money to initiate this and the ultimate control of the rings came from sources further up the hierarchy. Money from drugs was being used to finance this lucrative colony in a growing criminal empire.

Linda Coleman weighed Peach's words carefully before she chose to reply. 'I know nothing of this. It is ludicrous that you should try to connect me with such things.' The coffee arrived, served with biscuits on a wide metal tray by a slim and elegant Asian girl. Not a word was spoken whilst she was in the room. Their hostess watched the door close behind her before she picked up the coffee pot and poured. 'I did hear that your wife had been questioning some of our Asian friends about these allegations. I doubt if there is anything in them, but I should hate it if DS Peach came to grief. I'm told she's a pretty and enthusiastic officer. It would be a pity if anything changed that.'

Percy felt his pulses racing. This wasn't right for him; this was the kind of apprehension he had intended that Coleman should feel. He had not known that this woman was even aware that Lucy was an officer, let alone that she knew his wife was involved in the prostitution enquiries. He spoke as steadily as he could. 'That sounded very like a threat to me, Mrs Coleman. Note it down, please, DS Northcott.'

She glanced at Northcott, whose notebook looked tiny in his very large hands. 'It was nothing of the sort, DCI Peach. It was no more than well-meant concern for a police officer who might move out of her depth and into dangerous waters.'

'Who killed James O'Connor?'

She appeared not at all shaken by his abrupt switch. 'I've no idea. I should have come forward with the information as a good citizen if I had.'

'Was your husband involved?'

She smiled. 'Peter wasn't even there.'

'I know that. Was he involved?'

'What a preposterous idea! Of course Peter wasn't involved. He scarcely knew Jim O'Connor.'

'He handles what he calls security for the Lennon group of enterprises. We all know what that means: Peter Coleman deals in violence and sometimes in death. As the Lennon organisation is now planning to control the group of criminal enterprises formerly run by James O'Connor, it is perfectly logical that he should have eliminated the former owner. Or arranged his elimination.'

'He did neither. Place that on record, please, DS Northcott.' She savoured echoing Peach's direction to his bagman, then turned back to him. 'You have an over-developed imagination, DCI Peach.'

'My imagination is fine. What I at present lack is the evidence to support it. That will come, in time. So who did kill James O'Connor?'

'I've no idea. I never left the banqueting hall during that comfort break; my neighbours at the table will confirm that for you. I've always had a strong bladder, among other things. For the record, I hope the creaking police machine gets a result on this one. I liked Jim.'

Clyde Northcott drove the car down the drive between the immaculate lawns and back to the station at Brunton. He had the good sense to say nothing to Peach, who stared straight ahead with a face like thunder. Eventually Percy said, 'She's a dangerous woman, that one. And we made no impression on her. Linda Coleman is going to be a dire influence on Brunton, unless we can nobble her.'

Clyde braked sharply to avoid a Brunton cat which seemed bent on suicide, then waited his moment to pass a learner driver who was exercising extreme care. Only then did he say, 'She was very determined to let us know that she never left the banqueting hall during that ten minutes when the murder took place.'

'Indeed she was. And if we check it out with other statements, I'm sure we'll find it was exactly as she says. She wouldn't have drawn our attention to it otherwise.'

'No. Cast-iron alibi. It's almost as if she knew something was going to happen in those ten minutes.'

'Good thinking, Clyde. That's why you're a DS and not just a DC nowadays. I've always said you were more than just a hard bastard.'

It was only Percy Peach who'd ever called him that, but Clyde was much too astute to remind him of it now.

*   *   *

DS Lucy Peach was well aware of the dangers she ran. There was a heavy irony to them, in her view. The police regulations stated firmly that husband and wife should not work together, which meant that since her marriage she had needed perforce to undertake other duties in the CID section.

The nature of these meant that she felt in far more danger than she ever had felt whilst working alongside Percy. Brunton had an Asian population which now constituted almost thirty per cent of the whole. Amongst the tiny lunatic fringe of the Muslim fraternity, there lurked fanatical young men and a few ruthless older ones who directed them. Lucy Peach was ever more heavily involved in the campaign to frustrate these most dangerous forces. The anti-terrorism unit gathered more and more information and made itself more and more effective. Knowledge was power, but it was also a highly dangerous commodity, in this context.

There were also decisions which called for the most delicate of judgements. The policy was to let plots against the state and its citizens proceed as far as possible, as long as they did not risk injury or death to the public. Lucy and the officers who worked with her were aware at this moment of several embryo plots, over which they maintained a watching brief. They wouldn't move in to frustrate them unless it was felt that the safety of the public was in jeopardy. The reason for this was that they wanted to capture not merely the rabid young males who were prepared to sacrifice their own lives in pursuit of mistaken ideals, but the subtle and even more sinister men behind them who plotted the continuous 'war against the infidel' in which these were merely incidents.

It was a delicate balance. You wanted to intervene decisively, but at as late a stage as possible, in order to catch the generals as well as the advanced troops in this malevolent army. Lucy was too junior to take such decisions, but she felt her responsibility keenly. When you were front-line in these operations, it was often you who had to advise on when terrorist planning would actually explode into action. Wrong advice could result in the deaths of innocent people who might otherwise have been saved.

It was almost a relief today to be involved in a different

type of operation. Yet she was quickly changing her view about that. The people she was now investigating were almost more hateful than the terrorists, who were at least driven by a mistaken idealism. These people were preying on the young, selecting for their targets perhaps the most vulnerable of all people in a damaged society.

Lucy stared with undisguised distaste into the dark brown eyes on the other side of the square table. 'You were seen, Mr Atwal. One of our officers was watching you.'

Hostility flashed across the narrow face. He hated being questioned by a woman. He wouldn't underestimate her because of her sex, but something deep in his breeding said that he should not be forced to answer questions from her, that at least his adversary should be a man.

Lucy was well aware of that, but she would turn it to her advantage if she saw the opportunity. If there was a chance to humiliate him, she would take it, because resentment made people vulnerable, just as any other emotion did. Atwal said, 'This is mistaken identity. I was at home at the time. I can get people to swear to that and make you look stupid, DS Peach.'

He looked at her with contempt, which changed slowly towards a lust he did not trouble to disguise. She was an attractive woman, with flesh in the right places: buxom, the decadent English called it. She'd be good for one thing, and that wasn't strutting about pretending to be police. He let his eyes roam over her breasts, then slid his chair back a little and attempted to review that portion of her body she kept behind the table. She wouldn't come willingly, but resistance would give an extra spice to shagging her; he tried to convey all of this in his silent, brazen assessment of her charms.

Lucy knew what he was about. She wanted to tell him that she was proof against it, that she had endured all this and more from white youths who did not trouble to moderate their language or disguise their lecherous thoughts. Sexual insult was par for the course for her, even a little tedious by now. She spoke slowly and distinctly. 'You waited outside the council care home. You spoke at length to three of the girls who are resident there. You attempted to recruit them for prostitution. All of them were under age.'

'All of them were white trash who were prepared to sell themselves.'

'And how would you know this? You said a moment ago that you weren't there.'

He was shaken a little, but he didn't show it. 'I wasn't. I know these things, that's all. It's common knowledge. They wouldn't be in these homes if they weren't trash.'

'They're in these homes because they haven't got anyone to speak up for them or defend them. The very reasons why scum like you attempt to recruit them and exploit them. But I don't need to tell you that. It's because you know it that you hang around these places.'

'These girls are white whores. They're bred for it. They love it. They get paid for it.' He looked her up and down again, studied her red-brown hair for a moment, flashed her a predator's mirthless smile. 'There's plenty of older white women gagging for it, if they can get it.'

'We've got enough to charge you, Atwal. Do you want a brief?' At least it would be interesting to find where his lawyer came from and who was financing him.

'You won't be charging me. These kids won't go into court. They've got more sense than that.'

'But not enough sense to avoid scum like you? We'll give them protection, Atwal. And if you dare to—'

'You can't protect them! You and a whole bloody army couldn't protect them. Not against Lennon.'

The name was out before he could stop it. Anger had betrayed him, as Lucy had hoped it would. There was always a hope of that, with the thickos who operated down the order. His face telegraphed his mistake; for a brief moment fear flashed across his thin features, where there had heretofore been nothing but derision.

Lucy let the full implications of his blunder sink in for a moment before she said, 'I'm sure Mr Lennon and his muscle men would be interested to hear you quoting them in this context. We may need to call you as a prosecution witness, when this case comes to court. You could make quite a name for yourself, Mr Atwal, because there will be national publicity. I wouldn't like to be in your shoes afterwards, though.

Especially as I don't think you'd be a high priority for the police protection services.'

'You'll never make this stick, darling!' He tried to add menace to the last word, but it didn't really work.

'The best thing you could do is come clean right now. Luring minors into prostitution is regarded very seriously, and I don't fancy your chances inside. Some of the crazy villains in Strangeways take as strong a view as we do, and they aren't inhibited by the legal restraints that we have to observe.'

'I'm not worried by you, darling.' He glanced at DC Brendan Murphy beside her. The big, fresh-faced copper had said not a word, though he looked ready to use his fists at any second. Atwal blundered on blindly. 'You lot don't know what violence is. You lot don't know what we can do and get away with.'

Lucy Peach leaned forward a little and said with deliberate contempt, 'Murder, you mean? James O'Connor? Oh, I wouldn't be too confident you've got away with that. Not confident at all, in fact. I think your Mr Coleman may be helping our team with its enquiries at any moment now.'

A hit. A very palpable hit. Amazement and fear flashed across Atwal's mean features in quick succession. He uttered a few more phrases of ritual defiance before they returned him to a cell to stew for another couple of hours. Lucy watched him go, then contacted her husband on his mobile. 'I don't know quite where you're up to on the James O'Connor case. I'd go hard after Coleman and the rest of Lennon's muscle, if I were you.'

EIGHT

P eter Coleman was a contrast to his wife. She had been a smoothly finished product, well adapted to concealing her inner feelings. He was rough at the edges and apparently proud of it. He wasn't at all effective in disguising the fact that he traded in violence; indeed, he delighted in making it only too obvious to the people he was employed to threaten.

He chose to meet the filth in a builders' hut at the edge of a demolition site in the older sector of Brunton. The mill and the foundry which had once stood there were long gone. Now one of the last of the terraces of houses which had surrounded them was being removed to facilitate the building of new office blocks. Two hundred yards away, a new casino block with ample parking for its punters flashed its neon blandishments, even in the clear light of a May day. It was a depressing sight to anyone with a sense of history. The tawdriest of modern man's amusements was being set against the fresh air and clear skies which would once have turned thoughts of hard-driven mill workers to healthier pastimes.

This was very different from the way in which Mrs Coleman had recently received them. Coleman wrenched two stacking chairs from a pile of five in the corner of the shed and banged them down for his visitors, taking a third one for himself and placing it exactly opposite them, no more than five feet away. He scratched his left armpit deliberately, then said in a broad northern accent with a Geordie inflection, 'This canna take long. I've a work force to supervise. The buggers skive their arses off if they think I'm not around.'

Peach regarded the broad face steadily and without obvious emotion. 'They won't have to contend with you for much longer. Still, they might get someone who knows a little more about demolition and building and a little less about murderous violence, when you're off the scene.'

Coleman allowed himself a smile. He and Peach had clashed many times before, as each had risen up the ranks on opposite sides of the law. Peach had put him away for a year when he was in his twenties, for using a knife during an affray. Since then he had skirted the law and narrowly avoided conviction. It is one of the paradoxes of modern justice that as you rise higher in the criminal fraternity and become more dangerous, it becomes more difficult for those who attempt to uphold the law to charge you and make it stick.

You become a bigger player, moving away from street violence as you instruct others to do that for you. You have expert lawyers to insulate you against prosecution, as you did not have when you were taking on street fights against your low-level rivals. You cover your tracks and ensure by a variety of means that there is no one willing to bear witness against you, so that the Crown Prosecution Service lawyers tell indignant police officers that they are unwilling to pursue a case with scant chance of success.

The biggest danger is that you can begin to feel impregnable. Overconfidence is an Achilles heel for many men who live by violence.

Peter Coleman regarded DCI Peach with a smile flicking at the edges of his mouth. 'I don't know why you think I would involve myself in violence. Those days are long behind me. I was a wild lad, I admit, until I saw the error of my ways. I've now got myself a respectable job and a respectable wife.'

He couldn't resist brandishing his wife, that elegant creature they had recently left in the huge house her money had bought for them. But men were vulnerable through their women, as they were through anything for which they cared. Peach said, 'A rich wife, not a respectable one. You know where Linda's money comes from, so you shouldn't make that mistake.'

'Linda knows what she's doing. You shouldn't be jealous because she runs successful shops in the town.'

'Successful shop fronts. You know as well as anyone that she's laundering money from very different enterprises. Drugs and prostitution, principally, with you providing the necessary muscle.'

'You'll never make that stick. I should be recording this. You'd think twice about saying these things, if I was.'

But Coleman was rattled, in spite of his words. His broad, coarse-featured face was flickering with anger, even as he sought an easy defiance. Peach said, 'I'm sure DS Northcott has a cassette machine in the car, if you'd really like to have this on record. I don't think your brief would advise it. But we're not quite at the brief stage. Not yet.'

A bulldozer started outside, its powerful engine even more raucous in the silence of the hut, which shook a little as the machine began to move earth and stone which had been compacted by centuries of anonymous feet. Coleman said, 'I should be directing that machine. I told you, I've got better things to do than waste my time in here with you.'

'We know you killed James O'Connor.'

If he'd been rattled earlier, he was even more so now. Instead of denying it, he resorted to the villain's more desperate tactic. 'You'll never prove that.'

'We can and we will.'

'And who's going to stand up in court and say so? Get real, Peach.'

'I wouldn't dream of telling you that. I'm not giving you any targets for the sort of violence you deal in.'

'You're bluffing, Peach. I can see it a mile off.'

'Your vehicle was spotted. They're necessary evils, cars, don't you think? You need them to get there and get away swiftly afterwards, but they can be a dead giveaway once they're spotted.'

'You're bluffing, Peach,' he said again. 'I'd like you to fuck off out of it now. I've seen enough of you for one day.' But his tongue flicked quickly over his thick, dry lips. He was more used to threatening than to being threatened and he was very worried.

'Don't leave the area without giving us an address, please. But you'll find there isn't anywhere to run to, with murder on your hands.'

Coleman moved towards Peach as he stood up and turned away, causing Clyde Northcott to utter his only words of the meeting. 'Don't even think about it, Coleman! Nothing would give me greater pleasure than to give you the sort of beating you've dished out so often to others.'

The hard bastard had his uses, thought both policemen, as they removed their car from the path of the bulldozer.

Sarah O'Connor switched the lights on in the front room of the house, the dining room which was now rarely used. The police were working late on Friday night, but the dead man's widow wasn't going to give them any kudos for that. Instead, she said, 'I've been told I can't organise James's funeral yet. There will be a lot of people coming over from Ireland for it. Can you give me a date when the body will be released?'

DS Lucy Peach assessed her carefully. You had to be careful with grieving widows, but this one looked strong enough to take the truth. 'I'm afraid we can't, as yet. When we make an arrest, the defence solicitor will have the right to ask for a second post-mortem, if he thinks it might help his case. I think it is unlikely that he or she will do so in this case, but until the question is answered we cannot release the body. I know this is difficult, because the family needs to feel closure, but we do not have any choice in the matter.'

Lucy Peach watched the widow nod thoughtfully. She was doing her best to divine what this cool woman with the shining, freshly washed black hair was thinking, but not having much success. Percy had said it would be useful to have another opinion on the widow other than his own when he had been allowed to add Lucy to his team. She was surprised that he wasn't pursuing someone so close to the victim himself, as he usually did. Percy hadn't told her about Linda Coleman's scarcely veiled threats in connection with Lucy's child prostitution enquiries, which had shaken him more than he cared to admit even to himself.

Lucy glanced at Brendan Murphy and the DC seized his cue. 'I believe DCI Peach told you that we would need to speak to you again after we'd made other enquiries.' Sarah nodded coolly, assessing this fresh-faced young man and feeling that her considerably greater experience of life would give her the edge on him. As if he felt the stress of her judgement, he added, 'I should emphasize that you are helping the police voluntarily with this investigation.'

'As a good citizen should.' A smile spread her mouth wide as she nodded. 'I am well aware of the requirements of the law and of my duties as a citizen. I caught your name when DS Peach introduced you. You must surely be Irish yourself, with a name like that.'

'I'm afraid not. My roots are certainly Irish, but I've never lived outside Lancashire and never even visited Eire.' It was an explanation it seemed to Brendan he would have to make for the rest of his life. He tried not to show that he was well used to it.

'Don't be apologetic. I'm thoroughly English myself, but people often assume I'm from Ireland because of my marriage to Jim.' She stiffened a little as she turned towards DS Peach.

'I am anxious to have this matter cleared up as quickly as possible.'

This seemed to Lucy cold and formal phrasing for a woman who should have been stricken by the death of her husband. 'We know quite a lot more now than when DCI Peach spoke to you on Wednesday. We are moving towards an arrest, but we need to make sure we have the evidence to make a case stick before we prefer charges.'

'A curious expression that, I always think. I expect it's archaic, like much of the language of the law.'

She seemed to be demonstrating how in control of herself she was, how free she felt not only from guilt but from other emotions also. Lucy spoke firmly. 'In the aftermath of a serious crime like this, we have a large team and we follow the movements of many people. Most of this work produces nothing useful, but occasionally we discover something significant. That justifies the measures we take and the resources we allot to them.'

Mrs O'Connor looked at the small gold watch on her wrist, not troubling to disguise her impatience. 'I'm sure it does. Is this leading up to something?'

DC Murphy flicked open his notebook as Lucy said, 'I'm afraid it is. Forgive me if this sounds impertinent. You were followed last night as you drove out of Brunton.'

Sarah paused for a moment, determined not to reveal any emotion. 'A blue BMW is not the most inconspicuous of vehicles, I suppose. Does this mean I am under police surveillance?'

'No. It was a random sighting by one of our officers. It was his own initiative that made him follow you.'

She nodding, assessing the information and its implications. 'He was good: I'd no idea that he was following me. That is if it was a he – we all have to be careful about gender nowadays, don't we? I expect he followed me to the Grouse Inn.'

'It was a he, and he did.' Lucy tried not to smile at the notion of Clyde Northcott as a female. 'He saw who came to meet you there.'

'My brother-in-law. Scarcely an unusual meeting, for a woman who lost her husband three nights earlier.'

'But an unusual and remote place to meet. Almost as if you wished to keep the assignation a secret one.'

The broad brow furrowed as Sarah O'Connor showed her irritation for the first time. 'This is like living in a police state. Do I have to account for my every movement?'

'I'm sorry. I agree this is unusual and I can't force you to answer. But a murder investigation is by definition unusual. We are usually given a little more latitude, so long as it is clear that we are in pursuit of the truth.'

'And I would be regarded as obstructive if I chose not to answer your questions. It's a form of blackmail, isn't it?'

'It's not intended to be. Try to look at it from our point of view. We want to find the truth about everything. Ninety per cent of it will be irrelevant to the enquiry and will be discarded. You can't expect us to know which ten per cent will be relevant – even crucial.'

Sarah looked at the younger woman, wondering if she was more prepared to accept these explanations from a woman than she would have been from a man. Probably, she thought. She was sure she would have been more brusque with DC Murphy if he'd been offering her these thoughts. She said abruptly, 'I didn't initiate that cloak-and-dagger meeting last night. It was Dominic who said when and where he wanted to see me.'

DS Lucy Peach nodded, as if this was exactly what she had expected. 'And what was the purpose of this conference?'

She took a deep breath and looked at a point on the carpet exactly between her two CID visitors. 'Dominic thinks he knows who killed Jim. He wanted to check out a few things with me.'

Saturdays are quiet in police stations. The price of freedom is eternal vigilance, more now than it has ever been, so the law has to be upheld for seven days a week as well as twenty-four hours a day. But coppers like their weekends as much as other mortals, so that there is but a skeleton staff in the buildings on Saturdays and Sundays, even with a murder investigation in full swing.

The CID section was almost deserted at ten o'clock on this

Saturday morning, when Lucy Peach and Brendan Murphy conferred with the man in charge of the investigation and his bagman. There was a little tension between Lucy, who had been at Percy's side for several years, and Clyde Northcott who had now replaced her. Curiosity rather than tension, Lucy corrected herself; Clyde had been Percy's best man at their wedding and she had a huge respect for him. So she was merely anxious to see how Clyde was making out. But a small, unworthy part of her did not want him to be successful, did not want him to obliterate the memories of the cases Percy had conducted with her at his side. That was extremely petty, Lucy admitted to herself; perhaps she should get on with creating that baby and making her mother happy.

Percy said with some distaste, 'There are all sorts of things going on here as well as murder.' Peach liked things tidy. When you were investigating the most serious crime of all, you should be able to concentrate on it without the distractions of drugs and gambling and prostitution and all the subsidiary violence which accompanies them.

Lucy said, 'There's going to be a big case coming up about the procuring of minors for prostitution. Asian men have been raiding council homes in search of defenceless girls. Not just here but all over the north-west. These kids have been subjected to unspeakable degradation and repeated rapes. Our team is assembling more and more evidence. We'll be ready to present the case within weeks. It could happen now, but we want to get the big boys who are financing this as well as the men who've been procuring minors and arranging their clients.'

Percy nodded. 'The money's coming from the drug barons. They're expanding their enterprises, diversifying into other criminal businesses, as if they were legitimate entrepreneurs. They're dangerous men – and women.' He couldn't forget the image of Linda Coleman's smile as she casually informed him that she knew all about Lucy's pursuit of the young Pakistanis involved in this.

Clyde Northcott said, 'All this is muddying the waters around James O'Connor and his death. We know that he was moving further and further into local crime, but he covered his tracks well. He had successful legitimate businesses. His paper mills supply stationery and packing materials to some very big companies, and his betting shops and casinos appear to be perfectly legal earners. But he liked takeovers and it seems he was quite unscrupulous about what he acquired: so long as it was profitable, he was interested.'

Peach nodded. 'We have to be aware of that, because it is what surrounds our crime. But beyond that, we can be blinkered. Other teams are investigating the prostitution of minors and the sale of illegal drugs. Our concern is to determine who killed James O'Connor. Because there is so much other crime around this, questioning suspects is difficult. Too many of the people our team has spoken to have previous dealings with the police and are determined to reveal as little as possible.'

Lucy said quietly, 'The victim's widow says her brother-in-law can help us. She thinks Dominic O'Connor has vital information about James's death.'

Northcott said, 'I've been trying to contact him all morning, but there's no reply from his land line and his mobile's switched off.'

Peach frowned. 'I think you and I had better get out to his house this afternoon and see what he has to say for himself, Clyde.'

Dominic O'Connor lived on the northern outskirts of the town, not far from the road which ran out into the Ribble Valley and some of the finest country in England. Percy Peach, who had walked and biked through most of the area as boy and youth, was fond of telling anyone who would listen that there was no large town in the two hundred miles between Brunton and Glasgow.

They moved along an unpaved lane, past humble cottages which had been built here around 1850, well before the grander residences which had followed them. The younger O'Connor's dwelling was a solid detached house, late Victorian or Edwardian, in the smooth red Accrington brick which characterised the best local buildings of that era. It was less grand than the house of his dead elder brother, but it had a splendid view across the valley, over the once busy railway lines to the steep slopes opposite. There the North Lancs golf course, where Percy took his exercise, stretched away towards the wilder moorland beyond.

Percy studied the house and its surroundings for a moment before moving to the blue front door, which was flanked by Yorkshire stone bays. They could hear the bell ringing beyond the door, but no other movement. The house sounded very empty, but he pressed the bell twice more before accepting that it was not going to be answered. A man in the front garden of the adjoining house stopped working his border and leant upon his fork, watching them curiously.

Clyde Northcott went over to the low brick wall between the houses and showed the man his warrant card. 'We need to speak to Mr Dominic O'Connor. Would you know where he is, sir?'

'Nope.' The man seemed to find the negative very satisfying. 'I ain't seen 'im today. But I've only been here since two. I don't live here; I'm the gardener.' He lifted his head to look at the high elevations of the house where he was working, as if that should have been obvious to his enquirer.

'And have you seen anyone else coming or going from this house whilst you've been working?'

Their informant gave the question such consideration that they felt he must surely produce something. But all he said was, 'No. It's been very quiet all the time I've been here. I've been round the back part of the time, but I ain't seen no one. Lady of the house where you are always speaks to me when she sees me. Pleasant woman, don't know her name. But I ain't seen no one today.' He nodded his satisfaction over this glimpse into his social world, then resumed forking the border.

Peach tried the door to the passage by the side of the garage and found it unlocked. He and Northcott moved cautiously to the back of the house, where there was ample evidence of the era in which it had been built. The house extended a long way back behind the smooth brick of its high frontage. Now that it was obvious that the place was deserted, the two CID men peered through the windows of this rear section of the dwelling. Behind lounge and dining room, there was what had once been called a 'living kitchen', with the sort of huge black fire range which Percy's mother-in-law, Agnes Blake, would have coated with black lead in her youth. The old range, with an oven at one side and its hob for the sooty kettle, had long since been replaced in this residence by an attractive brick fireplace.

What had been a scullery with stone sinks when the house was new was now a well-fitted small kitchen; what had originally been a large wash-house behind this was now a spacious utility room. And still the buildings stretched backwards, into the garden which climbed away beyond them. Substantial buildings like this needed a lot of heating, but that had not been a major problem in 1900. Coal had been plentiful and cheap and the servants to carry it readily available. The rearmost building of all had once been a substantial coal store, capable of housing two or three tons of the shining black fuel if necessary.

It was a long time since this section of the house had been used for its original purpose. It now had a fine new entrance door, indicating that it had been converted into an office which could operate independently from the rest of the house. To their surprise, the door opened instantly when Peach turned the handle.

On this fresh May day of clear skies and high white clouds, their nostrils as they moved out of the clear air and into the room were assailed instantly by a scent both of them had known before and did not seek to smell again. Unnaturally sweet and characteristically foetid: the scent of human death.

Dominic O'Connor lay slumped over his desk with his head laid sideways upon it. The cord around his neck had bitten so deeply into it that it was scarcely visible beneath the darkening flesh. His eyes were wide and bulging, as if in astonishment at what had happened to him. He looked as if he had been surprised only minutes before they arrived.

Only the odour announced to them that he had been dead for several hours at least.

NINE

Peter Coleman was arrested and charged with the murder of James O'Connor at one o'clock on Saturday. Although a heavy police presence surrounded his house for the arrest, it was surprisingly low key and undramatic in the end. One of the thugs Coleman used to enforce security for the Lennon organisation disclosed the fact that his chief had driven to Claughton Towers with the sole aim of shooting the man at the centre of the evening's celebration. As Peach had forecast, the rat deserted his sinking master almost eagerly, once his own safety was threatened.

Chief Superintendent Tucker didn't like having his weekends interrupted. But Saturday was a quiet news day, so there was every chance that his media briefing would go out unedited on radio and television. When you had good news to impart to the public, you wanted maximum coverage; he always emphasized that to his staff. And it wouldn't do him any harm if the Chief Constable saw him broadcasting the news of a police triumph to the nation at large.

He had scheduled the briefing for four thirty, and the cameras and microphones, as well as the crime reporters from national and local press, were in position by then. Thomas Bulstrode Tucker spent a good twenty minutes with the make-up girls, removing his rimless glasses to allow them to powder and groom him before the single large mirror in their improvised set-up in the town hall. Tucker had designated this venue, in the belief that he would make an impressive figure at the top of the wide stone steps, as he announced his victory over the darker forces in society. A civic setting would give him gravitas. Gravitas was a very important element in the armoury of T.B. Tucker.

He liked to appear in a well-pressed uniform on these occasions, believing correctly that smartness added conviction in the public eye. Both BBC television and ITV microphones were here, he noted with approval. He nodded a friendly greeting to the young woman who was the BBC's weekend presenter in the north-west. 'Announce me as the man who directed this successful investigation of a major crime,' he whispered to her, as the director gave the one-minute warning.

Tucker had originally thought he would appear sitting behind a table, with lesser mortals in uniform alongside him to emphasise his status. But uniforms were thin on the ground on a Saturday, and he was secretly pleased that that insufferable man Peach had said he was pursuing an inquiry in the Wilpshire district of the town and wouldn't be around for this PR exercise. PR was emphatically not Peach's forte and he made Tucker nervous when he was anywhere in the vicinity. Peach might have produced this result, but it needed a man with his chief's gifts to put the right gloss on it and make the most of the situation. He would appear standing at the top of the town hall steps: that would give a greater sense of urgency.

The rather nervous presenter announced Tucker as he had requested: as the man in charge of this investigation into the brutal murder of a popular local businessman who was also a former international sportsman. She followed this with her first question, which Tucker had also set up for himself. 'We understand that a man is now helping you with your enquiries.'

Tommy Bloody Tucker smiled urbanely. 'That is correct, Jenny. But I think this is surely a bit of police jargon which we can dispense with on this occasion. Let us be honest and direct; I am here to tell you that an arrest has been made and that charges will be preferred within the next couple of hours.'

He paused, smiling modestly through the little flutter of reaction which followed his statement. Then he added, 'I shall not give you the offender's name at the moment. That will be released as soon as he has been charged with the crime of murder.'

He paused. The word still made its impact, even in this violent century. Jenny said, 'Did you make the arrest yourself, sir?'

Tucker gave her an avuncular smile. 'I don't see any need

for "sirs" here. I am a member of the police service who is proud to be a humble servant of the public.'

'Who pay your wages,' said the presenter, with a rather more acid smile.

'Who pay our wages and I'm sure are pleased to do so, when we produce results like this one.'

'So you led the enquiry and made the arrest yourself, Superintendent Tucker?'

'Chief Superintendent, Jenny. Not that we're going to stand on ceremony here, are we? Not with a result like this. Rejoice, as a certain fine lady said before me. Rejoice and be thankful for our success!'

'We shall, Chief Superintendent. Did you arrest this man yourself?'

Tucker's noble brow wrinkled a little with irritation at this nit-picking. He said with a lofty smile, 'I don't think you appreciate the way in which the system operates, Jenny. You couldn't be expected to, I suppose. I direct the team. I maintain an overview of order and disorder in the area. I estimate the place this particular crime occupies within that. I direct an efficient and enthusiastic team and ensure that it produces the desired results.'

'So you don't soil your administrative hands with anything as crude as the arrest of a violent criminal.'

There was a ripple of amusement among the cynical old hacks at the bottom of the steps. It was nothing as vulgar as hilarity, but rather the pinprick of merriment which pomposity brings upon itself. Tucker said loftily, 'I have confidence in my team. I allow my officers to get on with their work. And now, if there are no other questions, I am sure that we all have things to do.'

He had been nettled by his television interviewer into a further error. It was a mistake even to suggest questions from the seasoned hacks, who resented having to stand outdoors and be patronised by this balloon of self importance. Alf Houldsworth, former *Daily Express* crime reporter who was enlivening his retirement with part-time work on the local *Lancashire Telegraph*, enjoyed the occasional pint and exchange of information with Percy Peach. He knew all about

Tommy Bloody Tucker. He called from the edge of the crowd, 'So is the officer who has personally pursued and trapped this highly dangerous man here for us to congratulate?'

'My staff prefer me to speak in public for them. I am happy with their quality. Perhaps I should emphasise again that I have directed this whole operation and suggested the various strategies which have proved fruitful.' Tucker held up his hand as further questions were mooted. 'I cannot of course give any of the details of this hunt. That might jeopardise the success of future operations. But I have confidence in my team – as much confidence, I venture to suggest, as they have in me.'

There were more audible mutters of derision at this, so that the television presenter drew things to an abrupt close. Chief Superintendent Tucker insisted on having the last word. He said rhetorically to the audience he imagined beyond the cameras, 'I say again rejoice. Rejoice that our streets are safer today for the absence of the man who killed James O'Connor. Rejoice in the achievements of efficient policing!'

He jutted his jaw in his practised Churchillian mode until he was quite sure that cameras and microphones had been switched off.

He had wiped off his make-up and was getting into his car when the young policewoman approached him. 'Message from DCI Peach, sir,' she said impassively. 'Apparently another Mr O'Connor has now been murdered. Name of Dominic.'

It took some time to establish the whereabouts of Dominic O'Connor's wife. Eventually the police managed to contact her cleaner, whose number Clyde Northcott had found on a pad in the house. She told them that Mrs O'Connor had been planning to stay the weekend with her sister in Settle, forty miles to the north of her home.

Normally a junior female officer would have been dispatched to break the news of the death to the newly widowed woman. On this occasion, Percy Peach asked his wife to go. 'Take Brendan Murphy with you, if you can get hold of him. I want someone as experienced as you to be there when she gets the news. I want you to see how she reacts, whether she gives any indication that she was expecting to hear this. After all, she may have arranged to be conveniently away at the time of her husband's death.'

Percy didn't voice the thought that he had been worried about Lucy ever since Linda Coleman had uttered her threats about her involvement in the child prostitution investigation. He knew he would get short shrift for trying to protect her. Perhaps he did not care to admit his fears even to himself.

For her part, Lucy Peach was happy to be involved on even the periphery of a murder investigation. She ascertained by a phone call that Ros O'Connor was indeed staying at her sister's house, then collected DC Murphy and drove swiftly north towards Settle and the Yorkshire Dales. The house she sought proved to be a modest semi-detached on the edge of the small town. This was the residence of the youngest of Mrs O'Connor's three sisters. There were children playing in the rear garden, which shrilled with happy sounds that were wholly out of kilter with Lucy's grim police mission here.

They separated Ros O'Connor from this happy family environment and isolated her in the quiet front room of the house, shutting the door tight against that very different world beyond it. They had a little difficulty getting the lady to sit down, because she was anxious to have their news without even the slightest delay. At their insistence, she sat on the edge of the armchair and looked from one to the other of her visitors. 'Two plain-clothes officers. This must be important.'

Lucy sat down opposite her, not more than six feet from the small, concerned face. 'It is. And it isn't good news, I'm afraid.'

'Is it Dominic? What's happened to him?'

'It is Mr O'Connor, yes. And I'm afraid we are the bearers of very bad tidings.'

The blue eyes seemed to grow larger as she took this in. The noise of the children's voices behind the house seemed agonising in this instant of silence. The woman perched tensely on the edge of the armchair said quietly, 'Dominic's dead, isn't he?'

'I'm afraid he is, yes.' Lucy should have said that an unidentified male had been found dead in this woman's house, that nothing could be certain until identification had been confirmed, but reality cut through the formal phrases, when the facts were as stark as this.

It was an important part of the work of Brendan Murphy and Lucy Peach to study this woman and her reactions at this moment of revelation. The only unusual element in her reaction which they would report is that she did not seem unduly surprised by the news. Even that did not necessarily mean much, because shock affects people in so many different ways.

Ros O'Connor was in jeans and a light blue short-sleeved shirt. The smear of sand across the front of this seemed suddenly poignant as she lurched from noisy play with her niece and nephew to the news of death. She was slightly built; she was also very pretty, in the small-featured way which Lucy Peach, whose charms were more opulent and less subtle, always envied. This woman had a clear skin and good features; her face had the attraction and innocence of a kitten. A strand of fair hair escaped from the order around it and trembled a little over her left temple. Her air had an odd combination of control and vulnerability. She said with a strange calmness, 'Where did this happen?'

Lucy said reluctantly, 'He was found at your own house.' That always made things worse. It might seem out of proportion, but it was always worse for people when abnormal death, whether it be suicide or murder or manslaughter, took place in the family home. For most people, it tarnished the place where it had happened for the rest of their lives. Lucy knew that and tried to make this death as peripheral as possible. 'He was found right at the back of the building, in the rearmost room on the ground floor.'

'That's his office. That's where he worked. How was he killed?'

She was accepting immediately that he had been murdered, they noticed. They had come with the news of his death and she had assumed that someone had killed him. Lucy said, 'We are not able to disclose the details yet.'

'But someone came to our house and killed him.' Ros O'Connor settled back a little into the armchair and nodded twice. 'I told him he needed to be more careful.'

Brendan Murphy made a note, then said gently, 'Why was that, Mrs O'Connor?'

She shook her head gently from side to side, seemingly more in response to her own thoughts than to the DC's question. 'Dominic moved in dangerous circles, you know. He needed to be careful. When was he killed?'

'We're not certain of that yet. There will need to be a post-mortem examination.'

'Yes. Yes, of course there will. And I'll find out how he died, eventually.'

Lucy wanted to ask her about these dangerous circles in which she said her husband had moved. But this wasn't the time. Percy and his team would follow that up in due course. And in due course they would determine just how innocent this calm but bewildered-looking woman was. 'When did you come to your sister's house, Mrs O'Connor?'

The widow did not at first appreciate the significance of the question. 'Yesterday. Yesterday afternoon. Dominic was working late yesterday. It seemed a good chance for me to see Jane and the children.' She stopped abruptly, looking at DS Peach in consternation. 'You want to know whether I could have killed Dominic, don't you? When did he die?'

'As I said, we don't know that yet. And this is merely routine, Mrs O'Connor. We check the movements of all the people who were close to any death which is not straightforward.'

'Not straightforward. You mean murder, don't you? So why not use the word?'

Lucy risked a smile, trying even in these circumstances to lower the tension. 'We usually have to waffle on about "suspicious circumstances". We haven't established for certain yet that this is murder and I haven't visited the scene myself. But from what I've heard there doesn't seem to be much doubt that someone killed him. I'm sorry.'

The small, kittenish, curiously innocent face shook from side to side. 'It's not your fault, is it? I told Dominic he should be careful.'

Lucy stood up and Brendan Foster followed her lead. 'Someone will need to speak to you again, when we know more about this. In the meantime, I must ask you whether you have any idea who might have done this awful thing.'

'No. I have no idea at all.' She spoke as if she were repeating a formula.

'Are you sure of that? You say that he should have been more careful. Do you know where the danger was coming from?'

'No. I didn't like some of the people he had to meet. But I didn't want to know anything about them.'

'Well, as I say, someone will need to ask you more questions about this, when we have established some details. In the meantime, I think you should stay here with your sister and her family. I'm afraid your home will have become a crime scene, for the moment.'

Ros O'Connor nodded several times, as if trying to tap that fact into her consciousness. 'Will Dominic need to be identified? That's what happens, isn't it?'

'That is part of the legal process, yes. And you are the most obvious person to make the identification. But if you think it would be too harrowing for you, I'm sure we can find someone else to complete the formal identification.'

'No. I think I should do that.'

'Very well, I'll make the arrangements and we'll be in touch with you here. Thank you for your help and for your calmness today. If you think of anything which might have a bearing on your husband's death, please ring this number immediately.'

They left her staring hard at the card, as if Brunton CID might have more to offer her than the simple printed details.

Jack Chadwick was a persuasive man. As SOCO officer, he managed to get a team out on Saturday afternoon to comb the office at the back of the high house where Dominic O'Connor had died.

Peach also convinced the pathologist that this crime was of sufficient importance to warrant his absence from the crowd at the Lancashire League cricket fixture at Alexandra Meadows. He inspected the newly discovered corpse and lamented Peach's absence from the East Lancs team. 'They miss you,

Percy,' he said sadly as he opened his case. 'They were fifty-one for four when I left. And none of 'em scores at the speed you used to do.'

'Nice of you to say so,' said Percy. 'But distance lends enchantment, you know. I could be pretty stodgy myself, on early season wickets. Ball moves around a lot until the ground gets firm.' He glanced up at the blue sky and high white clouds. A glorious day for cricket. Nostalgia for his lost youth and the sumptuous feel of leather on willow hit him hard for a couple of seconds. He was only thirty-nine; perhaps his mother-in-law was right and he had retired a year or two too early.

He said firmly, 'I presume he died here?'

'Certainly. And in this chair. No one's moved him,' said the pathologist.

'Did he struggle?'

'No. Not to any effect, anyway. My guess is that he lifted his hands to the cable on his neck, but didn't get his hands on his assailant. I'll check his nails carefully when I get him on the slab, but there's nothing obvious beneath them to the naked eye.'

'And the murder weapon is obvious.' They were both assuming already that this was murder.

'Obvious and distressingly ordinary, from your point of view.' The pathologist looked at the cable which was still embedded in Dominic O'Connor's neck and would remain so until he was disrobed and anatomised in the pathologist's laboratory. 'This is standard electrical cable, the kind you get on a dozen appliances in every home. It was probably brought here specially for the job, but it would have been readily available around the place if this was a spur-of-the-moment killing. With a sharp knife or heavy-duty scissors, you could simply cut it off an electric radiator or a vacuum cleaner. Or even a computer.'

They looked automatically at the PC on the desk, but its cable connected it still to the socket in the wall. It was left to DS Northcott to ask the question to which everyone in the room felt they knew the answer. 'Could this have been done by a woman?'

'It could have been done by a child, I'm afraid. No great

strength is required if you take a sitting man by surprise from the rear, and I think that is what happened here. You throw the cable round his neck, twist it tight, and then keep twisting. This didn't take long and it didn't demand any great strength. My guess is that it was swift and ruthless. Not that I'm paid to guess, of course.'

He gave a sour smile and looked at the two members of the SOCO team who were on hands and knees in opposite corners of the room, using tweezers to lift hairs and threads which would almost certainly prove to have nothing to do with this crime. The photographer's camera flashed briefly as he took a careful picture of a faint print in the carpet. There was a brief pause as the CID men and the pathologist watched him and wondered if this was the footprint of the man who had been swift and ruthless in his despatch of Dominic O'Connor.

Then Peach said, 'We know how he died and where he died. Can you help us with when?'

'Not with any accuracy, at present. I shan't even disrobe him and take a renal temperature until these boys have finished examining his clothes. I'll have a better idea when I get him on the table. If you can find when he last ate, I'll give you a reasonably accurate time of death from the stomach contents.'

'But he hasn't died today?'

'Almost certainly not, I think. You'll have to wait for the official PM to give you anything you could quote in court, and rigor mortis isn't going to tell us a great deal, because the temperature in this room has varied so widely over the last twenty-four hours – not too far above freezing last night and up into the eighties with the sun blazing through that window today.'

'Give us a guess. We won't hold you to it.'

The pathologist smiled wryly. 'This man has clearly been dead for many hours. I'd say last night, but it could have been earlier.'

Five hours later, the street lights were on in Belfast.

The day in Northern Ireland had not been as sunny as in Lancashire. Now the clouds seemed to be dropping even lower over the city as darkness took over. There was a little light yet in the west, in the fields outside the city, but here a thin drizzle fell over river and streets and night had dropped in early.

This narrow street wasn't far from the Falls Road. It was little more than a hundred yards long, but there had been six killings here twenty years earlier, and a sectarian bitterness still ran deep in the veins of both sides. The houses seemed to carry the shadow of those killings still, so that the atmosphere on a night like this was as gloomy and hopeless as the black and starless sky above.

The man looked automatically over his shoulder at the corner of the street. He had no reason to think that he was being followed – indeed, he was certain that he wasn't. But old habits, as this furtive figure told anyone who cared to listen, died hard. And this was a man who was proud of what he had done during the Troubles, not ashamed of it. He carried the list of his killings in his mind like his own roll of honour. He still moved almost exclusively among those who had supported him then and who continued to feel as he did now.

There were few people abroad here at this hour. Fanaticism and bloody history had left their legacy. The non-violent and the uncommitted had left these streets as soon as they could. Twenty years ago, your very life had been at stake if you walked here at this hour. There was less violence now, though the occasional kneecapping settled old scores and reminded residents of how deep the playwright Sean O'Casey's 'murdering hate' still ran in this part of Belfast.

This section of the city was now largely occupied by an underclass who lived on the edge of the law and frequently beyond it. Petty thieves predominated, often with the added violence which accompanied muggings. There was also a growing amount of freelance prostitution, practised by women of various ages who were bold enough or desperate enough to ply their trade without the protection of a pimp.

The man who moved swiftly and close to the walls knew these streets and was not afraid. Courage was a quality he had always possessed. It had been taken for granted as he had shaped his violent career and risen through the ranks. His spell in the Maze prison had been a badge of honour when he issued orders to the younger men who had followed him into the Provisionals. And then, abruptly, he and his friends had been sold out, when Blair and the Irish traitors had reached their settlement.

Well, there were still a few good men left. And there was still work to be done. There were still Irish men and the odd Irish woman who needed punishing. They knew who they were. And when you got to them and dealt with them, you issued a lesson to others too. The cause was still alive. People who didn't recognise that needed regular reminders. You hadn't got the English army men here as your obvious quarry, as you'd had in the glory days. Today's targets were fewer and it took longer to get to them. But you had all the time in the world. When you'd fought for hundreds of years and now were almost there, you could afford to wait patiently for your opportunities.

This man enjoyed secrecy. He'd lived by it for many years now – since he was fifteen, in fact. It had become a way of life for him and he would have been loath to discard it now. He pulled the baseball cap more firmly over his forehead and thrust his hands deeper into the pockets of his shabby blue anorak. His right hand gripped the butt of the pistol he always kept there; he found the feel of it reassuring, even when it was not loaded. Not many of the old terraced houses he was passing had lights visible. Most of them were occupied, but people for the most part chose to live at the back of them, as if they knew that it was politic to mind their own business and maintain an ignorance of whatever else went on around them.

The door opened almost as he knocked, so suddenly that he almost lost his balance and fell forwards. The shaft of light from within the house flashed unnaturally bright across the wet flags, and then he was in and the door was shutting behind him. The man who led him through to the shabby room at the rear of the house was old. The grey stubble on his chin was a result of a failure to shave rather than an attempt at a beard. He had been driven for years by hate, which operated like a life force within him, far more important to his being than food or drink. He was diminished since the Good Friday agreement. His life was petering out, but he kept it going by the news he gathered from his old juniors, from the evidence they brought to him that violence could still be effective. The settling of old scores renewed his faith. Death or damage to those who had frustrated the cause operated like blood transfusions on his failing body.

The man who had come here understood all of this. He had operated under this man's command in the battles of the last century; he clung to the camaraderie of the glory days even in these less stirring times. There was a whisky poured ready for him on the table. He clinked glasses with the old man and they downed the Jameson's to one of the old toasts. Neither of them was really a drinker; they had seen too often in the dangerous years how drink had made others vulnerable.

The man slipped off his baseball cap. Despite the drink, it was his first real evidence of relaxation. He grinned at his old commander. He wanted to prolong the giving of his good news, but that wouldn't be fair. So he said simply, 'Dominic O'Connor's been seen off.'

Then he clasped the gnarled old fingers in his. The two men raised their linked hands skywards, in a hideous parody of the consecration in the Catholic Mass.

TEN

She'd been crying. That much was obvious. She had done her best to disguise it, but she was puffy around the eyes and unnaturally pale. These things are difficult to disguise, as she'd realised twenty minutes ago when she stood in front of the mirror in the cloakroom and studied her face.

But there was surely nothing wrong with a PA being upset by her employer's death. Dominic O'Connor had been a good employer to Jean Parker. They'd worked together for over four years. These were the first things she told the detectives when they came into the office to speak to her. She was a slim,

attractive woman. Her soft brown hair was cut short and her
dark grey eyes were very alert. She wore a lightweight grey
suit over a white blouse.

Peach watched DS Northcott note the facts Mrs Parker had
given him, then said, 'Your employer was killed methodically
and very deliberately by someone. This doesn't look to us like
a spur-of-the-moment murder or an argument which spilled
over into violence. We think whoever went to the house went
there with homicide in mind. Have you any idea who that
might have been?'

'No. I've been thinking about it ever since I heard the awful
news. I'm not naïve – I know you make enemies when you're
successful in business, so I've been thinking of possibilities
since I heard he was dead. But I haven't thought of anyone
who might have hated Dominic enough to kill him.'

Both Peach and Clyde Northcott noticed the use of the first
name and wondered what degree of intimacy it implied. But
relationships between employers and PAs were not as formal
as they had once been and nor were the titles used. 'Mr
O'Connor's brother was shot only a few days ago. Do you
think there is a connection between these two deaths?'

She allowed herself a small, bitter smile, the first one they
had seen from her. 'Shouldn't I be asking you that? You're
the ones with the experience of murder and the sort of people
who perpetrate it.'

'Indeed we are. But you're the one who knows the victim
and his associates. We are dependent upon you and people
like you for information. Apart from his wife, you probably
know more about this victim's life and the dangers it carried
than anyone.'

Both of them noticed a twitch of her face when the widow
was mentioned, but it came and went so quickly that it was
difficult even to guess at what it might mean. Peach said
quietly, 'It is your duty to be as frank as possible with us, Ms
Parker. The crime we're investigating is murder.'

'I'm Mrs Parker, please. Normally I wouldn't speculate
about my employer's marriage, but in these exceptional circumstances I will tell you that I think there were problems.'

These were phrases which she had obviously prepared

beforehand. Peach said, 'You are doing the right thing. You should be aware that we are normally very discreet. Anything you tell us which proves to have nothing to do with this death will not be made public.'

She nodded impatiently, anxious to tell her tale and have done with it. 'There's been a little gossip around the office. Mr O'Connor apparently had what one of the women here called a roving eye. Lots of men have that. The higher up they are in the system, the more they suffer from the gossip. People love to spread rumours about the boss. How much was just innocent flirting and how much was more serious than that I really couldn't say.'

'Couldn't or wouldn't, Mrs Parker?' Percy was quietly insistent, despite his smile.

'Couldn't, Mr Peach. I try to steer clear of tittle tattle. I see that as loyalty to my employer and thus part of my job. Dominic's business life, not his private life, was my concern.'

'Admirable, I'm sure. But a pity, nevertheless, from our standpoint, in view of what has now happened to Mr O'Connor.'

She shrugged her slim shoulders beneath the lightweight jacket. 'If you want my opinion, I think Dominic had affairs. I think that is why he had difficulties with his marriage. But that is no more than an opinion. I cannot give you any facts or any significant detail to support that view.'

'So he was a womaniser.' Peach waited for her reaction to the word. She frowned but said nothing. 'Not a good thing, from where we stand. Sex leads to passion and passion too often leads to violent and impetuous actions. But so, in our experience, does success in business. And his work is something you do know about, as you've already told us. Very few people succeed in business without making enemies along the way. No doubt you can identify for us some of the enemies Mr Dominic O'Connor made.'

Clyde Northcott flicked ostentatiously to a new page in his notebook and reflected once again on how his senior made bricks from however little straw was offered to him – this woman had said she knew only his working and not his private life and he'd immediately quoted that to make her speak.

But now Jean Parker picked her words carefully; Clyde couldn't be sure whether that came from a natural caution she had developed with her job or whether she was really trying to hide something. 'Dominic wasn't the owner of this business. He was the successful finance manager within it.'

'He was a partner. He became a partner two years ago. We've already checked that out.'

They thought in the pause which followed that she was going to say she hadn't known about that. But she eventually said, 'That is a tribute to his efficiency. I don't think you will find anyone in the firm who will say that Dominic was other than highly efficient.'

Was there a tiny suggestion of bitterness in her repetition of that last word? Peach let the thought hang in the air for a moment before he said, 'One man's efficiency is sometimes another man's dirty trick. Verdicts can alter with where you stand and how actions affect you. We'd like the names of anyone who felt aggrieved by any action taken by Dominic O'Connor.'

She was a surprising woman. They would have expected evasions, after what had gone before. Instead she said abruptly, 'Brian Jacobs. I'm not saying he had anything to do with this, mind. I haven't seen him for years. I think he still lives in the area, but I can't give you an address.'

'Did he work for a rival firm?'

'No. He worked here. He did the job that Dominic did, when the firm was smaller than it is now.'

'And he resented the way Mr O'Connor behaved?'

'You'd have to ask him about that. I don't know any details. I hadn't been here long, at the time.'

Northcott made a note of the name, then asked, 'Is there anyone else who had a grudge against Mr O'Connor?'

'No. There must obviously be a whole range of people in other firms who were business rivals, especially after he became a partner here, but I don't know that any of them would admit to having a grudge against Dominic.'

She came to the door and watched them depart, a slim, composed figure, with shrewd grey eyes and an air of being in total control of her office domain. They were half a mile away in the car before Peach said, 'Pretty formal in her attitudes, Mrs Jean Parker.'

'Yes. Goes with the job as a PA, I suppose.'

'Yes. But she slipped into calling her employer Dominic pretty quickly, didn't she? I appreciate that office conventions are more relaxed than they used to be, but I wonder just how close the very composed Mrs Parker was to her late employer.'

Back in the office they had left, Jean Parker was examining her reactions to their visit. She should have felt relieved. Instead she found she felt curiously empty, now that it was over. She'd told them exactly what she'd planned to tell them and it seemed to have gone quite well. Now she wanted to ring Brian Jacobs and warn him of what she'd said.

There was really no need for that. What she'd told the CID was what they'd agreed beforehand, no more and no less. It was Brian who'd said that they'd be determined to find out about him, that it was better if they heard it from her lips than dug it up for themselves. He'd planned it and he would handle it, as they both knew he could.

But Jean Parker felt deprived. She would have liked to be at Brian's side as he saw this through.

They didn't have much time for reflection when they got back to the police station at Brunton. The station sergeant stopped them at the front desk as they moved towards the CID section. 'God Squad's waiting for you in your office, Percy. Catholic priest from St Catherine's. What you been up to? I told you to keep away from them choir boys!'

Police humour is robust and predictable rather than subtle. Percy smiled sourly. 'If you've been rifling his poor box, George, your best chance is to admit your guilt and go for mitigating circumstances. I'd like to tell him you've been working hard and been under stress, but they might have me for perjury.'

When he reached his office, he reflected wryly that he should have learned by now not to form clichéd premonitions about occupations. He had been expecting a red-faced and portly middle-aged cleric with an Irish accent. The man who introduced himself as Father Raymond Brice was tall and slim and no more than thirty-five. He had a tanned face and a firm chin and he spoke English with a slight Geordie inflexion. 'I'm not sure if I should be here at all, DCI Peach. You must send me away quickly if you think I'm wasting your time.'

'We're glad of all the help we can get, Father.'

'I know the family. The O'Connors, I mean.'

'James or Dominic? They're both murder victims.'

'And I knew both of them. I'm here about Dominic, the younger brother. He's the one I knew well. I know the family – well, husband and wife. They weren't blessed with children. I suppose that might be a good thing now, with Dominic lying in the morgue.'

Percy decided to save time and take the initiative. 'We heard earlier this morning that this was not a straightforward marriage. Perhaps you can throw more light on that for us.'

Father Brice looked troubled. He sighed and said, 'That's why I'm here. I'm still not sure whether I should be.'

'You're worried about whether you should reveal the secrets of the confessional to us?'

The priest smiled and relaxed for the first time since they had arrived. 'No, it's not that old chestnut. Modern Catholics don't use the confessional as much as they used to, which may be a good or a bad thing. We priests still don't disclose anything revealed to us in that private little cell, which is one of the strengths of the system. If people don't believe they can trust us completely, they don't seek absolution for their sins. And forgiveness comes from God, not from us. That's another illusion many of the public have, that priests can forgive sins. We're just intermediaries between man and God.'

'Forgive me, Father, but I know all this. I began life as a Catholic.'

For a moment, it looked as if Father Brice might embark on a mission to retrieve the lost sheep, but something in Percy Peach's countenance made him think better of it. 'None of what I have to say here comes from the confessional. I have gathered it from other and less formal contacts. The modern pastor is expected to get to know his flock. I've learned quite a lot about Dominic and Ros O'Connor, both from themselves and from other people.' He sighed. 'We're expected to be counsellors as much as confessors, these days.'

'So what can you tell us?' Peach tried not to show his impatience with this well-meaning man who had obviously found it difficult to come here.

'It's Ros O'Connor.' The priest's relief at being pushed to reveal the name was obvious. It made it seem as if the detectives and not he had taken the initiative and given him no option. 'She's a good woman, but a woman under stress. I'm not a psychologist and I'm not sure how they would define the word, but I think she's unstable.'

Peach said quietly, 'You'd better give us the details.'

Father Brice leaned forward, clasping his hands and pressing them hard together. It was obviously a gesture he made which helped him to think. He looked slightly ridiculous, as if squeezing some imaginary orange in search of juice. But priests did not have wives to tell them to abandon ridiculous gestures; Percy had a sudden vision of the loneliness of clerical evenings, of the quiet desperation of a life lived alone with problems you could not reveal. Then Brice said, 'They're good Catholics, the O'Connors – whatever that means nowadays. They attend Mass each Sunday and receive Communion most times. That doesn't mean that they're not subject to the same pressures of modern life which others feel.'

Peach felt for the priest and saw the internal struggle this was costing him, but he now wanted whatever he could get from this to be delivered quickly. He said briskly, as if he already had the information from some other source, 'They weren't faithful to each other, were they?'

Again Brice looked as if being led was a relief to him. 'No. There were all sorts of rumours about Dominic.'

Clyde Northcott said eagerly, with pen poised over notebook, 'We need the details, Father.'

Brice glanced across at him as if he had forgotten for a moment that the DS was in the room, a difficult thing to achieve with Northcott's formidable presence. 'I can't give you details.'

'I appreciate that you cannot reveal the secrets of the confessional, Father, but you should be aware that this is a murder—'

'It's nothing to do with the damned secrets of the confession! I told you that!' The near-shout showed the strain the priest was enduring. He controlled himself with a visible effort and a very deep breath. 'Neither Dominic nor Ros confessed any sexual sins to me. It's embarrassing to parade your defects to someone you know, as you can probably imagine. Most people prefer to go to priests who do not know them when they have serious sins to confess. They feel the need for absolution, but they prefer a more anonymous intermediary between themselves and Almighty God than the man they know and the man who knows them.'

Peach nodded. He felt as if he himself was now assuming the role of therapist to this troubled man. 'But the O'Connors talked to you about this.'

He nodded eagerly. 'But not in the confessional and not together. And Dominic scarcely at all, except in the most general terms. But Ros is a tortured soul. She was quite frank with me when she felt desperate. And you hear rumours from other people, even when you don't want to hear them. They assume you know all sorts of things which you don't know.'

Peach prompted him. 'We already know from other sources that Mr O'Connor was a womaniser. He is now a murder victim and his womanising may be a factor in his death. Can you give us any information about his liaisons?'

Father Brice shook his head. 'I'm sure they exist and perhaps there have been several of them. But my only source is Ros and she isn't reliable when she speaks of this. She loses judgement and becomes hysterical. According to Ros, Dominic was bedding almost every woman he met, which was plainly ridiculous. I tried to point that out to her and she'd nod and agree with me, but then come up with something just as outlandish a moment later.'

'But you have some information for us about Ros herself. That is why you came here this morning.'

'She is a troubled soul and I fear unstable, as I said at the outset. I believe she has turned elsewhere for consolation, despite my advice. Sometimes I'm treated as a marriage guidance counsellor, when I have no training in such fields.'

'We need names, Father Brice.'

'Mrs O'Connor is not a promiscuous woman. She has acted rashly, under stress. I can give you one name, in strictest confidence. A man called John Alderson.'

He enunciated the syllables with obvious distaste, so that Peach said, 'He is obviously a man of whom you don't approve.'

'I couldn't approve any association outside marriage, could I? I haven't heard much that's good about Alderson from other people, but it's hardly fair for me to condemn a man I hardly know. But I can't approve his relationship with Ros O'Connor and I've told her that several times.'

'You said she isn't promiscuous. But is there any other person connected with her whom you think you should name here? Bear in mind that we are looking for a murderer.'

They could see him relaxing. Plainly he had rid himself of the burden he had brought here with him when he named John Alderson. He gave full attention to their question, but he was not wrestling with his conscience as he had been until now. 'There's no one else I know who is close to Ros. I'm sure there are several people who had reasons to wish Dominic O'Connor ill, in his private as well as his business life. But I cannot name any of them for you, because Dominic didn't confide in me as Ros did.'

It was a measured statement which he'd obviously thought about before he came to the station. Peach looked at him hard, but eventually believed him. He didn't give undue weight to the cloth clergymen wore any more, but Father Brice was patently sincere and genuine, a man who had found it hard to come here and had done so from a sense of duty, not personal interest. Percy thanked him for his help and then, with their meeting all but concluded, pointed out, 'You've twice used the word "unstable" about Mrs O'Connor. You clearly have an incident or incidents in mind.'

Raymond Brice nodded, regretful and relieved at the same time. He wanted this out. It was what he had come here for, to pass the burden of knowledge on to the appropriate temporal authority whilst he wrestled with its spiritual implications. 'Ros said she could kill her husband.'

Peach smiled. 'It's the kind of thing many wives say under

stress. I think I've even heard it said about someone as innocent as me, in moments of wifely stress.'

Father Brice smiled back automatically, but then his mouth wrinkled with irritation. 'Give me credit for a little understanding of the way people think and talk, DCI Peach. Killing Dominic was mentioned several times over a period of months and it wasn't humorous. On the last occasion, Ros O'Connor said she was fearful of what she might do.'

Peach was on his way out of the station when the summons came. He considered ignoring it, but he had always chosen to face bad things quickly rather than put them off. Ogres always grew more fearful with anticipation. And there was no greater ogre in Peach's world than Chief Superintendent Thomas Bulstrode Tucker. He climbed the stairs to the penthouse office of Brunton's Head of CID with a steadily sinking heart.

Tucker regarded him balefully over his rimless glasses, as if waiting for the abject apology which was not Percy's forte. 'So,' he said eventually. 'We have an arrest for the murder of James O'Connor.'

'Peter Coleman has been arrested, charged and remanded in custody this morning, sir. Be good to see one of our least savoury residents put behind bars for a very long time, don't you think? Even the CPS wankers are happy with the case we have delivered to them.'

When you mentioned lawyers, one of the banes of police life, you could usually rely on a moment of agreement even with Tommy Bloody Tucker. A moment for the mutual casting of eyebrows to heaven would certainly have been in order. This would have been followed by congratulations from the chief on a swift success in a high-profile case, if there had been any justice.

But this was T.B. Tucker and there wasn't. He shook his head vigorously and said, 'It won't do, Peach.'

Percy strove to keep a check on his blood pressure. Tucker in bollocking mode was one of life's more stringent trials. 'What won't do, sir?'

'What's happening on our patch won't do! I call a media conference and trumpet our success in solving the murder of a popular local businessman and former rugby international. I tell television, radio and press how efficient we have been. Good PR, Peach! Something you know very little about. But the next thing I hear is that you've landed me with another murder, before I can even catch my breath. It won't do!'

'Is that me or the CID unit as a whole that's landed you with another murder, sir?'

'Don't be impertinent, Peach. I'm not in the mood for it.'

'Then perhaps you will explain to me how we are responsible for the death of Dominic O'Connor, sir.'

Tucker's hands rose and fell at his sides. He repeated the gesture, reminding Percy of a portly young blackbird who had but lately left the nest and had not yet learned the full secrets of flight. 'Detection is not merely about reacting to crime, Peach. You should anticipate things and nip them in the bud.' His face brightened as a phrase surfaced suddenly in the heaving swamp of his mind. 'A decent Detective Chief Inspector needs to be proactive, not reactive.'

He drummed his fingers on the shining desert of his desktop to emphasise his point, whilst his junior wondered which management course had provided him with this phrase. Percy's face brightened as if illuminated by an unexpected gem of thought. 'Perhaps your comprehensive overview of crime in the area should have revealed the prospect of a second O'Connor killing to us, sir.' Percy beamed his satisfaction at that idea.

'Don't be ridiculous, Peach. What is the connection between the killing of these two brothers?'

'There may not be one, sir.'

'May not be one? But surely . . .' Tucker passed appealingly into goldfish mode.

'Or on the other hand, there might.' Percy nodded gnomically, as if the weight of philosophy involved in this observation pressed heavy upon his noble brow.

'Now look here, Peach! We need facts, not speculation.'

'Enquiries are proceeding, sir. I've already had the local Catholic priest who claims to be their pastor in here and given him a thorough grilling.'

He forbore to smile at the thought of earnest Father Brice

and his genuine desire to help. Tommy Bloody Tucker's reaction was as predictable as he had expected. 'You must tread very carefully whenever religion is involved, Peach. How many times do I have to tell you that?'

'You don't, sir. The man came here himself. Presented himself for our inspection. A bold move, I think you'll agree. I wondered if I should give him a bit of the third degree treatment over sexual assaults on minors, in view of his church's deplorable record over the last few years.'

'You'll do no such thing, Peach! I expressly forbid it!'

Peach's face fell as he abandoned his enthusiasm. 'Very well, sir. I hear you. Perhaps that line of questioning would be better left to you. I'm sure your overview will enable you to put any local clerical assaults in the context of a more national picture.'

'Who killed Dominic O'Connor, Peach?'

Percy's eyes widened as his eyebrows rose impossibly high beneath the bald pate. Then he allowed a slow chuckle to spread through his torso. 'You don't lose your sense of humour, do you, sir? Enquiries are proceeding, as you would no doubt tell the media. No stone is being left unturned. That is the official line. In private police parlance, I haven't a fucking clue, sir. Not as yet.'

Percy didn't swear anything like as often as most modern police officers, male or female. But he found as he descended the stairs that this particular lapse had given him disproportionate pleasure.

What DCI Peach had said to his chief was quite true: he didn't yet know whether the deaths of the two O'Connor brothers were connected. It seemed an almost impossible coincidence that they wouldn't be, but what he had heard from Dominic O'Connor's PA and from Father Brice suggested that the second death might be a more complex mystery than the first one had proved.

Clyde Northcott still hoped the same man might have dispatched both brothers. He voiced that thought as they journeyed to Strangeways to interview Peter Coleman, who had been remanded in custody after being charged with the murder of James O'Connor. 'Let's hope it's him. Be nice and simple, that would. Help our clear-up rates. It would even please Tommy Bloody Tucker.'

'There's no pleasing Tommy Bloody Tucker,' said Peach gloomily. 'You might as well try to please a camel with indigestion. But I know what you mean. It would make life a lot simpler if we could get Coleman to admit this one as well and save us chasing our tails around.'

Peter Coleman looked a different proposition from the truculent hard man they had seen when they'd interviewed him three days earlier. He'd been confident then, defying them to arrest him; now he looked every inch the criminal he was. The warder set him in his chair and stood impassively behind his man, but there seemed little chance now of this powerfully built man offering any physical aggression. His hair was cut close, emphasising the size of his head and his neck, but the anonymous prison garb made him look smaller and less formidable than when they had confronted him in the hut on the building site.

When Peach did not speak but merely stared at him and assessed him, Coleman could not withstand the silence. 'I've nothing to say to you, Peach. I'll deal with you when I get out of here.'

'We could both be old men by then. DS Northcott might still enjoy knocking you about, though. He might still be a hard bastard, if he keeps himself in trim.' He glanced appreciatively at the formidable black presence beside him.

'I've got a good lawyer, Peach. We'll see you in the Crown Court.'

Peach's grin suffused his whole countenance, a frightening sight for any criminal, let alone one accused of the most serious crime of all. 'I shall look forward to it. Especially as we have witnesses and evidence that are proof against even the best defence counsel. When he sees the prosecution case, he'll be telling you to plead guilty and scratch together some sort of mitigating circumstance – though what that might be, I can't imagine.' He hit Coleman with the confident smile of a man with three aces in his hand and a spare one up his sleeve.

'It's circumstantial. It won't stand up. Not when Patterson

gets to work on it.' He threw in the name of the man who had conducted numerous complex and lucrative defence cases over the last ten years. Then he tried to trump Peach's smile with one of his own. In that contest, he failed abjectly, as many had done before him.

Percy said abruptly. 'You were seen parking your car and slipping over the wall of Claughton Towers twenty minutes before the killing. You were seen scrambling into it and driving away five minutes after it. You were in charge of Lennon's muscle and you're known to have killed before. We'll produce people who worked for you to send you down. Rats desert sinking ships very fast, Pete. You'll go down on the vermin vote.'

'We'll bloody see about that,' said Coleman. But it was a ritual defiance. His voice carried no conviction and his coarse face was pale.

Peach judged that he'd done enough softening up to move now to the reason for their visit. 'We're here about your second murder. When we add the death of Dominic O'Connor to that of James, they'll be able to throw away the key.'

'I didn't kill Dominic. You're not pinning that one on me.'

'Be easy to do that, I should think, after they've nailed you for Jim. Jury's going to be well set to have you for Dominic as well, after they've heard about Jim.'

'But I didn't do it. I couldn't have done it. Your lot arrested me on Saturday. Burst in on me whilst I was still in bed with Linda, the way you pigs like to do. Your boss was telling anyone who'd listen that you'd arrested me for murder by Saturday lunch time.'

'Heard about that, have you? He does a good line in boasting, our boss does.' Peach's voice hardened. 'But it doesn't get you off the hook, Pete boy. Dominic O'Connor was murdered on Friday night, when you were still at large and obeying your latest orders.'

'But I didn't do it. What happened to innocent until proved guilty, Peach?'

'Nothing at all, Pete boy. It remains a basic principle of the English law. And an admirable one, no doubt about that, despite what frustrated coppers might say. But it doesn't always operate in practice. I'm no lawyer, thank God, but my guess is that when we've got you banged to rights for one murder, the jury and everyone else in court will be more inclined to think you guilty of another. Especially when they're looking at a man who's made his living by violence for years, like you.' Percy nodded two or three times, then let a smile steal slowly over his round face at his happiness in that thought.

'I was with my wife on Friday night.'

'Ah, the old wife alibi. Suspicious but difficult to disprove.'

'You ask Linda. She'll tell you.'

'She might. Unfortunately for you, she might be in clink herself by the time your case comes to court. We know all about her involvement in the procurement of minors for prostitution and worse. We'll be delighted to put her away. That won't make her a very reliable witness for you, though, will it?'

'I didn't kill Dominic O'Connor. I'm not worried what you do.'

'Ah, the joys of a clear conscience! But it must be a long time since you knew anything about that, Mr Coleman. Best thing you could do about this second murder is admit it and put in a plea for mercy, I should think. The court might appreciate your honesty if you did that, but I wouldn't rely on it. We'll leave you to think about it. Lot of time for thought in here, I expect.'

It was a relief to move through the old prison entrance and out into the bright sunlight of the May day. They were well on the way back to Brunton when Clyde Northcott, who was driving, said, 'You gave him a fair going over in there.'

'Yes. Quite enjoyed it. I don't feel any obligations towards scum like Coleman. Or his wife, for that matter; you can't get lower than pushing kids from care homes into prostitution and making them victims of gang rape.'

'Peter Coleman won't come out for a long time. We've got a safe case on the murder of James O'Connor.'

'Yes.' Peach looked away thoughtfully over the moors as they slid by on his left. 'He didn't kill Dominic O'Connor, though, did he? We've got a whole new can of worms to deal with there.'

ELEVEN

The widow of the elder O'Connor brother was coping well with his death. It was a week now since James had died. Sarah had coped with the pressures of sympathy from those around her and those at a distance. She had composed a standard letter of thanks for the messages of condolence which had poured in from England and Ireland – Jim's death at Claughton Towers had been too dramatic and well-publicised for people to miss it.

The most difficult thing for her to handle had been her daughter's grief. Clare had been the person in the world hit hardest by Jim's killing. She had been close to her father as she grew up, in the way that daughters are. He had been away from home a lot when she was young, but he had been able to indulge her when he appeared, in the manner which was customary for doting dads.

Clare had taken Jim's death hard and the fact that she was an intelligent girl had made it more difficult for her mother. Her daughter had seen through Sarah's conventional protestations of grief, been sceptical about the prayers and the trappings of religion behind which she had tried to retreat. 'You didn't feel like I did about Dad. I'm sure you had your reasons. But, Mum, don't pretend you're devastated by this when you aren't. That would make it much worse for me to bear.'

They'd had an uneasy weekend, but Clare had gone back to university now. No doubt she would find her consolation with the thin and pimply youth who had been with her at Claughton Towers on that fatal Monday night. Jim had been baffled by what his daughter saw in that tongue-tied youth who was in so many ways still a boy; he'd been unable to divine what it was that attracted Clare. Probably the lad was good in bed; Sarah certainly hoped he was. She hoped he would provide consolation and diversion for Clare, rather than allowing her thoughts to dwell on the mother who seemed so little affected by her husband's death.

No one knew the full story of their marriage and she had every intention of keeping it that way. These things were private and it was much better for all concerned if they stayed private. It was the same with grief. Sarah had a greater grief than Clare thought she had for Jim. But her mourning for him was for times long gone and what might have been, not for the man he had been at his death. Her task now was to keep control of herself until the world resumed its normal rhythms.

She decided on Tuesday morning that she would tidy the bathroom and remove all Jim's stuff from it. It had to be done and she needed a task to occupy her. She took the waste bin with her and began to pitch male toiletries into it. She had scarcely begun when the phone rang. For the last few days, she'd been letting it ring and waiting until the evening to listen to whatever messages people left. But normal service must be resumed at some time. She went into the bedroom and picked up the receiver there.

An impassive female voice told her that Detective Chief Inspector Peach would like to speak to her as soon as possible. She told the woman that he should come to the house now. Best get it over with, she told herself as she put the phone down. But she could feel the pulse in her temple beginning to race.

The post-mortem and forensics reports on Dominic O'Connor didn't offer the CID team anything they hadn't expected.

He had died quickly, throttled within seconds by means of a cable thrown round his neck, almost certainly from behind him as he sat at his desk. The victim had lifted his hands in an attempt to drag the cable from his neck, but had not reached as far as his attacker, for there was nothing useful found on his hands or beneath his fingernails. The death weapon was available but uninformative. Forensics had already examined the cable which had been embedded in the corpse's neck and found it to be the sort of electrical cable attached to millions of household machines around the country. The assailant had probably brought it with him, but even if he hadn't the five-feet length applied would have been readily available on appliances within the house.

The report pointed out that the criminal could possibly have been a woman; the victim appeared to have been taken by surprise, in which case no great physical strength would have been required. The ends of the cable bore signs of being twisted hard and fast between someone's hands, but there was nothing useful in the way of fingerprints: the attacker had almost certainly worn gloves.

In the hours after O'Connor's death, the door of the room which had been his office had been shut, as had the large, south-facing window. The room temperature had varied from near-freezing overnight to almost ninety degrees Fahrenheit as the sun had poured through that window before the body was discovered on Saturday afternoon. Therefore any deductions from the progress of rigor mortis must necessarily be highly tentative, which made the establishment of a time of death very difficult.

However, analysis of stomach contents indicated that a substantial cold meal of sandwiches, fruit and fruit cake had been consumed some two hours before death. An almost empty flask of coffee had been found in the bottom drawer of the desk. O'Connor had died more than twenty – and anything up to thirty – hours before he was discovered at 16.07 by DCI Peach and DS Northcott. Establishing the time when he had last eaten would pinpoint the time of death.

Forensics had found fibres on the corpse's person which were from someone else's clothing, as well as hairs which were quite certainly from someone else's head. These might of course have no connection with the murder. A locked drawer contained personal letters which had been fingerprinted by forensics and had now been passed to the man in charge of the investigation.

Peach and Northcott immediately found one of these very relevant.

Peach thought Sarah O'Connor looked rather more upset than she'd been six days earlier, when they'd interviewed her about the murder of her husband. Her face was composed but very white beneath the shining black hair; her dark eyes glittered deep in their sockets. She looked as if she had not slept well. There was nothing necessarily significant in that. Shock can be delayed as well as immediate.

James's widow remembered not only Clyde Northcott's name, but his detective sergeant rank, which was unusual.

The CID men looked round the big comfortable room with its luxurious furnishings and fittings. As if she read their thoughts, she said quickly, 'This place is far too big for me. Clare's off at university and I'm rattling around in this mansion. I shan't stay here, once Jim is buried and I can feel closure.'

Peach nodded. 'We should be able to release his body quite soon now. You will have heard that we've made an arrest for his murder.'

'Yes. A man called Peter Coleman, they said on the radio this morning. Not a name I know. But I kept well clear of Jim's business deals.' She sounded as if she was deliberately distancing herself from both her husband and his death.

'You've missed nothing by not knowing Coleman. He's a violent man who's committed other crimes. We shall get him for this one. He's going to go down for a long time.'

'That's good. You're used to hearing threats of violence, when you're married to a prominent Irishman, but you somehow don't think it will ever happen to anyone close to you.'

'And now your brother-in-law has been killed as well. Only a day after you'd met him in the Grouse Inn on the side of Pendle Hill. That must have been another terrible shock for you.'

'It was. A woman officer called Peach interviewed me on Saturday about Dominic. Would she be any relation to you, DCI Peach?'

He smiled. 'Detective Sergeant Peach is my wife, Mrs O'Connor. We used to work together, but police procedure dictates that partners cannot work together as a pairing. Lucy was excellent at distracting susceptible males, among other things. DS Northcott doesn't do that; he is able to offer a more physical presence, whenever it is needed.'

Sarah smiled at the big black man, who inclined his head an inch forward in acknowledgement. Then she said, 'Your wife is quite a looker, DCI Peach.' She waited unsuccessfully for a reaction. 'Still, you might be better with your new partner in a crisis.'

'Yes. It seemed rather a strange time for you to be meeting alone with your brother-in-law.'

She thought of saying that she'd already told his wife her reasons for that. But she decided that it was better for her to be as cooperative as she could be. 'There were some nasty people around Jim, at times. Dominic thought he knew who had killed him. That's why we met.'

'I see.'

'He wanted to check a few things out with me. Whether certain people who were at Claughton Towers last Monday night were there at Jim's invitation or mine, for instance. He thought he'd glimpsed the man you mentioned, Peter Coleman, just before Jim was killed. He knew the people Coleman worked for and he wanted to check on one or two of the invitees for that reason.' She had been so composed that it was a surprise when her voice broke suddenly on her next words. 'He . . . he knew far more about the people Jim worked with and the people who were his business rivals than I did. Dominic steered clear, but he knew a lot of things about Jim.'

'Do you think that is what cost Dominic his life?'

She was shaken by the question. 'I don't know, do I? I don't see why – Dominic didn't fish in the same murky pools as Jim.'

'But two brothers killed in the same week. It would be amazing if there wasn't a connection between the two deaths, don't you think?'

'I suppose it would. I hadn't really considered the matter before.'

Peach doubted that, but he didn't pursue the notion. 'Policemen have to keep open minds. We're doing just that.'

Sarah stared down at the elegant navy leather shoes beneath the dark blue trousers which clothed her long legs. 'You know your own business best. I hope you find who killed Dominic as quickly as you did Jim's killer.'

'We shall need to know much more than we do at present about the months before his death. I think you can help us with that.'

If he had expected to startle her, he was disappointed. She continued looking down at her feet and allowed herself no more than a small, controlled sigh. 'And why would you think that, Mr Peach?'

'We're still investigating the victim's possessions. We found personal letters in a locked drawer in his desk. One of them was from you.'

Now at last she looked at him, with a mixture of fear and resentment on her white face. 'I had nothing to do with Dominic's death.'

'You had been conducting an affair with Dominic. You've chosen not to disclose that to us. Secrecy is never a wise policy after a murder. It excites suspicion.'

'It was all over.'

'It doesn't seem so, from what you said in your letter.'

Her eyes had tears in them, but she brushed the moisture away angrily before it could run down her cheeks. 'This is humiliating.'

'I appreciate that. But we need the details of this. We need to know when this close relationship with your brother-in-law began, how intense it was, when it finished, if indeed it did end as you claim. It is one strand of our enquiry. There will be many others. If your relationship has nothing to do with this death, what you tell us will go no further.'

Being the wife of a powerful industrialist had brought privileges to Sarah O'Connor over the last decade. It was years since she had been called upon to account for herself, years since anyone had treated her other than deferentially. She folded her arms deliberately and made herself look at this aggressive and insistent man. Then she forced herself to speak slowly and evenly. 'I slept with Dominic for the first time last summer. That would make it about ten months ago. I expect it seems shocking to you because he was as you say my brother-in-law. That was a mere accident: I don't think either of us considered it at the time. We were both deserted by our spouses and both lonely. You ask about intensity. The relationship became close and very intense by the beginning of this year – more so than either of us had intended it to be. It ended just over a month ago.'

They looked at each other for a few seconds, with Peach's inquisitive eyes glittering even darker than hers. He said quietly, 'Thank you. Who decided to end the affair?'

She resented his second use of that word, but she wasn't going to react to it. She said between tight lips, 'He did. Now you'll want to know why. I can't tell you that. Perhaps Dominic had found someone else. Perhaps he just tired of me. I expect if he were still alive he'd tell you that he'd never intended the relationship to last indefinitely. He didn't tell me that and I didn't feel like that.'

She felt as if she was stripping away her clothes and exposing herself. That was what she was doing with her emotions, she supposed. Peach, watching her closely, felt he only needed to prompt to learn more. 'You resented the break. The letter from you which we found was quite threatening.'

'Dominic was a heartless bastard when it suited him. I knew that, but I never thought I'd see that part of him turned against me.'

The age-old complaint of the lover whose judgement had been blinded by love. *I knew he was like this but I never thought it would be applied to me*. Along with the idea that you could eliminate vice and change character by the power of your passion, it was the oldest of all love's illusions. Peach said, 'It is plain that you were and still are very resentful about the way he treated you.'

'Yes. I should have just shrugged my shoulders and gone away, shouldn't I? Perhaps I'll be able to do that, now that he's dead.'

'Who else knew about this liaison?'

She said with a bitter smile, 'I think I prefer "liaison" to "affair". No one else knew, as far as I was concerned. Jim was far too busy with his own concerns to notice what I was doing and Dominic's wife Ros is far too self-centred to follow what he was doing. I know lovers are often too sanguine about what people know, but I'm certain none of the people close to us knew about Dominic and me. We were discreet and we didn't meet that often; we probably averaged about once a week.'

'Thank you for being so frank.' But Peach wondered as always what she had concealed beneath her apparent openness. Clever people told you as much as they chose, and he had already decided that Sarah O'Connor was a clever woman. Capable of murder? Certainly, but that didn't necessarily mean she had committed this one. He said, 'The letter from you which we found was threatening. It implied things would be the worse for your late lover if he continued to ignore you.'

'I expect I did threaten. I felt frustrated and very violent when I wrote that letter.'

'Sarah, did you kill Dominic O'Connor?'

It was the first time he had used her forename and it distracted her more than she would have expected. 'No. As you imply, I felt as though I could kill him when I wrote that letter, but I didn't.'

'Where were you last Friday, please?'

'I was here in the house with Clare. She was very upset by Jim's death. More than I was, as you can now appreciate.'

'But she can vouch for your presence here at that time?'

Sarah pursed her lips again, as she had found herself doing repeatedly over the last fifteen minutes. 'Clare went out in the evening. I encouraged her to visit one of her friends. To be honest, we needed time away from each other.'

The three were silent for a moment in the big room, digesting the implications of this, wondering if she would offer any thoughts on the disappearance of her alibi. Then DS Northcott said in his deep, calm voice, 'What car do you drive, Mrs O'Connor?'

'A blue BMW Z4.'

'Did you go out on Friday night?'

'No. And I had no visitors.'

She saw them out of her house and then came back into the lounge and sat down in the biggest armchair. She spent a long time staring into space and trying to control her racing mind.

* * *

He wasn't happy with telephones. They weren't secure, in his view. When your employment and sometimes your very existence depended on security, that was important. But he needed to keep on the right side of the law. He took a deep breath and rang the police station.

'I need to speak to you. It's in connection with the death of Mr Dominic O'Connor.'

'What is your name, sir?'

'It's Davies. Colin Davies. No one will know it at Brunton police station.'

'I see. May I ask the nature of your business?'

He pictured the woman on the switchboard, felt his resentment rising at the safe tedium of her job. No doubt she sat there day by day and played it by the book, whilst he was out taking risks. 'I've told you. It's connected with the death of Dominic O'Connor. That should be enough.'

'We get a lot of calls, sir, when a crime gets the publicity that this one has received.'

'You get some odd calls, I know. People who claim to know things they can't possibly know. Even nutters who want to confess to the crime when they were nowhere near it. I'm not going to confess and I'm not a nutter.'

'I didn't suggest you were, sir. I'm merely trying to get a little detail from you to pass on to DCI Peach.'

'He's the man in charge, is he? I've heard of him. Tell him I was working for Dominic O'Connor until quite recently. Tell him that I know things which might help to pinpoint his murderer.'

'Thank you, sir. That is the kind of detail I need. I'll pass it on to DCI Peach as soon as he's back in the station.'

'I'm sure you will. And I'm equally sure he'll want to see me. Tell him I'll come in to see him at four o'clock this afternoon.'

'I'll pass on your message, Mr Davies. I'm not sure that DCI Peach will be available to see you at that time. However—'

But the phone had gone dead several seconds earlier.

TWELVE

'You should keep me out of this.'

'I don't think I'm going to be able to do that.'

Dominic O'Connor's widow inspected her carefully manicured nails as she held the phone. The varnish on one of them was chipped away at the end. How could that have happened?

'It won't help either of us if I get involved, Ros. It will only complicate things.'

She could picture John Alderson at the other end of the line, gripping it like an anxious teenager, looking automatically over his shoulder even when he knew there could be no one there. She said with a smile, 'I need support, don't I? You're always saying I'm not fit to be out on my own.'

'That's just me teasing you. You're perfectly capable of looking after yourself when you need to. You're my special girl.' He threw in the familiar phrase, but it sounded out of place now, lame and rather desperate.

'That's right, I am! And when this is all over and the fuss has died down, we'll be special together. We won't have to skulk about then. We won't need to be hole-in-the-corner. We'll be a pair. It's going to be brilliant!'

'You mustn't get too far ahead of yourself, Ros. Live in the present. You'll need to have all your wits about you, over the next few days.'

'And why would that be, darling?' Ros felt in control of things now. She was quite enjoying his apprehension. It was the first time she could remember calling the shots – she rather liked that dramatic cliché.

'The police will be all over this. They're bound to be. They'll question everyone and everything. You mustn't be overconfident, even though you're innocent, or it could land you in trouble.'

'Innocent, yes. You don't think I killed Dominic, do you?'

'Of course I don't! But that's the kind of thing I mean. You shouldn't even be voicing the idea. It might set other people thinking.'

'Did you kill him, darling?'

'Don't be ridiculous! And don't even think that way, Ros. I need to be kept out of this, for both our sakes. You must remember that.'

'Very well, my darling, I'll try to remember! Can't guarantee success, of course, but I'll try very hard. I always try hard to do what you say, don't I?'

She rang off before he could react to that. John Alderson stared at the silent phone in frustration and fear.

Brian Jacobs didn't look like a man down on his luck. He might have been treated badly by Dominic O'Connor, as the latter's PA suggested, but he seemed to have made an excellent recovery.

He was around fifty and looked alert and healthy. He was running a little to fat, but the excellent cut of his dark blue suit disguised that efficiently. His dark hair was plentiful and a little untidy. He welcomed his CID visitors into his office, instructed his PA that they were not to be disturbed, and watched her shut the door carefully behind her. Then he came round his desk and sat opposite the two men he had already invited to sit in armchairs. There were four of these, making what was in fact a large room seem slightly crowded, with the other furniture it contained.

As if he felt a need to explain this, Jacobs said, 'I like to have flexibility in my office arrangements. Sometimes we have informal exchanges among small groups in here; I find that pushes things along much more quickly than more formal meetings, with agendas and minutes.'

Peach said with an immediate air of challenge, 'You've moved on from the days when you worked with Dominic O'Connor.'

A brief, scarcely detectable flicker of pain flashed across his equable face at the mention of the name. 'I've left him and Morton Industries well behind me. I can't imagine why you wish to speak to me about Dominic O'Connor.'

'Because he was callously murdered on Friday, Mr Jacobs. Because your name was given to us as that of a person with good reason to hate Mr O'Connor.'

'That's over-dramatic. I didn't like O'Connor. I had a serious working dispute with him and he treated me badly. I can't even say that I felt very sorry when I heard that he was dead. That is as far as it goes.'

DS Northcott never looked very happy in armchairs. His tall, lean frame seemed made for more active things. He now said, 'It's good that you're being so frank, Mr Jacobs. Perhaps you'd care to be equally frank about your criminal record and the nature of your dispute with the late Dominic O'Connor.'

Brian Jacobs had been concentrating on the round, inquisitive face of DCI Peach. He switched to the very different countenance of the detective sergeant and tried to keep calm. 'It is a long time since anyone has mentioned my criminal record. I doubt if any of my present acquaintances knows about it.'

'And there's no reason why it shouldn't remain that way – unless of course it turns out to have a bearing on this case.'

'I can assure you that it doesn't. But you're policemen: you won't accept statements like that.'

Peach gave the blandest of his many smiles. 'Unless someone is kind enough to confess to us that he killed Dominic O'Connor, we can't do that. I'm glad you understand the situation. You must have had a good lawyer in 1989.'

'I did. My father saw to that.'

'Affray and assault with a knife. Very serious charges.'

'With mitigating circumstances.'

'As there always are, in the view of defence counsels. We only have the bare facts of the case in our files. It seemed when I read those that you were lucky that you hadn't killed the man. You wouldn't have got away so lightly on a manslaughter charge.'

'I was attacked. Or rather we were attacked. I was part of a group.'

'Yes. The only member of the gang who was carrying a knife. Which meant that you'd gone there prepared for serious violence.'

'We were attacked. We defended ourselves.'

'That's not what the witnesses said. Not the majority of them. Especially the ones who knew you best – they said you went there nursing a grudge and were bent on revenge.'

'This is irrelevant to your present enquiries. It's all a long time ago. I'm a very different man now.' Jacobs looked round the pleasant, well-lit office with its expensive furnishings, as if they should take that as evidence of the difference.

'Perhaps. There is a saying about leopards and spots. It's very popular in the police service.'

'I expect it is. You don't believe people can change.'

'We're always happy when they do, providing it's for the better. We have to pay attention to the statistics of crime, which show us that the overwhelming majority of serious offences are perpetrated by people who have committed crimes before.'

'Well, I'm happy to tell you I'm one of the reformed sinners. I learned my lesson. That knife incident is ancient history.'

'I see. I believe the judge said in his summing up that you had a violent temperament which could be your downfall. Temperaments rarely change. Yours meant in 1989 that you retained grudges and tried to get revenge by violent action. Would you say you still have that same temperament, Mr Jacobs?'

Brian Jacobs gripped the arms of his chair very hard. He could feel a vein pulsing in his temple; he wondered if it was visible to this man who was so calmly baiting him. 'I didn't expect something which happened when I was twenty-two to pursue me through life. I am an accountant: we're hardly noted for fisticuffs, let alone murder! I'm sure the people who work with me would regard it as ludicrous that you should even be questioning me like this.'

'What happened between you and Dominic O'Connor?'

'He made out that I'd been dishonest. He told the Managing Director that I'd been cheating the firm.'

'And had you?'

Jacobs glared at Peach, who did not drop his eyes or move a muscle in his face. 'No, of course I hadn't. But even the whiff of corruption is enough to finish you, when your business is finance. In effect, it was his word against mine. He was younger and he'd made himself the owners' blue-eyed boy. I got out and made a fresh start. It tore me apart at the time, but it was the right decision.'

'The people who worked with you at Morton Industries remember you as feeling very bitter against a man who is now dead. I believe you threatened him with violence.'

Jacobs was silent for so long that Peach thought he was not going to react. Then he said evenly, 'I told Dominic O'Connor at the time that he wouldn't get away with what he'd done. I told him that, however long it took, he was going to suffer the consequences.'

'Thank you. Perhaps you can now understand our line of questioning.'

'What I said to Dominic O'Connor four years ago was rhetorical. It was said in a red mist of fury. I don't think he felt threatened by it.'

'I would have done, if it had come from a man who'd previously almost killed an enemy with a knife.'

Jacobs' nostrils flared and his face reddened beneath his floppy dark hair, but his voice remained controlled. It was a strangely disturbing combination. 'I'm no longer violent. You may not wish to believe that, so consider what I had at stake. Common sense would argue against me taking retribution now, however much I might desire it. I've got too much to lose.'

'That is a convincing argument, here in your office. But logic doesn't always win, when passion takes over. Where were you on Friday night, Mr Jacobs?'

He was shaken anew by the sudden question. He ran a hand quickly through his hair, making it look even more out of control. Then his face brightened. 'I left work early and went and played a round of golf at Brunton Golf Club.'

Tommy Bloody Tucker's club. Peach didn't ask if Jacobs knew the superintendent; you shouldn't allow yourself to be prejudiced against any suspect. 'What time did you finish your game?'

'It was a four-ball. It would be around six when we finished, I suppose. Then we had a round of drinks.'

Clyde Northcott recorded the names of Jacobs' three companions in his notebook and they watched their man relaxing in his chair. Then Peach said, 'What time did you get home in the evening, Mr Jacobs?'

He was suddenly tense again. 'That's when he died, isn't it?'

'That seems the most probable time at the moment, yes. We'd like to know when you left the golf club and when you arrived home.'

In case there is too long an interval between the two, he thought. Dominic O'Connor's house was only a couple of miles off his route and they must surely know that. 'I can't be certain of the times. I didn't know then that I was going to be questioned about them by a DCI, did I? Most people left the golf club before us, apart from a party who were eating there. I think I left at about half past seven, but I couldn't be precise. I'm pretty certain I was home by eight o'clock.' He tried to banish the graveness from his face with a smile, but didn't succeed. 'And I didn't kill Dominic O'Connor on the way!'

'So who do you think did kill him? If you're innocent, it's obviously in your interest to give us your thoughts on the matter.'

'I agree. But I can't help you. I've not been in close touch with him for the last four years.'

It was over, at last. They left him with a card, so that he could contact them if he thought of anything useful. He shut the door behind them and went and went slowly back to sit behind his desk, staring for several minutes at the chairs the CID men had lately occupied.

The young officer was studiously incurious about Colin Davies. It wasn't her business to size him up. She was waiting at the station sergeant's reception desk and she ushered the visitor swiftly through the labyrinth of the CID section and into DCI Peach's office. 'Mr Davies to see you, sir,' she said stiffly, and then was gone.

Peach rose and shook the man's hand, noting a firm, sinewy grip and a few grey hairs in his visitor's short-cut crown. Probably mid-fifties, Percy thought, but fit for his age and without an ounce of surplus fat. One of those enviable men who would be the same weight when he was sixty as he had been when he was sixteen. Percy said, 'This is Detective Sergeant Northcott, who will be as interested as I am in whatever you have to say.'

'Your bagman.' Davies nodded affably at the big black man and sat down in the chair which had been set ready for him.

'You're ex-job?'

'No. I've never been in the police service. But I worked for many years in state security. I used to protect politicians and the occasional royal. I can provide proof of that, if you think you need it.'

Peach wasn't surprised by this. Over the last thirty years, the protection of VIPs from terrorism had employed more and more people and been a greater and greater drain on the resources of the country. No one save a privileged few had any clear idea of the vast cost of this security. It was an immense burden on national finance which politicians and others chose not to publicise. He said, 'I imagine you were eventually pensioned off. I need to know you weren't dismissed for other reasons.'

Davies smiled bitterly. 'You have it in one. The powers that be think you need to be as young and fit as an SAS man to look after the great and the good. In most situations, experience and judgement are more valuable qualities than youth, but people like to have clear rules: it saves them having to think.'

'And why are you here?'

'To give you whatever sparse information I can. It concerns Dominic O'Connor.'

'Then thank you for coming in. You know enough about police work to realise that we'll be glad of all the help available at this stage.'

Colin Davies wasn't a man for small talk, which suited his listeners. 'I haven't retired. I operate in private security work. There's plenty of work around for people like me, as you can no doubt appreciate from what you see. Dominic O'Connor had used my services in the past. He was about to use them again. I was due to see him today, with a view to resuming employment with him.'

'So you've a good idea who killed him.'

A thin smile, a sharp shake of the head. 'I can't tell you who did that. I think I know why he wanted me back. I think he felt a threat, but I can't guarantee that he was right. In other words, I can't be sure that his death came from that source.'

'We'll be glad to have your information. We need your expert view on this.' Peach wasn't being ironic, as he might have been with some outsiders. This man knew his work and was no time-waster.

Davies relaxed a little as he realised he was being taken very seriously. 'Any Irishman who has grown up in Eire and attained a prominent position is of interest to the provisional IRA. People here think that all danger has passed with the Sunningdale Agreement and subsequent settlements, but that isn't so for all Irishmen. Both James and Dominic O'Connor were regarded as traitors by the extremists in the republican movement. I'd guarantee that both their deaths are being cele- brated in Dublin and Belfast at this moment.'

It was Peach's turn to shake his head. 'Jim O'Connor was killed by a man employed by an industrial rival. We're confi- dent that we've arrested the right man.'

'I accept that. And the same may be true of his brother. But it was my duty to inform you that action by the provisionals is at least a possibility.'

'It was and we're duly grateful. Can you give us any more detail?'

'A little. The numbers of the provisionals are much dimin- ished since the settlement. But as you would expect the ones who remain active are extremists. They haven't forsworn violence; on the contrary, they constantly seek opportunities to use it. They argue that in taking revenge on people they think have let the Cause down, they are keeping the neutrals fearful and preparing for their final revolutionary push, which will secure a free Ireland without divisions. Dominic O'Connor was one of the people they thought had let the Cause down. He was sympathetic to their aims as a young man, but he rejected violence as a way of securing them. That meant that the more successful he became, the more prominent a target he made himself for revenge.'

'And how exactly does this operate?'

'They have five people, three in Ireland and two in this country, whom they actually title Avengers. Both the administrators and these men themselves seem to like that title, which they think adds drama and excitement to what many English people would see as mere terrorism, the brutal killing of innocent people.'

'And Dominic O'Connor felt in danger from one of these men?'

'That's where this gets frustrating, for me and for you. I simply don't know. I'd have found out today. When he used me a few months ago, he was protecting himself against threats from some of the people working around his brother Jim. They weren't particularly close as brothers, as you may have discovered, and Jim operated in very shady circles. There's evidence of that in the way he died. Four months ago, Dominic was afraid of the same sort of death. He also knew that both he and Jim were possible targets for the rump of the IRA provisionals. So he retained my services. I found out what I could for him and I stayed at his side for eight weeks. There was no threat to him during those weeks and he eventually decided that he could dispense with my services. Broadly speaking, I agreed with him. There is never *no* threat, but by the beginning of March it seemed minimal in this case.'

'But he was about to re-engage you.'

'It seems so. You may know of some threat from the people who killed his brother a few days earlier. Otherwise, I think he must have been thinking of the Irish danger.'

'We're investigating various other possibilities, but the one you're talking about seems the strongest one of all at this moment. We know the IRA people you're talking about are fanatical killers.'

'And trained and experienced as well. They've picked off seven people that we know about, over the last couple of years.'

Clyde Northcott had his notebook open. He now spoke, for the first time since he had been introduced to this slight, intense visitor. 'You mentioned these men who style themselves avengers. Is there a particular one who operates in this area?'

'They take turns, operating for a few months each to mini-mise the chances of discovery and arrest. They regard their killings as executions: they're zealots operating on behalf of other fanatics, as you say. According to my information, the man shadowing targets in this area at the moment is a man named Patrick Riordan.'

Northcott made a note of the name and said in his deep voice, 'Presumably he's killed before.'

Davies nodded. 'He's been killing since the worst days of the conflict. That was in and around Belfast. But in recent years, he's killed at least two people and probably more as an avenger. He's a dangerous man with nothing to lose. You need to approach him with extreme care.'

Peach gave him a grim smile. 'Unfortunately the system doesn't allow us to employ you, Mr Davies. I should certainly do that, if it were possible.'

'I can give you an address. He'll bear no grudge against you, because you've no connection with the Irish conflict. That's the theory, but men like him are volatile. He regards himself as a soldier with a right to protect himself when fighting for the Cause.'

Percy looked at the address Davies had scribbled on his desk pad. 'Do we take an Armed Response Unit with us? That might escalate a simple interview into a major incident, putting innocent people at risk.'

'It's your call, but I think you've answered your own ques-tion. We know he's killed, but we haven't the evidence for an arrest. You might find that, if you can prove that he killed Dominic O'Connor. At present Riordan is officially an innocent citizen.'

They shook hands whilst Davies wished Peach luck. Two very different men were united for a moment by this danger from a man neither of them had ever seen.

The mortuary attendant had seen all kinds of reactions. This brittle control and near-giggling was unusual, but not unique.

He said, 'Would you like a few minutes to compose yourself, Mrs O'Connor? I can rustle up a cup of tea in no time if you'd like to sit down.'

'No. I'll get it over with, I think. It's only a formality, isn't it?'

The mortuary man didn't answer that and didn't offer any further comment. He wasn't the most imaginative of men; it didn't pay him to be, in this job. He said, 'We've completed all the forms now, apart from the final signature. You can go ahead whenever you're ready, Mrs O'Connor.'

Ros nodded and moved quickly to the spot where he told her to stand. It was strange seeing the body paraded before her like this. So flat, so cold, so still. Quite solemn, but not frightening at all, really. They'd tidied him up very well; you could hardly see the line under his hair where they'd peeled the scalp back, and the sheet was well drawn up over his torso to conceal the cuts beneath it. There was still the death mark where the cable had bitten into his neck, but they'd done their best to disguise even that.

She took a long moment to look at what had once been her husband. It felt almost like an anti-climax. She found herself wishing that it could last a little longer. Then she said, 'That's him. That's my late husband. That is Dominic Francis O'Connor. If you'll show me the right place on the form, I'll sign it now.'

Ros looked round into the solemn face of the man standing behind her and gave the little half-giggle he had already heard twice before. 'It doesn't take long, does it?'

THIRTEEN

Dominic O'Connor's widow chose to meet them in the front part of the big late-Victorian house, even though the office at the rear was still cordoned off with the blue-and-white plastic ribbons which forbade entry to a scene of crime. Ros had the high red front door open as they arrived. Peach and Northcott could see down a long hall into the kitchen, where a variety of crockery and utensils lay on sink and units, waiting to be washed. They noted this, as they noted the coat flung carelessly over the banister of the stairs. CID officers acquire the habit of observation early in their careers.

Ros O'Connor saw these things also, but did not seem at all upset. 'I've not got myself properly organised since this happened.'

Peach hastened to reassure her. 'That's entirely understandable in these circumstances. And it's still only just after nine in the morning.'

'That's true and it's nice of you to make excuses for me. Truth to tell, I'm a bit of a slut about the house. Dominic used to say that. Well, he did when we were younger and closer.'

She led them into a dining room which looked as if it had not been used for months and invited them to sit on the opposite side of the table from her. 'There's dust on this table, isn't there? I really am a bit of a slut, you know. Mrs Rigby comes in to help me clean on Wednesdays, but I haven't used her in here for ages.' She sat down, then half stood again. 'Do you want to see where Dominic died? It's at the back of the house. I can easily—'

'That isn't necessary, thank you, Mrs O'Connor. It was Detective Sergeant Northcott and I who found him on Saturday.'

Her hand flew to her mouth. 'Of course it was! I remember now. You must think me a very stupid woman!'

'We don't think anything of the sort, Mrs O'Connor. This is a time of great stress for you and we understand that. Now, I know that my wife saw you at your sister's house in Settle on Saturday to break the news, but we need to ask you a few questions.'

'Of course you do! I understand that. The spouse is always the first suspect, isn't she, until you can clear her? John told me that.'

'John?'

'Oops! There I go again. John specifically told me he didn't want to be involved in this, and I drag him in straight away. Well, it might be all for the best in the long run. I'm sure you'd have found out about the two of us sooner or later! You can call me Ros, by the way. I think I'd prefer you to do that.'

Peach wanted to tell her to calm down and listen quietly, but you had to be tactful in the face of what might be no more than a manifestation of grief. He slowed his own tone, hoping that she would take her rhythm from him. 'A murder victim can't speak for himself. We'd like to piece together Dominic's last day, if we could.'

'We were here in the morning. Dominic was working at home. We haven't any children, you know. Dominic used to say that it might have kept us closer together if we'd had them, but I don't know about that. I thought he might go up to Settle and see Jane with me, but he said he had a lot of work to do.' She leaned forward confidentially. 'Between you and me, I think Dominic used to find my nieces and nephew a bit of a trial. He wasn't good with kids. Might have been different if we'd had our own, I suppose.'

Northcott opened his notebook, perhaps hoping that the gesture of formality would slow down this fluttering bird. 'Can you tell us exactly what time you last saw him on Friday, Ros?'

She smiled at the big black man, so that Peach thought for a moment that she was going to compliment him on his appearance or his voice. Her small features were very animated, like a kitten's when it is concentrating all its attention on playing with a ball. She frowned suddenly. 'We had lunch together before I left. We didn't talk a lot – I rather think Dominic read the paper for most of the time. That would be about one o'clock. I looked after him quite well as regards food, you know. So I'm not entirely a slut!' She gave a gay little laugh which rang oddly in the unused room. 'He said he was going to be busy, so I made him some sandwiches and left him a large orange and a flask of coffee. Oh, and a big piece of fruit cake: he was very fond of fruit cake.'

Northcott made a careful note of this, noticing how it tallied with the pathologist's report on the stomach contents. 'Can you remember what time you left him during the afternoon?'

'It must have been about three o'clock, I think. I know I was with Jane and the kids by around half past four.'

Peach tried to be as casual as he could. 'So you finished your lunch at around half past one. When would you think Dominic would get round to eating this tempting and substantial cold meal you'd left ready for him?'

Her face creased in thought for a moment, then lit up as she felt able to help. 'Almost certainly at around half past six, I should think. He loved sandwiches and fruit and cake – liked stuff like that much more than bigger meals, he said, because he could eat it wherever and whenever he fancied. And he liked to listen to *The News Quiz*, that programme on Radio Four, which is on after the six o'clock news. I reckon he'd almost certainly stop his work to listen to that and eat what I'd left for him at the same time. That was one of the ways he liked to relax.'

That would put the time of death at around nine: approximately two hours after he'd finished eating the sandwiches and fruit, the PM report had said. 'Thank you. This is very useful for us; you're helping us to piece together his last hours just as we hoped you would.'

'That's good, isn't it? Perhaps I'm not such an airhead as I thought I was.' She brushed a strand of blond hair away from her left eye and sat back in her chair, like a schoolgirl who has been congratulated on speaking well.

'You mentioned John at the beginning of our conversation. Would that be John Alderson?'

Peach had thought she might bridle at the name, but she seemed quite pleased to have it set on the table between them. 'You've been talking to other people, haven't you? Who told you about John? Oh well, it doesn't matter. I think it's better that I tell you all about John, whatever he thinks.'

'So do just that, please.' Peach allowed himself a touch of acerbity. You had to make great allowances for grief, but he thought the widow might just be exploiting her position a little.

She looked at him silently for a moment, then put her hands together on the table in front of her and stared down at them, as if the physical movement was an aid in marshalling her thoughts. 'My marriage to Dominic was less than perfect. It's no use trying to disguise that, because other people are going to tell you about it – perhaps they already have, if you know about John. Dominic had lots of affairs. Most of them were with women I never even knew and he was careful not to leave much evidence around. He wasn't sentimental, like me;

Dominic didn't keep things. But I knew about his women, all the same.' She smiled knowingly and rocked gently backwards and forwards on her chair, pressing her hands on the table to facilitate the movement.

Peach said gently, 'You were starting to tell us about John Alderson.'

'I was, wasn't I? Well, I was lonely and John was kind to me. Neither of us intended it, but over two or three months we became what used to be called an item. Can a married woman be part of an item?'

She stopped and looked at Peach in what seemed genuine enquiry, her small head with its perfect miniature features held a little on one side. But all he said was, 'Carry on, please.'

'We've been sleeping together whenever we could over the last six months – well, we've not managed to sleep together all that often, but we go to bed whenever we can. I'm sorry if that shocks you: I got used to the idea a long time ago.'

Peach gave her a wry smile. 'Policemen are trained to be professionally unshockable, Mrs O'Connor.'

'Ros, please. Well, there isn't much more to tell. I realise now that I should be married to John, not Dominic.' She lifted her curiously childlike visage and looked her examiner full in the face. 'We'll be able to do that now, won't we? Get married, I mean. After a few months, that will be. Mustn't shock Father Brice and the church folk, must we?' Her laugh tinkled round the room again. The two men with her found it an uncomfortable sound.

Peach allowed silence to seep back into the room before he said, 'Who do you think killed Dominic, Ros?'

'I don't know that. He was all right when I left him. And he ate his meal, so he must have been all right much later than that.'

'You've said that your marriage wasn't going well. Perhaps it was over, as you imply, but that isn't our business. You still know far more about a murder victim than any of us and you must help us to find out who killed him.'

The kitten-like head nodded earnestly and repeatedly. 'Yes, I can see that. But I can't help you. I've thought about it ever since I heard Dominic was dead, but it's a mystery to me.' A contented smile stole over the delicate lips, as if she found that a satisfactory state of affairs.

'We shall be questioning John Alderson in due course. Do you—?'

'He won't like that! John wanted to be kept out of all this. But it's rather exciting, isn't it? Much better to be part of it than left outside it. Well, that's my view, anyway!'

'I was about to ask you whether you thought Mr Alderson had anything to do with this death. I'd like you to answer that question, please.'

'Sorry! My mind runs away from me sometimes – I've got that sort of brain. No, of course John had nothing to do with this. He's not that sort of man at all.'

'We shall speak to him and form our own opinions. But from what you have told us in the last few minutes, this death is very convenient for the two of you. It means that there is no longer any obstacle to you and Mr Alderson marrying, if that is what you wish to do.'

'That's true. We've both got a motive, haven't we?' Ros hugged her folded arms against her chest in what seemed like physical delight. 'And Dominic was a practising Catholic who didn't believe in divorce. He'd have made it very difficult for me to leave him.'

'But you weren't involved in his death. And as far as you know, neither was Mr Alderson?'

'No, certainly not. And I can't imagine who else might have done it, but I'll go on thinking about that.'

As Peach drove back to the station, Clyde Northcott looked at the facts he had recorded in his notebook. Then he said in his deep, usually confident, voice, 'I'm out of my depth with women like that. I've never had to try to make sense of an interview like that one before.'

Peach grinned as he conceded right of way to a cheerful-looking Brunton mongrel. 'All part of your widening education, DS Northcott.'

'Do you think she's unbalanced?'

'If that's a technical term, you'd need to define it. But no, I don't think she is. I think she's a strange lady. I think she'd drive me up the wall if I had to live with her. But beneath the girlish mannerisms and the pretty face, there's a brain at work and she's used to getting her own way. We shouldn't under-estimate her, because that's probably what she wants.'

Northcott nodded over his notes. 'Well, she's given us a time of death. All we have to do now is find out who was there last Friday night.'

Peach arranged to see John Alderson at three thirty. He was due to see Tommy Bloody Tucker to update him before then. Wednesday was becoming a bizarre day. When he climbed the stairs to meet his chief, it rapidly became more bizarre.

Tucker wasn't there when he arrived, which was unusual in itself. Percy pulled up an armchair in front of the huge empty desk and sat down to wait in comfort. He wasn't delayed for long. Tucker came to the top floor in the lift and bade a noisy goodbye to some anonymous fellow-traveller. He fumbled a little with the door handle, then half-fell and half-stumbled into the room.

He seemed glad to reach the haven of the big leather chair behind his desk and slumped thankfully into it. 'Ah, Percy Peach!' he said affably, belatedly sighting his DCI. 'How the devil are you, sir!'

He's pissed, thought Percy. Tight as Andronicus. Tommy Bloody Tucker's pissed! There must surely be mileage in this.

But it was Tucker who took the initiative, as drunks often do. 'Bloody awful job this, isn't? Glad to get away from it 'casionally, tell yer the truth!'

'It is a little taxing at times, sir. But you asked me to—'

'Been saying goodbye to an old mate, Perce. Member of the Lodge anallthat! Movin' away, you see.'

'Yes, sir, I do. But if you remember—'

'Did us proud.' He leaned forward confidentially over the big desk. 'Might just 'avad a bit too much, you know.'

Percy recoiled hastily from the spirit fumes. 'Really, sir? I'd hardly have noticed. You carry it so well, you see.'

'I do, don't I?' Chief Superintendent Tucker tried to lever himself to his feet, then thought better of it and slumped back contentedly into his pilot's chair. A look of astonishment stole slowly over his face. 'I feel bladdered, Percy.'

'Pleasantly pissed, I'd say, sir,' ventured Percy daringly.

'Presently pissed, that's about it!' said Tucker contentedly.

'Perhaps I'd better come back when you feel—'

'We had some good jokes today. Private room, you see. Now listen to this, Perce. Man 'as a gorilla to work for him. Thirty bloody stone. Cleans the 'ouse, digs the garden, lifts the piano across the room for 'im. Where does it sleep?'

'Anywhere it fucking likes!' said Percy, with the air of a man answering a routine question.

'You've 'eard it!' said Tucker, deflated with a huge disappointment.

'About 1993, sir, I think. It was a good one, in its time.'

'Man said you need the swear word to give it the right ring. The proper effasy – no, the proper effany . . .'

'The proper emphasis, sir?'

'Thassit! Whatyersaid. Thassit.'

'Good. Now in the matter of the Dominic O'Connor case, sir. We—'

Tucker leaned across the vast acreage of his desk and made a frantic effort to grasp the lapels of his DCI. He failed by several inches. His wildly gyrating hand grasped empty air as he fell heavily back into his chair. 'Bugger Dominic O'Connor, Percy! Bugger work! Bugger the Chief Constable, if it comes to it!'

'I think I'd prefer the second prize, sir, if you don't mind. Meanwhile—'

'Meanwhile?' Tucker was as outraged as if he had been accorded the vilest epithet know to man. 'Meanwhile? There's no bloody meanwhile, Percy Peach! You need to learn to live a little. Thassanorder, Perce.'

Percy decided this was way beyond black coffee. 'I think you should go home, sir. I'm going to go downstairs and get someone to drive you. You won't go away, will you?'

'Not going away.' Tucker shook his head and lifted his right hand in what looked like some sort of blessing.

DC Brendan Murphy was unfortunate enough to be checking facts at his computer. Percy seized upon him, outlined the problem, and directed him to drive home the stricken head of Brunton CID. He then returned to the penthouse office and managed to lead Tucker to the lift.

The chief superintendent threw his arm round his DCI's shoulder and used the privacy of the lift as the opportunity for a confidence. 'We don't always hit it off, do we, Percy? But underneath it all, I reshpect you.' When Peach failed to react to this, he clutched his resisting torso to the chief superintendal breast and insisted, 'I love you, Pershy Peace. You know that, don't you?'

A small group of CID officers witnessed the departure of their chief, belted securely into the back of the police Mondeo behind DC Murphy. Tucker waved at them like departing royalty as he disappeared between the high brick pillars of the exit.

Percy decided that Mrs T.B. Tucker might need to know what to expect. It wouldn't do for this apparition to disrupt one of her bridge afternoons. He rang Brunnhilde Barbara and apprised her of her spouse's impending arrival.

'And why do you disturb my day to tell me this?' came the formidable enquiry.

She scarcely needed a phone, thought Percy, holding the receiver six inches away from his ear. 'He's been saying goodbye to an old friend. You may find that he's – well, a little the worse for wear.'

'You mean he's DRUNK?' Both the volume and the outrage were Wagnerian.

'I suppose he is, yes. But DC Murphy will see him safely into the house.'

'There will be no need for that. I shall see to him MYSELF.' The tone indicated that the Valkyries were saddling up.

Percy went back into the squad room and the hushed group awaiting him there. He announced, 'He's going to get a seeing to from Brunnhilde Barbara.'

A hush fell over the little conclave. A passing uniformed officer removed his hat and stood reverently erect.

Peach wasn't sure how he had expected John Alderson to look, but this wasn't it.

The house was a modest 1930s' terraced with a small garden at the front, where the buds of roses were swelling and spring-flowering pansies were giving of their best at the edges of the single big bed. The owner met them at the door. He was slight, balding, fiftyish, and he walked with a limp as he led them indoors.

He sat them facing the light in the small, tidy living room and said, 'We won't be disturbed. I live alone here.' He watched Clyde Northcott as he produced notebook and ballpen, noting how small they looked in the DS's huge hands, but offering them neither refreshment nor further comment.

'I gather that you didn't intend that we should have this meeting at all,' said Peach aggressively. Best to get the latest episode in a trying day off on a combative note, he thought.

If Alderson was shaken, his narrow features didn't show it. 'I didn't see any point in wasting your time. I knew I couldn't help you, so I thought it was better if I was kept out of it.'

'So you won't be at all pleased to find that Mrs Ros O'Connor immediately volunteered your name to us.'

He hoped his verb would annoy Alderson, but the man didn't show any irritation. 'Ros is an impulsive creature. She doesn't always think before she speaks. But I wouldn't have it otherwise.'

The kind of sentiment lovers often voiced but rarely meant, in Peach's experience. He said, 'Mrs O'Connor probably wasn't quite herself after her husband's death. She seemed a little erratic.'

He smiled appreciatively. 'Erratic, yes.' He rolled the syllables round his mouth and apparently found them acceptable. 'That's rather a good word for Ros. She's certainly impulsive. That's what brought us together.'

'I think we should know a little more about what brought you together, Mr Alderson.'

'Do you really? I'd say that it's a private matter and that the details should remain private.'

'And then I'd remind you that a man has been brutally murdered and that you are the lover of his wife. In these circumstances, you are a man who warrants full CID investigation, which is what you are going to receive.'

Peach gave him a satisfied smile. If the man preferred the confrontational approach, that would suit him admirably at this stage of the day. Alderson's grey eyes narrowed, but he didn't flinch. 'I suppose I should try to see this from your point of view. What is it you want to know?'

'You could tell us a little more about your relationship with Ros O'Connor, for a start. Other people are going to do that, so it would be as well if we have your account now.'

'We're lovers. We have been for the last few months. We don't flaunt it, but I expect quite a few people know about our situation. People whose own lives are empty love to gossip about others.'

The timing tallied with what Ros had told them earlier. 'How much did Dominic O'Connor know about this?'

Alderson took a packet of cigarettes from his pocket, extracted one, then tapped it against the back of his hand thoughtfully, first at one end and then at the other. But he didn't light it. Having examined it carefully, he returned it to the packet. It was a curious performance and it wasn't clear how conscious he was of his actions. He said, 'On the face of it, Dominic knew nothing. But he was an intelligent man who was alert to the world around him. Perhaps he didn't want to know. Some men don't like to face the fact that they've been cuckolded.' He glanced at their faces, searching for a reaction to the ugly old word, but receiving none. 'It's more likely that Dominic was preoccupied with his own amours. If you've found out anything about your victim, you'll know that he conducted a string of affairs.'

'We have been told that, yes. Do you think any of them was connected with his death?'

'It's possible. *Cherchez la femme*, they say, don't they? But I can't help you. His love life didn't concern me and I wasn't interested in the details of it.'

'Except that it left the way clear for you with his wife.'

'You make me sound like an opportunist.'

'Perhaps that's how it looks from the outside. If you think things are different, this is your chance to enlighten us.'

Alderson stared hard, first at Peach and then at Northcott, searching for a reaction he did not get; both men remained impassive. 'Perhaps you're not so far wide of the mark. I found a lonely woman, who didn't quite know what she'd done wrong to be so neglected. I'm used to being on my own, though I'm no monk. I was divorced ten years ago and I've played the field as it suits me since then. I'm not proud of that: I'm telling you because you could find out easily enough, if you chose to.'

'What we're interested in is the investigation of a murder and how you fit into it. It's your present affair with the victim's widow which we need to know about.'

Alderson weighed this and apparently found it acceptable. 'I suppose I thought of Ros as just another opportunity, at first. She's a pretty woman. She was also a lonely woman in search of sex and companionship. You'd be surprised how many of them are available. Or perhaps you wouldn't.'

'So it isn't a deep relationship.'

Peach made it a statement: he was still keen to provoke this acute man into some impulsive reaction. He didn't succeed. Alderson eyed him coolly, assessing what the implications of his answer might be for himself. 'We're close now. It's probably true to say that neither of us thought of it as more than a fling when it began. But you can never forecast how these things will develop.'

'That sounds like a cautionary note for the promiscuous.'

'Maybe it is. I think sex was a big part of it for both of us when it began. It goes deeper than that now.'

'Mrs O'Connor thinks that the two of you will now marry.'

'It's early to make long-term plans. I haven't seen Ros since I heard about Dominic. I expect she's still reeling from the shock.' He looked at his two visitors for a long moment, teasing them with the thought that he might be about to cast aside his lover. Then he said, 'But I expect we shall marry, after a suitable interval. There isn't any need to formalise things quickly, in modern society. And even Ros's Holy Mother Church can't object, now that Dominic's dead and she's a free woman.' He let a little flare of contempt into his tone as he mentioned religion.

'What do you do for a living, Mr Alderson?'

'I expect you already know that, through your efficient police research machine. I'm a consultant. I advise on engineering problems.'

'At present unemployed?'

'Yes. The work comes and goes. It's generally quite lucrative, when it's around. You may have noticed that the country is at present enduring a prolonged recession.'

'Indeed we have. It's even affecting the police service. No doubt Mrs O'Connor will be a rich woman now.'

'Which will be very convenient for me as well as for her. I can't help that, DCI Peach.'

'It makes this a very opportune death for both of you.'

Alderson shrugged his slim shoulders and raised his hands palm-upwards for a moment. He allowed himself a small smile, but he didn't speak. Peach regarded him steadily, then gave a tiny nod to Northcott, who said, 'You worked in Middlesbrough before you settled in Brunton, I believe.'

'You believe correctly.'

'Where you were involved in some unpleasantness.'

Alderson forced a smile. 'I like that word, "unpleasantness". It's very English. The facts are that we were involved in a very nasty industrial exchange. One small firm took business away from another, by means we didn't like. They undercut us far beyond what you could call fair competition. They were non-union, so we couldn't even ask the union to help us. We'd no choice but to take matters into our own hands.'

'With serious injuries resulting.'

'Broken arms and a couple of broken jaws. Nothing life-threatening. You may have noticed that I walk with a limp. It dates from that time.'

'But you dealt out more than you received.'

'How well-informed you seem to be.' His voice was mocking as he looked from Northcott's earnest black face to Peach's round white one. Then his tone hardened. 'I grew up on a sink estate in Newcastle. I learned to take care of myself early in life.'

Clyde Northcott nodded. 'So you could have taken care of Dominic O'Connor, when you found that he stood in your way.'

John Alderson looked hard at Northcott. 'I reckon you could handle yourself, if you needed to. Well, good for you! And yes, I might have harmed Dominic, if it had come to a direct contest between the two of us. But sneaking up on someone the way the papers say this happened isn't my way. Make a clear note in your little book that I deny all connection with this murder, will you, please?'

Peach said quietly, 'Where were you on Friday evening, Mr Alderson?'

'I was here all day on Friday, apart from a visit to my local shop for bread, milk and a paper. And before you ask, I was alone. That's the way of things, when you're unemployed and single. Perhaps I would have tried to see Ros, but I knew she was going up to Settle to see her sister.'

'What car do you drive?'

'A metallic grey Ford Fiesta. It's in the garage, if you wish to inspect it. And it was there all day on Friday. I don't know who killed Dominic O'Connor, but if I have any useful thoughts on the matter I'll be in touch with you immediately.'

'The vice squad's moving in tomorrow on those Asian men who are procuring minors from care homes. We've passed on our evidence to them,' said Lucy Peach to her husband as she dried the dishes.

'And about time too.'

'We needed the evidence. We've got it now. No one's going to walk on this one.'

'Including Linda Coleman, I trust?' Percy couldn't get the image of that affluent woman threatening violence to Lucy out of his mind.

'Including her for certain. She and her cronies have been financing the whole business, setting up the big-money clients and creaming off the best of the profits.'

They watched indifferent television for an hour or so. Eventually his arm stole around her shoulders and she leant contentedly against him, her head on his chest. He loved the clean, outdoor smell of her hair, as well as its softness and its rich red-brown colour. He nuzzled it softly, wishing that he could remove her for ever from all physical danger. 'How's your mum?'

'She's fine. What brought that up?'

'Aren't I allowed to ask after Agnes? She's my favourite seventy-year-old.'

'I shouldn't think there's a lot of competition for that honour. At least I don't feel jealous of Mum.' She ran her fingers along the back of Percy's hand and up his forearm. 'Wonder what's happening to poor old Tommy Bloody Tucker?'

Percy sat upright beside her. 'Wash your mouth out, Lucy Peach! That name is not to be mentioned in this house. I shall ravish you as a penalty!'

'Ooer! Am I allowed to join in?'

'Only if you do that thing you did last week.'

'All right, then. I'm not sure what it was. I might have to run through my entire repertoire to find the bit you want.'

'Bloody 'ell, Norah! You know how to turn a man on. Even a man in terminal sexual decline like me.'

He watched from between the sheets whilst she disrobed, producing his usual guttural groans of sexual anticipation as more and more of the delicious flesh was revealed. 'There's no call for that!' said Lucy.

'It's expected of me. I can't let down my audience of one,' said Percy.

She leapt between the sheets and was immediately enveloped in his arms. She gasped and giggled almost simultaneously. 'I swear you've got more than two hands at times.'

'Standard issue when you make DCI. But I do appreciate a good handful of buttock.' He took two handfuls for good measure.

'Buttock! You make it sound like the fatstock market!'

He kissed her urgently; it seemed the simplest method of shutting her up. Later, much later, he said sleepily, 'She has some good ideas, your mum. It's fun trying to produce these grandchildren.'

FOURTEEN

Manchester's Moss Side is now world-renowned as a dangerous area. Even the police tread carefully there. They do not care to venture into the narrow old streets after dark, unless it be in numbers and on a particular assignment. This raises all sorts of questions about the law of the land and its enforcement. Anarchy is perilously close, when criminal forces control an area and the police tacitly acknowledge it.

Things were different in daylight. Or DCI Peach hoped they were. This was unfamiliar territory for him. He knew all about Moss Side, but it was largely by hearsay. He said to Northcott as the big man drove into the area on Thursday morning, 'You'll feel at home here, Clyde. There are more black faces than white ones.'

'There's every shade here, sir. And every shade of soul.' They were silent for the next five minutes, though observant of their surroundings. Percy wasn't sure whether he was more surprised by the title of 'sir' or the mention of soul. Neither was common between the two of them.

There were lace curtains at the windows of number twenty-two, the house they wanted. They were cleaner than they might have expected. 'My mother had lace curtains at one time. She got rid of them when I was in short trousers,' Peach told Northcott. The big man didn't comment. He wasn't used to seeing Percy Peach nervous: it was almost a first.

Peach decided after close examination that the woman who opened the door was probably around sixty. She looked seventy-five. Her face had the grey pallor of someone who saw little daylight and no open skies; her features carried the shiftiness of a being who kept a constant watch on the other creatures around her. Percy had abandoned his jacket for a sweater and scuffed the usually immaculate toecaps of his shoes to come here, but he was sure from the look in her tired eyes that this woman recognised them as coppers.

But she didn't comment. She gave them nothing save a few terse phrases. She wouldn't get involved. You asked only the questions you really needed to ask round here. They told her whom they wanted to see and she said, 'Up the stairs. Second door on the right on the first landing.'

Northcott tapped lightly on the scratched brown paint of the door. It opened immediately, which meant that the room's occupant had probably been listening to the exchanges in the hall below. He nodded them inside, then took the single chair whilst they perched uncomfortably on the side of the newly made bed. He was in his fifties, with short-cut, grizzled hair and deep lines in his face. It was two days at least since he had shaved. His narrowed brown eyes watched their every move, as if challenging them to make a wrong one.

'Patrick Riordan?' said Peach.

'Pat to my friends. You can call me Mr Riordan.' It would have been a small, hostile joke if he'd smiled, but he didn't.

They showed him their warrants. He held them for a moment under his eyes, as if he wished to retain the information, but his expression didn't change. Peach studied him in turn for a moment. Silence was a weapon he used to build tension with many of the people they interviewed. It wasn't going to work with this man. He said, 'You work for the IRA Provisionals.'

'I don't work for them: I'm a member of the army. I believe in the Cause. We shall have the united Ireland Parnell fought for and Gladstone promised us. It's almost with us now.'

He'd been watchful and alert since he'd opened his door, but this was the first sign of animation he'd shown. Peach said, 'May we ask what you are doing in this country?

'You may ask, but you won't get a reply. I don't have to answer your questions. Arrest me, if you fancy it. I still won't answer and I'll have you for wrongful arrest.'

'Oh, I don't think you'd do that, Mr Riordan. You don't want a high profile. It wouldn't help your work and your masters wouldn't like it.'

The brown eyes looked at him balefully. 'There's nothing for you here.'

'I'll tell you why you're in Moss Side, since you aren't inclined to reveal it yourself. You're here to kill people.'

'I would deny that. Of course I would. I'd say you hadn't got the right man. But I'd agree that the Cause needs revenge. There are people who've been traitors to the Cause. They need to be eliminated. That is justice. We kill as an example for others as well as to bring to traitors the punishment they merit.' He was mouthing phrases he'd used many times before, but his lined, mean face was suddenly alive with passion.

'And Dominic O'Connor was one of your victims.'

'Both the O'Connor brothers were traitors. They were in positions of power and they ratted. They failed the Cause.'

'And now both of them are dead.'

'They got what they deserved.'

'We've arrested a man for Jim's murder. We're here this morning to talk to you about Dominic's death.'

'Nothing doing. Someone got to him before us, same as they did with Jim.'

'You don't wish to claim the death of Dominic O'Connor as a glorious victory for the Cause?'

Riordan didn't seem to notice Peach's contemptuous irony. He looked for a moment as if he would indeed like to claim this success, like a Battle of Britain fighter pilot notching up another Luftwaffe victim. His head lifted and his eyes were raised towards the dusty ceiling for a moment. Then caution reasserted itself and he said, 'You can't have me for this.'

Peach looked round the narrow, shabby room, with its chipped sink and its ancient Baby Belling cooker. He looked at the wardrobe with its door askew, at the small attaché case on top of it. He was wondering where this man kept his weaponry, whether indeed he had more than one killing tool. A pistol and an Armalite, perhaps? He didn't know what was standard issue for an IRA avenger. He turned back to the watchful face with its black stubble. 'You were seen in Brunton last week. You were seen near Dominic O'Connor's house.'

He was pushing the scanty information Colin Davies had been able to give them as far as it would go, chancing his arm a little on times and places. Riordan said sullenly, 'I'm a free citizen. I can go wherever I like.'

'You were making your preparations for what happened on Friday. Dominic O'Connor had arranged to hire a bodyguard. He knew that you were around and were planning to kill him.'

'I don't have to tell you what I was doing. This is a free country. It's just not my country.'

'You watched and you waited. And when your moment came and he was alone, you twisted a cable around the neck of your target and killed him.'

'It's not our way, that. We prefer the bullet through the traitor's brain. The soldier's way.'

'The coward's way. Soldiers fight face to face. You'd have been happy enough to twist the life out of O'Connor with a cable, so long as you got clear away afterwards.'

'You're right! I'd like to have done just that. I'd like to be the patriot who choked the life out of that cheating traitor! But some sod got there before me. I hope you never catch him.'

Patrick Riordan, assassin, was buoyant at last. He was breathing hard, glaring at the men who had come here in pursuit of him, trumpeting his warped form of patriotism rather than troubling to disguise it. But was he indeed the man who had killed Dominic O'Connor, his declared target, or had someone else got there before him as he claimed?

Clyde Northcott said in his quiet, deep voice, 'It's much better that you confess to this now if you did it, Pat. You'll get the glory back in your own country. The men you work for will make you into a hero. You'll be on rolls of honour. Maybe your name will be remembered a hundred years from now.'

It was a strange prospect to hold out to him in that shabby room in Moss Side, but for a moment it seemed to beguile Riordan. The deep-set brown eyes glittered with the light of military glory. Then he looked at Peach and his face changed. 'You might get me for a killing at some time, but it won't be this one.'

The stocky man who sat ridiculously on the edge of the bed was ready for this. 'That sounds like a challenge, Riordan. I like a challenge. You're right in the frame for this. We shall go away and set about gathering the evidence for an arrest. Don't leave the area without letting us know your new address.'

It was a useless instruction to a man like Patrick Riordan, of course. He would move when he wished and where he wished. But the routine instruction seemed to drag him more firmly into the middle of the case. He was a man who would have killed O'Connor without a vestige of conscience. Neither of the CID men could decide as they journeyed the thirty miles swiftly back to Brunton whether he was guilty, but both of them hoped he was.

The police machine had produced a little more information

for them by the time they reached the station. Patrick Riordan had hired a car in Manchester for four days, from Wednesday to Saturday of the previous week. It had been sighted in Brunton on Thursday and on Friday and returned to its Manchester base on Saturday.

Job done?

The late Dominic O'Connor's PA was keeping things going in his section of the firm, as all good PAs seem able to do. The managing director at Morton Industries had his own office staff, but after the death of his Financial Director he needed Mrs Jean Parker to hold the fort in that division, during the confusion which inevitably followed.

The MD said four days after the death of Dominic O'Connor, 'You've done splendidly, Jean. You've kept our clients happy and explained things very well to them. But I know it's a holding operation and that you can't take decisions. We'll need to appoint a new financial director as quickly as possible.'

They were the words Jean Parker had been waiting for. Once she was sure she was alone, she made a brief phone call and arranged a lunchtime meeting in the pub by the Ribble where they had often met before. It was a big, rambling place, but there were not very many people there at a wet Thursday lunchtime, and the many nooks and crannies of the place afforded privacy for those who sought it.

Brian Jacobs felt no qualms about putting his palm firmly on top of his mistress's hand as they sat together at the small round table.

It was curious how that still gave her a thrill, Jean thought. Sex was a strange thing. It was an important – perhaps the most important – part of life. Yet after all the things they had done in bed, after all the intimate things they had muttered to each other and repeated to each other over the years, she still felt that little surge of warmth running through her body when Brian simply put his hand on top of hers. Love was a curious business, at once complicated and very simple.

She said, 'We're muddling through. People have been very understanding. I've managed to postpone most of the meetings he'd arranged.' She wouldn't refer to Dominic O'Connor by name; Brian was still absurdly sensitive about that. He couldn't bear to hear her pronounce the name of the man he had so hated.

'Yes. People will be very accommodating, for a while. Then they'll get impatient. You can't do without a Financial Director for very long. Not with the scale at which Morton Industries now operates.' It was the nearest he would come to acknowledging the success of his late rival's work with the firm.

Jean Parker smiled at him, then brought up her other hand to clasp his. 'That's why I thought we should meet. The MD came in to see me this morning. He thinks as you do that the firm urgently needs to make an appointment.'

Jacobs gave her a small, contented smile. 'Great minds think alike.' He had no baggage with the MD at Morton's, who had been appointed after he had left the firm. He'd met the man on neutral ground and got on well with him. 'He's right. You need as seamless a transition as possible, and that means a swift appointment.'

'It might carry a partnership, if they replace exactly.'

'Yes, I'd forgotten that. He'd worked himself a partnership in the firm, hadn't he? He knew how to feather his nest, after he'd done his cuckoo act and tipped any rival out of it.'

It was a good metaphor, she thought, but it was absurd that he wouldn't even mention Dominic O'Connor. You couldn't go on hating a dead man; there was no substance in it, nothing left to hate. She said, 'I think if you applied, you'd stand a very good chance.'

It was an outrageous idea. But he'd known the suggestion was coming, known from the moment he'd received that excited phone call two hours ago. 'They say you should never go back.'

'They aren't always right. Especially if the reason you left no longer exists.'

'The new man won't want me. He'll think I left under a cloud.' He was ticking off the objections that others, not he, might make.

'But you didn't. As far as the records are concerned, you were an ambitious man who wanted more responsibility and sought it elsewhere. You needed to spread your wings.' After the cuckoo had pushed you out, she'd nearly said. She was pleased to push the bird metaphor along. It seemed to keep them on the same wavelength – or was that a different metaphor? The brain was a strange organ. Why should she be concerning herself with metaphors, at this key moment in her life?

'I'm not sure that I'd want to put in a formal application. It might compromise my position with my present firm.'

'I think Morton's might be prepared to approach you, if I said you were available. I'd have to plant the idea subtly, of course, let the MD think it was his notion. I'm only a humble PA who is at present without a boss.'

Brian grinned at her. 'Behind every successful man there is a clever woman. And you're the clever woman I want behind me, Jean Parker.' He squeezed her small hands between his, pouring more emotion into that small contact than into many a coupling between sheets.

'The MD's going to pop in to see me at the end of the day. I'll suggest tentatively that there might be a man available who's already enjoyed success at Morton's and knows the ways of the firm. And who's gone on to broaden his experience through success with another firm. Or let him come up with those ideas for himself.'

'This man sounds the ideal candidate, whoever he is. I can't see how Morton's could turn him down.'

'I can only plant the thought. My humble station doesn't allow more than that. But there's nothing to be lost, is there?'

'Nothing at all, my darling. You go ahead and be the clever woman behind me!'

She left discreetly before him. Brian Jacobs looked at his watch, bought himself another drink, and settled back comfortably into his chair. He'd told that bastard at the time that he'd suffer for what he'd done. Well, you couldn't have more complete revenge than this. Your enemy lying stiff and cold in the mortuary, his widow bedding another man, and you yourself about to step into the job and the partnership he had left behind. Cheers, Mr Dominic O'Connor!

They were becoming familiar with the impressive modern mansion where James, the elder O'Connor brother, had lived.

Drugs and prostitution were lucrative industries to add to your more respectable portfolio, thought DCI Peach, as he and DS Northcott drove past the gardener and up to the main entrance of the house. Well, James O'Connor would never have to answer to the law for his sins now.

His widow seemed even more composed than when they had seen her previously. Her long dark hair was lustrous and impeccably groomed. Her face was skilfully made up and had more colour in its cheeks than when they had seen her on Tuesday. Peach wondered whether she had chosen the bright blue dress especially for them. It looked to him elaborate for this time of day, but perhaps it was her habit to dress to impress. Lucy would have had an opinion on that; he wouldn't ask for Clyde Northcott's view.

He said once they were seated, 'We shall be able to release your husband's body in the next few days. You can begin to plan the funeral.'

'Thank you. Both I and my daughter will be glad to have closure. For different reasons, of course. I told you on Tuesday that I'd ceased to be close to Jim by the time he died.'

'You told us that you'd taken to sleeping with his brother. It's Dominic's murder we are now investigating.'

'It wasn't a casual shag, as you imply.' She watched him for a moment, as if assessing the impact of the harsh word from her well-groomed lips. 'As far as I was concerned it was a serious relationship. Dominic apparently thought differently. But he isn't here to defend himself, so you have only my account of the liaison.'

'Precisely. And it's my opinion that you were very bitter when Dominic O'Connor chose to end it. He may well have known things about your husband's death when you met last week, as you claimed. But I think you were also hoping to revive your affair when you met Dominic at the Grouse Inn last Thursday evening.'

'I can't prevent you thinking whatever you choose to think. It hardly matters, now that Dominic is also dead.'

'He died within twenty-four hours of that meeting.'

Sarah O'Connor showed the first signs of strain she had allowed them to see. 'You're surely not suggesting that I had anything to do with that? Not the old "Hell hath no fury" cliché, for God's sake. Don't waste my time and yours!'

'It's a cliché because it is so often true, Mrs O'Connor. We've seen it operate many times. Where were you on Friday night, please?'

'I've told you that before. I was here. My daughter Clare was with me during the day, but she went out in the evening.'

Peach looked at her steadily. 'I'm giving you the opportunity to revise that statement, in the light of information we have now received.'

'I have no wish to revise it. You can't change the truth.'

'And you're still telling us that your car didn't leave the garage on that night.'

'I am.'

Peach glanced at Northcott, who said immediately, 'Your car was seen at eight fifty-five on Friday night, Mrs O'Connor. It was reported as being less than a mile from Dominic O'Connor's house at the time.'

'There must be a mistake. Did your observer note the number of the car?'

'A blue BMW Z4 was reported. It is a very distinctive motor car.'

'Yes. That is one reason why I was attracted to it. Distinctive, but not unique. My car was safely garaged here on Friday night, DS Northcott. And now, unless you have any more relevant questions, I shall bid you good day.'

'I think we should go to the Lake District. Have a long weekend together to celebrate our freedom. I'm a good walker, you know. You'd be surprised. You might think I'm a fragile little thing, but I can put on my boots and tackle the fells. You haven't seen that side of me yet!' Ros O'Connor stretched her slim legs out in front of her in the passenger seat of the car and inspected them.

'I'm sure I will, my darling. And I can limp along with the best of them on the hills: it just takes me a little longer. But not yet. We don't want to excite too much interest, do we?' John Alderson tried not to look as nervous as he felt.

'I don't see why not. Let the old biddies gossip all they

want! Give them something to occupy them, I say. Father
Brice might not approve of the way we got together, but he'll
have to marry us in church, when we choose to ask him.
I shall enjoy watching his face!'

John grinned. He would rather enjoy upsetting Father Brice
and any other representatives of Holy Mother Church. But it
was too soon for that. 'We need to be confident the police
have finished with us before we make any moves, don't you
think? And I was divorced, you know. It's a long time ago,
but the Catholics might not want me to have a church wedding.'

'Oh, things have changed a lot in the last twenty years. I'm
sure I'll be able to square it. If Father Brice doesn't cooperate,
we'll go over his head. Perhaps I should sound him out now,
so that we know where we stand.'

'I don't think you should do that, Ros. Really I don't. I
want you to trust me on this.' He took her hand in his and
looked earnestly into the small, feline face, trying to still the
round eyes which were so mobile. 'We've nothing to lose by
waiting. The police are anxious to make an arrest. If we excite
their interest, they won't leave us alone. And who knows, they
might even decide that one of us killed Dominic, if they can't
get anyone else for it.'

'Oh they wouldn't do that, I'm sure. This is England, not
Russia, you know.' The blue-green eyes fastened on his, the
small, humorous mouth creased into the winning smile he
found so hard to resist. 'I feel quite guilty. I'm glad Dominic's
dead and out of our way, you see, and I don't really care who
knows it.'

'You mustn't go round saying things like that. You really
mustn't.'

'Only to you, my darling. Those thoughts aren't for public
consumption.'

'I'm glad to hear it. But it's better that you don't voice them
at all. Better that you don't even think them.'

She took his hand. 'You're a cautious old thing, aren't you?
But I wouldn't have it any other way. I wouldn't change
anything about you.' She rubbed her small, chiselled features
hard against his shoulder.

The sun was setting brilliantly over the sea twenty miles

west. They were sitting in John Alderson's car on Jeffrey Hill, high above the vale of Chipping, which looked at its serene best in the light of evening. He looked round, making sure they were unobserved, that they had the spot to themselves. Then he slid his arm round Ros's shoulder and held her hard against him. 'I wouldn't change anything about you, either. Except maybe your impulsiveness. I'm just afraid you might get yourself into trouble if you celebrate our freedom too obviously. We live in an imperfect world, you know.'

'You sounded almost like a priest when you said that, John. But you're right, of course, you always are.' She kissed his cheek softly, then looked at the long, soft shadow on the other side of the valley. The late spring night was stealing in slowly over a scene which had changed little in centuries.

Ros O'Connor allowed a small, silent giggle to shake her slim body, to show this was not a serious thought. 'It wasn't you who put Dominic out of our way, was it, John?'

FIFTEEN

Jean Parker surveyed herself in the mirror and decided she looked as composed as ever. That was the way a good PA should always look, and she was jealous of her reputation as a good PA. You should be like a swan moving serenely along, Dominic O'Connor had once said. However frantically your limbs were working beneath the surface of the water, you shouldn't let the watchers see them.

It was strange that the image should come back to her now, when she was trying to put Dominic out of her mind. The police would be here again soon, though what they wanted to come back to her for she couldn't imagine. The woman who'd arranged the time with her on the phone had refused to give her any details. No idea what it was about, that neutral voice had said. Jean had used the tone and the idea often enough herself to recognise that she wasn't going to learn anything. She opened a sales file on her computer and busied herself solemnly with its details.

They came precisely at nine thirty, the time that impersonal voice had specified. The bouncy little man with the bald head and the tall black man, the same pair who'd come here on Monday. She wished obscurely that different officers had come. That would have made it seem more impersonal and more safely distant, as if they were starting again. She said breezily, 'Here after more information? I'll help in any way I can, of course. I suppose I'm not allowed to ask how the case is going?'

'You're allowed to ask. We might be more inclined to answer if you'd been frank with us four days ago.' Peach's refusal was calm but uncompromising.

'I can't think what you mean by that. I gave you all the information about Dominic O'Connor which I had available.'

'Maybe you didn't tell us lies. But you withheld certain facts. That can impede an investigation just as effectively as lies. You intended to deceive.'

'I was frank with you. You have taken away my computer files which relate to Dominic's business dealings, as well as the contents of my filing cabinet. And I told you that he had conducted a series of affairs – I gave you whatever I could of his private life.'

'But not of yours.'

The grey eyes hardened beneath the soft brown hair. 'I am entitled to my privacy.'

'I'm afraid that isn't so. No one is entitled to privacy during a murder enquiry. Not if his or her private life has a bearing on the case. Whatever the rules say, that's the way it works out.'

'What I choose to do away from here has nothing to do with your case.' She was trying desperately to keep calm; it was a long time since anyone had spoken to her so aggressively.

'We need to be satisfied about that before we leave you to get on with your life. When you take a deliberate decision to conceal things, it excites the suspicion of cynical coppers like DS Northcott and me.

She suddenly hated this odious little man, with his

immaculately creased trousers and his highly polished shoes and his confident, overbearing manner. Yet she was obscurely conscious that he might be delighted by that. If she lost her temper, she was likely to give him more than if she remained calm. 'Perhaps you had better make yourself clear instead of speaking in riddles. What is it that I am supposed to have concealed?'

'I think you know that perfectly well. I think you're playing a little game with us. I should warn you that the stakes for you might be dangerously high. And also that you might endanger Mr Jacobs rather than help him by trying to conceal his involvement in this.'

'I don't understand. I specifically cited Brian Jacobs to you when you asked me if Dominic O'Connor had any enemies.'

'You did. You prompted us to interview him. It was an interview for which he seemed well prepared.'

'Brian is a very well organised man. I don't see why he should apologise for that. It's been an asset to him in his work for many years now. You need to be well organised, if you're handling a company's finances.'

She hadn't known she was going to say that. She heard her pride in her man coming out in her words. Peach gave her what she regarded as an odious smile before he said, 'No doubt Mr Jacobs was well briefed last week on the actions and movements of our murder victim. No one was better placed to give him that information than Dominic O'Connor's PA.'

'You're barking up the wrong tree.' She felt the lameness of the cliché even as she delivered it. But more original and effective words wouldn't come to her. 'Brian Jacobs didn't kill Dominic O'Connor.'

She lapsed into 'Dominic' for her dead employer whenever she was under stress. Peach wondered if at some time she had been one of the string of women everyone said O'Connor had bedded. 'You won't expect us simply to accept a statement like that, Mrs Parker. Especially as you chose to conceal your relationship with a man whose bitter and permanent enemy has now been brutally murdered.'

'Brian was certainly his enemy. But I didn't disguise that.

I gave you Brian's name when you asked me for enemies of your murder victim.'

'Yes. It seemed very frank and helpful of you at the time. As it was no doubt intended to be. But you deliberately withheld the information that you had a close relationship yourself with Brian Jacobs.'

'I'm not ashamed of that! I've been divorced for three years. One of the things everyone tells you is that you have to pick yourself up and live the rest of your life. That's what I'm doing, and you aren't going to stop me, DCI Peach!'

Clyde Northcott regarded her steadily as she glared furiously at his boss. 'Where were you last Friday evening, Mrs Parker?'

For some totally illogical reason, she found she wanted to explain why she'd kept that name, wanted to tell him defiantly that she would be changing it soon to Jacobs, wanted to tell him that Brian would be back in charge of the financial division at Morton's if everything went according to plan. She swallowed hard and controlled all of these impulses. 'I was at home in my own house, the one I have lived in since my marriage failed and I received it in the settlement. I live there with my son, but he was out on Friday evening.' She piled on the irrelevant details, as if hoping she could convince them of more vital facts by accuracy with this useless surrounding data.

'Is there anyone who could confirm this for us?'

'No, there isn't! You've got me down as a suspect for Dominic's murder now, have you? Just because I chose to regard my relationship with Brian Jacobs as a private matter when we spoke on Monday?'

Northcott responded with a calm smile. 'We'd like to eliminate you from all suspicion, if we could, Mrs Parker. It would make our job easier, as well as helping you.'

'Well, you can't!' She heard herself sounding like a petulant child and knew she wasn't doing herself or Brian any good here. 'Look. Brian hated Dominic O'Connor and in my view he had good reason to do that. I'd even be prepared to admit that Brian was a little unbalanced about it. But that doesn't mean he killed him.'

Peach came back in immediately on that. 'It gives you

both a good motive. Having Dominic O'Connor off the scene is convenient for both of you. Perhaps more than convenient. Is Brian Jacobs hoping to replace this man he hated here?'

She thought furiously. They or their team had talked to lots of people in the firm in the last couple of days, including the MD. Probably someone had told them about this idea she had planted on Brian's behalf, so she had better not deny it. 'He may well do that. I've spent the last few days stalling callers on my phone, so that I know better than anyone that the firm needs someone urgently. I can't think that they are going to get anyone better than Brian, who knows this business well and now has experience elsewhere to add to that knowledge.' She said it defiantly, making a case for her man because it was what she wanted to do, irrespective of whether that was the right strategy here.

'And where was Mr Jacobs last Friday?'

'I expect he was at work in the afternoon and on his own in the evening. You'd better ask him.' Suddenly, she wished she'd said they were together at the time of the murder, but it was too late for that now.

Peach smiled at her, as if she had made some kind of mistake. 'Someone will ask him that, Mrs Parker.' He glanced at his watch. 'Someone may be asking him that at this very moment.'

And checking whether our stories tally, she thought. She was a novice at this game, whereas this man had played it many times. She tried to force confidence into her voice. 'Brian's got nothing to fear from you. He didn't kill Dominic O'Connor.'

But for the first time, Jean Parker had a small, secret doubt about that.

The Vice Squad moved in like a small army. It had been a huge operation and it had gone on for several months. But on Friday, May 10, the Asian men who had been luring and sometimes virtually kidnapping under-age girls from care homes into prostitution and worse were taken into custody. On the same day and at the same time, there were arrests not just in Brunton but in two other towns, one in Lancashire and the other in Yorkshire.

The Asian men looked thoroughly sinister in the photographs secured by the press. As the men who had fronted the operation, they received most of the publicity, which was appropriately damning. These were shocking crimes, involving multiple rape for the most unfortunate of these girls and dreadful suffering for all of them. It was the most despicable sort of crime, practised on some of the most vulnerable members of a troubled society. It was right that the criminals should be seen in the harshest spotlight, however untypical they might be of the Muslim community which had harboured them. But these arrests and the accompanying publicity weren't going to do much for race relations in Brunton, with its thirty per cent Asian population. Percy and Lucy Peach were glumly aware of that.

DS Lucy Peach had been no more than a small part of the vast organisation which had secured this result. But she was determined to be involved in the arrest of Linda Coleman; when you had worked hard to secure a collar, you wanted to witness it personally. She supervised the arrest and charging of two young Asian men, who had treated her with the contempt they accorded all working women when she had questioned them during the earlier stages of the investigation.

One of the most satisfying factors in the arrests which were carried out on that Friday morning was that the shadowy figures who had financed this grim business were also brought to justice. Too often the major criminals who put up the money for vicious enterprises like this got away with it, because of lack of evidence. They had skilful and highly rewarded lawyers and they often sheltered behind the respectable façade of more legitimate businesses. But this time the links had been established early in the investigation. Moreover, the Asian men they had paid to handle the dangerous processes of recruitment soon split on the people who had financed them, once they found that their own arrests were inevitable. Fear of long jail sentences and what might happen behind the high walls of British jails loosened tongues. The attitudes of the men who had treated the care-home girls so abominably turned suddenly from arrogant to desperate.

Linda Coleman, whose husband was already awaiting trial for the murder of James O'Connor, was arrested on the same morning as the men she had paid and directed to recruit the under-age girls to this squalid servitude. Her conceit was her Achilles' heel. She had believed until the last minute that she was unassailable, that her lawyers insulated her from anything as sordid as arrest. She left it too late to try to get away, in the belief that her wealth and what it bought for her would keep her secure.

Lucy Peach, who had worked for months to secure this outcome, witnessed not only Linda Coleman's arrest but the preferring of charges which would put her away for a long time.

'You'll suffer for this!' Coleman snarled at Lucy. 'That face of yours won't look quite as pretty when it's had a razor across it a few times!'

'Record that, please,' DS Peach said to the custody sergeant, who had just outlined the charges against Linda Coleman at Brunton police station. Lucy spoke more calmly than she felt. But the Lennon criminal group, in which Linda Coleman had been a major figure, had been crippled by this, with its major figures arrested along with her. Lucy said calmly, 'Your husband's going to go down for the murder of James O'Connor. You might be inside for almost as long as him, when this comes to court. You wouldn't like to indicate who killed his brother Dominic, would you, Mrs Coleman? We're offering no deals, but it might get you a year or two off your eventual sentence, if you were seen to be cooperating.'

'Get lost, you cocky young bitch! That's one killing you can't pin on us. We had nothing to do with seeing off that randy sod!'

That was probably true, from what Percy had told her, Lucy thought. But even negative information had to be useful, when you were narrowing your field of suspects.

John Alderson's small front garden looked as neat as it had when they had visited it two days earlier. More so, if anything, since its owner was working diligently in it when they pulled up outside the terraced house.

'It's as colourful as anything in the street,' said Peach as they stood on the flagged path beside him.

Alderson looked up and down the long, respectable road, as if testing the verity of that. 'The trouble with so-called winter pansies is that they're really spring-flowering. You have to pull them out when they're still at their best to put in summer bedding plants.'

It was as if he was trying to assert himself as a bona fide gardener; perhaps he thought that would give him a harmless respectability in police eyes. 'It's south-facing here, sheltered by the houses. We shall have flowers open on the roses in a couple of days. That's very early, for Brunton.' He looked at the police car outside his house, then at the two men who had ridden here in it. 'I suppose you'd better come inside.'

He limped a little as he led them into the small, tidy bachelor's living room where he had spoken to them on Wednesday. There were black-and-white pictures of a couple who might have been his father and mother on the sideboard, a nineteenth-century watercolour of Whalley Abbey on the wall opposite the window. There were eight books between the marble bookends, but four of them were reference books and the other four were from an ancient book club. There was nothing contemporary about this room, nothing they could see which might give them a clue to the personality of its occupant.

They sat down, refused the offer of afternoon tea. Peach studied his man for a moment, then nodded to Northcott, as if he hoped to rattle Alderson by the use of a different questioner. The big detective sergeant opened his notebook carefully, then dropped his bombshell as if it were no more than an introductory conversational gambit. 'Your car was sighted outside Dominic O'Connor's house on the morning of the day when he was murdered.'

John Alderson smiled hard into the unsmiling face of DS Northcott. 'My car is a silver metallic Ford Fiesta. There are a lot of them around.'

'There is only one which has your registration number. Are you denying that it was there at that time?'

'No. I wouldn't wish to do that. I didn't go into the house, though.'

'Why did you choose to conceal this visit, when we spoke to you on Wednesday?'

'I didn't conceal it. You asked me what car I drove and I told you.'

'And you chose not to tell us that you had used this car to visit a murder victim on the day he died.'

'Whoa there! I didn't visit a murder victim. I didn't even go into the house. If I had done, Dominic O'Connor wouldn't have been there at the time. I knew that, or I wouldn't have gone near the place.'

Northcott glanced at the watchful Peach and then returned his attention to Alderson. 'Perhaps you'd better tell us what the purpose of this visit was.'

'Perhaps I had. It's quite simple. I was returning Ros O'Connor to her home. She'd spent the night here.'

'And Dominic O'Connor?'

'Dominic had spent the night in Birmingham. Ostensibly on business – whether there was a woman involved or not, Ros didn't know. And frankly by this time didn't really care. It was because we knew Dominic was going to be away that I picked Ros up on Thursday and brought her here. You could say that we were taking advantage of an opportunity.'

'But you chose to tell us nothing of this on Wednesday.'

'No. It had no bearing on Dominic's death. And tell me frankly, would you have chosen to tell two curious policemen that you'd been in bed with the wife of a murder victim on the night before he was killed?'

'I don't have to answer hypothetical questions, Mr Alderson. When did you last see Mr O'Connor alive?'

The suddenness of the query shook John Alderson, but he strove not to show that. He retreated behind a smile, trying to look as though he had expected this, wondering exactly how he would answer it. He decided that he couldn't risk trying to deceive them about this. If they'd spotted his car at the other end of Brunton, then they'd probably seen Dominic O'Connor's much more noticeable red sports Jaguar outside this house. Perhaps the CID men were hoping he'd deny this, so that they could immediately expose him as a liar. He certainly couldn't afford that.

'I saw Dominic on that same Friday morning. But much later – about three hours after I'd dropped Ros off. It must have been at about half past eleven. He came here to see me.'

Peach had so far done nothing save study him closely. Now he said, 'You'd better tell us about this meeting.'

John nodded, trying to look perfectly at his ease. 'I think that would be best, now that you know that he was in this house. He came here to tell me that he knew about Ros and me.'

Peach nodded, wondering how he was to shake this very cool opponent. 'You're taking care to sound very calm about this. I imagine you had a fierce exchange over the matter.'

'Then your imagination misleads you. It certainly wasn't a friendly exchange. I didn't like Dominic because of the way he'd treated Ros. And I don't imagine he was feeling friendly towards a man who was bedding his wife. But within those limits, what we said to each other was civilised. There was never any prospect of blows being exchanged.'

'And within a few hours the man who came to see you was killed. It must be obvious to you that we need to know exactly what was said during that late-morning meeting on Friday.'

'I can see that.' John was now extremely uncomfortable, though he was trying hard not to show it. He didn't want to tell them what had passed between him and O'Connor, because it wouldn't show him in a good light. But he was shrewd enough to know that these men had a large team who were experts at digging out information which people wished to conceal. If he didn't tell them the truth and they discovered it from someone else, it might land him deep in trouble. He tried to stall them a little whilst he decided exactly what he was going to say. 'What took place was a private exchange between two men. Dominic wouldn't have wanted me to talk about it now, any more than I do.'

Peach said with the air of a man whose patience is wearing

thin, 'And Dominic is now dead, murdered by person or persons as yet unknown. That alters things quite drastically, as you are surely aware.'

'Very well. Dominic O'Connor came here to warn me off – to tell me that I wasn't going to benefit financially from any association with his wife.'

'And how did he propose to do that?'

'He said what I already knew: that he was a Catholic who didn't approve of divorce and wouldn't consent to it. When I said that that would represent no more than a delaying tactic, he told me he was planning to change his will. Ros would inherit nothing. And she would get nothing if she left him whilst he was alive.'

'And your reaction to this was?'

'I told him that I didn't think the law would allow him to behave like that. Women have rights to property, even in a divorce which they have initiated. He conceded she might get the house, or a share of it. But he was a rich man, a partner in a prosperous firm, and he'd get an expert lawyer onto the task. He would deny Ros and me every possible penny. He said he thought I should know this, since it would undoubtedly change my intentions towards his wife.'

'It must have shaken you.'

'It didn't. Well, not as much as you might think. I wasn't really surprised that he knew about Ros and me. Discretion isn't Ros's strong point – if he challenged her, she'd be likely to scorn deceit and come out strongly about her feelings for me and her feelings for him. I think he was eventually more rattled than I was. I said I was sure he couldn't leave Ros as destitute as he planned to do, and that even if he succeeded it wouldn't alter my feelings in the slightest.'

John Alderson stopped on that. He was almost challenging them to dispute what he said, because it was important to him that he asserted the depth of his love for Ros. Peach said reasonably, 'But this meeting must have shaken you to some degree. The discovery that the man was hell-bent on denying you the financial benefits you could have expected from a long-term relationship with Ros must have altered your expectations about the rest of your life.'

'No. Dominic O'Connor thought he could make me back off. He thought that if I was told I wasn't going to make big money on the deal I'd drop his wife like a used coat. He looked round this place and assessed it, the way you did when you came here on Wednesday. He said that I was unemployed and anything but prosperous. Then he said he was sure I wouldn't want to take on an enemy like him, that I'd see sense and back off.'

'And did you agree with him?'

John was shrewd enough to know that Peach was trying to nettle him, to make him reveal more of himself than he wished to do. He took his time, trying to estimate what reactions his words would excite in these men who wanted an arrest. 'I surprised myself a little, I think. I told him that I didn't want him as an enemy. I said that I could understand that he must feel humiliated that someone like me now had the affection of his wife. But I also pointed out that he'd brought this upon himself by taking a string of lovers and treating Ros with contempt. I told him that I wasn't in this for financial gain and that it was insulting of him to presume that I was. I said that the lady would decide on this and that I was confident that Ros would come to me, whatever the financial set-up might be. I then asked him to leave my house.'

'You sound very organised. You sound as if this is a statement you prepared in case we came to interview you about this meeting.'

John smiled for the first time since they'd mentioned O'Connor's visit here. 'It wasn't as cool and as logical as this at the time. There was passion on both sides and a good deal of shouting. I've given you the gist of a very animated half hour.'

'So he came to threaten you, but was met with defiance and sent away without satisfaction. But you now knew that he was determined to deprive you of whatever financial benefits he could. So you thought about it and decided that you had better act quickly, before he could implement his threats. Knowing that his wife would be away visiting her sister, you went there on the evening of the same day and killed Dominic O'Connor.'

'No. I know it looks bad, which is why I didn't want you to know about that meeting on Friday morning. But the money or lack of it wasn't going to alter my intentions one jot.'

He hadn't realised how hard he was breathing, how emotional he felt, until the CID men rose to leave. He was dimly conscious of Peach warning him coldly that they might require a statement about the events of Friday morning. Then they were gone and he was standing in the empty hall of his house, pressing his forehead hard against the coolness of the long mirror on the wall.

SIXTEEN

DCI Peach had not been back in the CID section for two minutes when there was a summons from on high. 'I need to be put in the picture. I can't form a satisfactory overview of the local crime scene unless you put me in the picture,' complained Thomas Bulstrode Tucker. The Chief Superintendent sounded rather petulant on the internal phone.

Percy looked at his watch. Two minutes to four on Friday afternoon. Par for the course, then: Tommy Bloody Tucker preparing to depart for his weekend whilst a murder hunt continued without him. Peach climbed the stairs with a stoic resignation and watched the lights beside the door flash a succession of commands when he pressed the button beside them. He donned an artificial solicitude as he sat down on the uncomfortable upright chair in front of the directorial desk. 'Feeling better today, sir, are we?

'Better?'

'You were somewhat under the weather on Wednesday, sir. I was glad to hear you got home safely.'

'Ah, yes. Wednesday. I was overworked.'

'As a newt, sir.'

'I suppose I may have been a little – well, unwise.'

'As a newt, sir.'

'Look, I don't mind telling you, Percy. As a friend, I mean. I think I might have – well, overindulged a little on Wednesday. Of course, I was perfectly happy—'

'As a newt, sir.'

'Look here, Peach, we're not going to get anywhere if you keep repeating that ridiculous phrase. Wednesday is over and done with. Part of history. Do you understand that, Peach?'

Percy was glad to hear that his forename had been abandoned. He felt much happier with the state of armed neutrality which prevailed when Tucker used his surname. 'Was Mrs Tucker able to minister to your needs satisfactorily, sir?' Percy's face was suddenly suffused with the blandest of his inquiring smiles.

Tommy Bloody Tucker shivered visibly. This was a novel and pleasing phenomenon for Percy. He even felt a momentary spurt of sympathy for his chief at the thought of Brunnhilde Barbara's ministrations to her stricken husband. He didn't think helpless drunkenness was a quality of which she would approve in her spouse, even though Wagnerian scales of excess should have been within her tolerance.

The chief superintendent forced out a concession. 'It was good of you to see that I was taken home safely on Wednesday.'

'No trouble, sir. DC Murphy is an efficient chauffeur who can be trusted to maintain silence about the episode.'

'Good. That's good. It was a bit of an overreaction on your part, of course. I was perfectly capable of making decisions and of driving myself home, but I know you meant well.'

'I did indeed, sir.' Percy tried to dismiss the vision of himself acting as Jeeves to this unlikeliest of Woosters. 'I expect Mrs Tucker was overreacting as well, when she rang in and accused me of sending you home as drunk as a lord.'

'As a lord?'

'I paraphrase, sir. I think the expression "piss artist" passed between her fair lips, but she seemed to be under considerable stress at the time. Perhaps you could disabuse Mrs Tucker of the notion that I was responsible for your condition on Wednesday. It might keep me out of the stocks.'

Tucker glanced fiercely at his watch. 'Look, I've no time for any more of your fripperies. Put me in the picture on the progress of your enquiries into the Dominic O'Connor murder.'

'It's a complex situation, sir.'

'It shouldn't be.'

Percy was accustomed to his chief's curious reluctance to accept the world as it was. 'There are several candidates for this one, sir.'

'Huh! You already have a man in custody for the murder of James O'Connor. The death of his younger brother is surely a connected crime.'

'That is what we expected to find at first, sir. It appears more certain with each passing day that the second murder has no connection with the first. Dominic O'Connor was six years younger than James and by his own declaration had not much in common with his brother. He had a different circle of friends and business acquaintances. It is possible that there is a connection between the deaths, but we now think that unlikely.'

'But you still admit it's possible the deaths may have a connection. My experienced nose tells me that we should explore this first.' He jutted the sensitive proboscis aggressively towards his junior. 'So give me your connection, and let me be the judge of the matter.'

'Patrick Riordan, sir.'

'Eh? Who? An Irishman, by the sound of it.'

'You go to the heart of the matter with your usual perspicacity, sir. Mr Riordan is a former IRA killer who was released from the Maze under the general amnesty, sir. He was a known zealot who cared little for his own safety at the height of the Troubles. Because of that, the security service thought it politic to keep tabs on him, long after the Sunningdale Agreement and the peace settlement which most people on both sides accepted thankfully.'

Tucker showed unusual excitement. 'Dominic O'Connor was Irish, you know.'

'Yes, sir. His name and the fact that he was the younger brother of a famous Irish international rugby player rather suggested that to us. He was planning to employ professional protection at the time of his death.'

'Was he really? Well, it looks as if this Riordan fellow got there first, doesn't it?'

'It was because of that thought that DS Northcott and I journeyed to Moss Side, Manchester, to interview Riordan on Tuesday, sir. Our findings were summarised in the email I sent you on Wednesday. But you were indisposed on Wednesday sir, weren't you? As indisposed as a newt, one might say. You probably didn't get round to reading my report.'

'So tell me now, Peach,' directed Tucker, between teeth which were dangerously clenched.

'Pat Riordan is still working for the unofficial IRA. He regards himself as an avenger. I think he even uses that as an official title. It summarises the work he undertakes. He hunts down men whom the IRA regards as traitors and dispatches them. He regards this as legitimate vengeance and he claims it will encourage others to heed the message and rally to the Cause.'

'He's a dangerous man, Peach. You need to handle him very carefully.'

'I shall take note of that, sir.' The adjectives *blindin'*, *bleedin'* and *obvious* flashed in quick succession through his active brain. 'Riordan was seen in a hire car in Brunton shortly before Dominic O'Connor was killed.'

'Then you have him, Peach! Pull him in and charge him! I'm happy to have been of service to you in this.'

'I expect you are, sir. Unfortunately, we need evidence. The CPS would never sanction a prosecution on what we have at present.'

'Bloody lawyers, Peach! How much simpler our job would be without bloody lawyers!'

'It would indeed, sir. However, in this case there is also the fact that neither DS Northcott nor I were convinced of the man's guilt. The bullet through the head is much more the approved method of terrorist dispatch than garrotting with electrical cable. People like Riordan seem to favour the bullet as being the soldier's method. But we haven't ruled him out. We're still seeking evidence.'

'I can't think you've got anyone else who's as strong a bet as this man Riordan. However, I'm a fair man.' He looked truculently at Peach, as if expecting him to debate that. 'I'm willing to listen to whatever other suspects you may care to parade before me.'

'Very well, sir. As you are aware, sir, Dominic O'Connor was, on all the evidence we have, the victim of a surprise attack from the rear. Because of that, his killer could well have been a woman.'

'Ah! A cowardly attack from behind. Could well have been a woman, as you suggest, Percy.'

Peach didn't like the return of his forename with this anti-feminist assertion, but he bore it manfully. 'O'Connor was a womaniser, which has the effect of increasing the female field. The widow of his elder brother, Sarah O'Connor, is a definite possibility. She's quite a looker and she's one of her brother-in-law's more notable conquests. As you know, Dominic O'Connor ended their affair abruptly. Sarah O'Connor is not the kind of woman who would calmly accept being cast aside by a lover. She drives a distinctive blue BMW Z4 sports car. Such a car was seen within a mile of Dominic O'Connor's house at eight fifty-five on Friday night.'

Tucker nodded sagely, slipping into his elder statesman mode. 'Devious creatures, women. More devious than men, in my experience.'

Percy wondered what half the world would make of this profound philosophical proposition. 'It's circumstantial, sir. No more than that. Sarah O'Connor denies that her car left its garage on that night.'

'Pull her in and break her down is my advice.' Tucker shook his head, firmly rather than sadly. 'Devious creatures.'

'She denies that she was anywhere near the scene of the crime on Friday and says she has no connection with this death. The victim was a former lover and no more than that, as far as the law is concerned. Unfortunately, we don't have the registration number of the Z4 which was seen in the area – we have to accept the possibility that this was a totally different blue BMW.'

'I'm directing you to keep an eye on the woman. That is my official order.'

'Right, sir. Keep an eye on Sarah O'Connor, the deceased's sister-in-law and former lover. Your overview is every bit as useful as ever it was.'

Irony wasn't a strong suit for Tommy Bloody Tucker. He said sagely, 'I've always found that women couldn't be trusted.'

Percy said, 'I've made a note of that for the female members of the CID section, sir. There are two other women to consider. Womanisers like Dominic O'Connor tend to leave a trail of female suspects behind them. His PA might have been sweet on him at one time.'

Tucker nodded, frowning with concentration. 'Men often leap into bed with their secretaries, you know. You should bear that in mind.'

'What a useful piece of know-how, sir. I'll relay it to the whole team at my next briefing. In this case, it may be the lady's association with a different man than O'Connor which has a greater bearing on the case.'

'Another man? This woman must be a real harlot. That makes her a promising suspect, you know.'

Percy was silent for a moment, contemplating the idea of the trim and efficient Jean Parker as a harlot. Then he roused himself and explained, 'Mrs Parker was formerly PA to Dominic O'Connor's predecessor as head of the financial division at Morton Industries. A man by the name of Brian Jacobs. He moved elsewhere after a bitter dispute with O'Connor, who seems to have done the dirty on him in a successful pursuit of his job. Jacobs has been eminently successful with his new firm and we believe he now plans to regain his old post and possibly a partnership at Morton Industries.'

T B Tucker leaned forward. 'This makes him a suspect, you know. Have you considered that?'

Percy cast his eyes mentally to heaven but maintained an attentive visage for his chief. 'In our view, it brings both Jean Parker and Brian Jacobs into the frame, sir. Either separately or in collusion. She admits to being his mistress and it seems they intend to marry. Neither of them has a satisfactory alibi for the time of death.'

Chief Superintendent Tucker wrestled for a moment with these complex possibilities. But all he produced was, 'It's a Jewish name, you know, Jacobs.'

Percy wondered if the man was about to add anti-Semitism to his other prejudices. He said hastily, 'I believe it is, sir, yes. Brian Jacobs seems to have established an excellent reputation in financial matters. We've interviewed him and what emerged strongly was his almost pathological hatred of our murder victim. It is quite logical that he should dislike him, in view of what happened at Morton's, but his bitterness goes well beyond the bounds of logic. It's the kind of unbalanced hatred which often drives men to murder.'

'They sound a thoroughly unsavoury pair, these two. You're right to have them well in the frame.'

'I shall bear in mind your informed opinion, sir. However, Mrs Parker and Mr Jacobs are not the only pair we have to consider.'

'Really? This is getting very complicated. I expect you to be more efficient than this, you know.'

'I do know, sir, yes.' Percy heaved an extravagant sigh which was wasted on Tommy Bloody Tucker. He wanted to say that the number of suspects derived from the case itself, not the man investigating it, but he didn't have that sort of time to waste on Tucker. He said dolefully, 'We still haven't spoken of Dominic O'Connor's widow.'

'Aaah!' A long-drawn out exhalation of satisfaction from the head of Brunton CID. 'The spouse is often the prime suspect in domestic crime, Peach. Did you know that?'

'Yes, sir. It was pointed out to us in our first fortnight of police training. Several years before I entered CID.'

Irony was once again wasted on Thomas Bulstrode Tucker. He nodded his satisfaction and said, 'You would do well to remember that.' When this produced no reaction from his junior, he stared fiercely at the wall behind Peach and said resolutely, 'Devious creatures, women. Unpredictable, in my experience.'

Percy resisted the temptation to explore the murky pool of

Tucker's experience with women. 'This one is certainly unpredictable, I'd say. Even a little unbalanced, perhaps. But it's difficult to say how much is genuine and how much is an act put on for us.'

'I told you. Devious creatures.' Tucker nodded his satisfaction at this immediate vindication of his conviction.

Percy wanted to say that humanity, or at least that section you met of it in CID work, seemed to be generally devious, that gender scarcely entered into the equation. But he hadn't time to explore that philosophical avenue with the dense presence which was Tucker. 'Ros O'Connor didn't like her husband – probably with good reason, from everything we've heard about Dominic O'Connor from her and others.'

'Don't trust everything she says, Peach. She may well be devious.'

'Thank you, sir. That possibility had occurred to us. That is why we've checked out her every movement around the time of her husband's death.'

'Good thinking, Peach.' Tucker drummed his fingers on the desk, happy to have given a little praise where praise was due.

'The body was discovered on Saturday afternoon by DS Northcott and myself. Because of variations in temperature from near-freezing during the night to around ninety degrees during the day, we can deduce little about the time of death from the state of the body or the progress of rigor mortis. However, the pathologist's analysis of stomach contents tells us that O'Connor died approximately two hours after consuming a meal of sandwiches, cake and fruit. Ros O'Connor says that she left him with this meal in his study at the back of their house. His habit would be to eat it at around half past six, whilst listening to a favourite radio programme. That would mean that he was killed at some time during the evening, most probably between eight and ten o'clock.'

'Clever chaps, these pathologists. They're even prepared to stand up to the lawyers in court.'

This was clearly the highest proof of competence that Tucker could envisage. Percy had never seen his chief in court, but it must have happened, earlier in his chequered career. He shuddered at the thought of Tommy Bloody Tucker under cross-examination. 'Ros O'Connor was with her sister in Settle from teatime onwards.'

'Settle?'

Percy sighed again. 'It's a pleasant market town in the Yorkshire Dales, sir. About forty miles from the scene of the crime.'

'Yes, yes, I know where Settle is, you idiot! I used to camp there as a boy scout, many years ago.'

Percy thrust away the insistent image of Tucker in khaki shorts and shirt, looking for his good deed of the day. 'I see, sir. Part of the youthful experience which hardened you for your police career and taught you to be always so well prepared. The point of Settle for us is that it seems to give Mrs O'Connor a cast-iron alibi for the time of death.'

'Then why on earth have you got her still in the frame? Why on earth are you wasting my time and yours by talking about her?' Tucker thumped his desk violently to emphasise this unusual percipience on his part.

'Because she may be an accessory to murder, sir.'

'Ah! I told you she might well be devious, if you remember.'

'I do remember, sir. It is one of the more consistent of your theories. Ros O'Connor has formed a serious association over the last few months with a man called John Alderson. I believe they were fellow parishioners at their local Catholic church, though Alderson seems to be rather sceptical about what he calls Holy Mother Church.'

'They'll be shagging each other.' Tucker produced the crude word with relish, as if it might restore his status as a proper policeman. 'That's the modern way, you know. Leap into bed at the drop of a hat.'

'Or even other, more intimate, garments, sir. I believe your surmise is correct. However, we are assured that this is not a casual affair but a more serious and long-term passion. The two seem attached to each other and make no secret of the fact that they now intend to get married, after a decent interval.'

'Decent interval my arse!' Tucker seemed to have acquired a sudden taste for vulgarity. 'You grill this Alderson fellow,

Peach. I've a feeling in my water that he might have done this. Where was he on Friday night?'

'He claims that he was at home, sir. But he has no one who can substantiate that.'

'There you are then! It's almost an admission of guilt, don't you think?'

Percy had a sudden, awful vision of Tucker as a JP, a sudden fleeting sympathy for the petty villains of the country whom he normally pursued so vigorously. 'John Alderson lives at home. He knew that the woman who is to become his partner was away in Settle on Friday evening, sir. It means that he cannot easily establish his innocence, but not that he is indisputably guilty.'

Tucker stared at him, then nodded sadly. 'Tricky thing, the law. Always found that. And the lawyers are a damned sight worse than tricky!' He paused for a moment, hoping Peach would join him in the universal police whinge about lawyers. 'I suppose we've got to gather more evidence before we put away this Alderson fellow.'

Percy noted the chief's first use of the word 'we' but thought it no more than a rhetorical flourish as he anticipated an arrest. 'We do know that the victim went to Alderson's house on the morning of his death, sir.'

'I told you! This looks to me like our man!' Tucker was almost as pleased as if he had discovered this meeting for himself. Percy was almost reluctant to go on damning the man, but there was no alternative. 'According to John Alderson's account, Dominic O'Connor went there to warn him off his wife. He told him that he would make any divorce as difficult as possible, since both he and Ros were practising Catholics. He also said that he would deny Ros as much of his wealth as was humanly possible if they split up. Alderson says that he told him in effect to get knotted. He said that whatever O'Connor did wouldn't make any difference to the way he and Ros felt about each other.'

Tucker could hardly wait for him to finish. 'You can surely see what this means, Peach! It gives this man Alderson an even stronger motive. He got to O'Connor and killed him that very night, before he could implement any of these threats to impoverish his wife.'

'I can surely see, sir, yes. I put that very thought to Alderson, about an hour ago.'

'And how did he react?'

'He reiterated his story that he hadn't left his house on that night, sir.'

'He would, you know, he would.'

'Yes, sir. I appreciate that. But we still have to find the evidence to support your view that he's guilty, before we can arrest him.'

'Then you should get about it, Peach. Use all the resources of your team to secure the arrest of Alderson by the end of the weekend. Or the arrest of someone else, of course.'

Covering himself with that blanket injunction, T.B. Tucker departed majestically to the pleasures of his weekend, leaving DCI Peach to gather his frayed resources for an assault upon the crime face.

SEVENTEEN

Cafferty wasn't important. He was just the driver. His skills might mean life or death for his passenger, but he wasn't a soldier. He wasn't fighting glorious battles for the Cause. He wouldn't have the glory of this latest achievement. That would rightly go to the soldier.

Patrick Riordan's thin chest swelled automatically with the vision of glory as the car moved swiftly through the city streets. The fight would go on until the vision was fully achieved and Ireland was freed for ever from the English yoke. The whole of Ireland, not just the present Eire. Those mealy mouthed politicians on both sides might think they'd made a settlement with their Sunningdale Agreement and all the subsequent climbdowns, but this period was no more than an interlude. The real Irishmen like him felt closer now to a united, independent Ireland than they'd been for centuries, and it would be men like him who would scale the last barriers. He would be one of the real patriots who achieved the final victory. His name would go down in Irish history.

He did not realise that it is the men with the ideas, not the soldiers who force them through, who go down in history. The men who for centuries have used people like Patrick Riordan never tell them that.

Pat had known tonight's target well, thirty years and more ago. They'd grown up in the same Belfast suburb, attended the same primary and secondary schools. Fitzpatrick was six years older than him, so they hadn't spoken much at school. 'Fitz' had been a hero of the rugby team, towering above all others in the line-outs, shrugging off tackles, forcing his way over the try-line with lesser bodies clinging ineffectively around his shoulders. Schoolboys remembered that kind of picture long after others had been forgotten.

But Riordan remembered much more vividly how Fitzpatrick had spoken for the Cause, how bright and articulate he had been for Ireland in those heady days in the Eighties and Nineties, which were long gone but sometimes seemed but yesterday. Seamus Fitzpatrick had stood head and shoulders above his peers, morally as well as physically, and his eyes had blazed with the righteousness of the Cause as he urged young Irishmen to join him.

He was James Fitzpatrick now, not Seamus. He had made his peace with England and taken the tyrant's gold. He had condemned the IRA when they conducted the great bombing of the centre of Manchester in 1996. He had turned traitor to the Cause he had once espoused. He was a prominent supporter of the Labour Party now, a man who spoke at conferences and had risen steadily through the council ranks of local politics. People had spoken of him as a possible Labour MP and it had looked for a time as if he might take that route.

But local eminence was more his line. He wanted to be a big man in the city of his choice, Manchester. This was the place where he had made a name for himself through his successful business and his well-publicised work on the council. This was where he had gained much publicity and secured the moral high ground locally by his instant condemnation of the IRA bombing which had devastated the city centre. He had been prominent in much of the subsequent redevelopment, securing central funds, driving through the plans, and suggesting the architects who had seen proud new buildings rise from the debris.

Well, nothing came without a price, in Patrick Riordan's view. And tonight the man who had grown up in Belfast as Seamus Fitzpatrick was going to pay the price of his treachery.

Cafferty was nervous. It didn't affect his driving, which came to him automatically, but he was crouched tensely over the wheel. He answered Riordan's questions in monosyllables; eventually he made it clear that he didn't want to talk at all unless it should be absolutely necessary. 'Suits me, Mick!' said Pat Riordan, smiling a superior smile in the passenger seat. You couldn't expect men who weren't soldiers to be as cool and confident as he was.

James Fitzpatrick was speaking at a Labour party meeting about future policies. The party committees were anxious to be prepared for the next election, which wasn't due for another couple of years but might come at any time, with Europe in chaos over its currency and the economic recession showing little sign of abating. It looked from the opinion polls as if Labour would walk in on the back of the discontent which economic troubles always brought to an existing government. But you needed to have policies formed and a manifesto prepared against the possibility of a snap election. You couldn't trust those Tories: that was one of the few old saws guaranteed a chorus of approval at a Labour party gathering.

The meeting wasn't in any of the city's major meeting places. Crowds at party gatherings were thin. Except in the months before an election, only the keenest attended. The attendance at this one was a little bigger than usual, because James Fitzpatrick had a loyal local following to add to the surprising number of party officials who felt it their duty to be there. But the numbers didn't warrant a major hiring fee. This gathering would be in a large, single-storey building, some way from the city centre.

Pat Riordan had examined the place carefully three

days ago and concluded that it leant itself admirably to assassination.

In truth, he would probably have decided that whatever the venue. Like many a man bent upon glory, Riordan was impatient for action at almost any price. Glory is a dangerous aspiration. It upsets the judgement. Men in pursuit of glory are careless of their own lives as well as of those they plan to terminate. The delusion of an honourable death makes men careless of danger and leads to reckless decisions. The man who thought himself so cool made one of those now.

The large, shabby building was a former storage facility. It had large doors at the front, but no other means of entrance or exit. A man planning murderous violence should have preferred at least one more entrance, which would have accorded him a greater element of surprise and a better possibility of a swift getaway.

The building was also at the end of a cul-de-sac. No professional killer liked that. Psychologically, it made you feel trapped: with only one exit, you felt like a rat running along a single drainpipe. It faced you with an immediate tricky decision. Did you park your getaway car near the entrance, risking curiosity and suspicion? Or did you park it outside the cul-de-sac altogether, on the busy main thoroughfare at the end of it? This made you much more anonymous, but meant you would have to race the best part of two hundred yards on foot to your waiting car, probably with people in frenzied pursuit.

Patrick Riordan decided that they would park beside the entrance to the hall.

This meant they had to be there early, to secure the place they wanted. They parked an hour before the scheduled time for the meeting. Cafferty reversed the VW CC GT carefully into position, eight yards from the high doors, facing straight down the narrow little street. It was a stolen car, and it was the sort he'd wanted, fast and sleek. And its owner was away for the weekend, so that its absence would not be swiftly reported.

Riordan stuck the red rose sticker which was the Labour Party emblem predominantly on the side of the windscreen. That would insure them against any challenge as to their presence here, he thought, and he was right. No curious eyes moved any further than that cheerful English symbol. He and Cafferty disappeared swiftly from the scene.

The car was in position, but its occupants must maintain a low profile until the time for action came. They found a pub on the corner of a neighbouring street and bought themselves two halves of bitter. Cafferty wanted a whisky chaser, but Riordan wouldn't allow it. Soldiers didn't drink much, if they wanted to remain alert and efficient, and neither would their drivers. The English troops in the trenches might have been dosed with rum to make them go over the top, but they were English and merely cannon-fodder, not dedicated men like him.

You needed to have your reactions razor-sharp for what he was going to do tonight. And you didn't want any confusion in your driver; it would be foolish to throw away your triumph through any bungling of your escape. In any case, this pub probably wouldn't have Irish, he told Cafferty, and they shouldn't attract attention to themselves by asking for Jameson's. He fancied a whisky himself, but he'd have it later, as a celebration.

The minutes ticked by very slowly. The two tense men found conversation increasingly difficult. Eventually they ceased to attempt it. At one minute to seven, Riordan and Cafferty were back in the car.

It was a warm May evening, so that the loose brown anorak the killer now had to adopt looked a little out of place. Most of the men they'd watched going into the meeting wore only light sweaters; some were in shirt sleeves. There was even the odd young woman in a summer dress, though youth was rare in this gathering. But Pat needed the anorak to conceal the Armalite. He slipped quietly into the back of the hall without anyone taking much notice of his dress. This was Manchester, after all, not Torquay, and people were accustomed to caution about the weather.

The place looked bigger inside than out. There were thirty-two rows of seats, with thirty chairs in each row. The hall could accommodate 960, Riordan calculated, though there were less than a quarter of that number here tonight. He made these calculations because he had no interest in what was being said on the raised wooden stage at the front of the hall. He sat in the penultimate row and made his preparations – in a thinly populated arena, you attracted attention to yourself if you sat isolated from everyone else on the last row of all.

There were boring introductory speeches from two Labour Party worthies, one very bald and one very portly. They said conventional things and received conventional applause. Riordan found himself at once bored and tense. It was a strange combination, which he didn't believe he'd ever encountered before. He was totally uninterested in what was being said, but feverish with expectation of the action to come. He felt the pulse in his temple racing as he made his hands move together in the polite applause which greeted the opening speeches. You wanted to be unnoticed, so you made yourself a part of the tapestry by producing the same reactions as the other unsuspecting extras around you.

There was a quickening of expectation as Seamus Fitzpatrick rose to speak. Or James Fitzpatrick, as they called him here. Pat curled his lip with contempt at that; the name emphasised how the man had sold out to the enemy. He tried to shut out the content of what his target was saying. He didn't want to hear any of it, in case it upset his concentration as the moment approached.

But he had to admit that Fitzpatrick remained an effective and persuasive speaker, as he had been in his youth when he had spoken for the Cause. He acknowledged the men who had introduced him, by means of gracious words and a half-turn in their direction. They had many years of faithful and diligent service to the Labour cause, he said, making Pat start by his use of that word. Fitzpatrick said that people forgot that nothing was achieved without hard work, and these men had toiled hard and selflessly in years past. The triumphs of the 1997 election and the two which had followed were due to the work of men like them.

Then he turned to the future and what they must all do now. He made a couple of little jokes which got the audience on his side and showed that he had the common touch. He moved more sombrely into the present recession, which thanks to the

Tories was now a double-dip one and the most serious setback
the nation had suffered since the great slump of the 1930s.
He made a couple of cheap cracks about the government and
its distinctively Etonian cabinet, which was safe ground for
an Irishman in a Manchester socialist meeting. He touched on
the establishment and how out of touch they were with the
harsh reality of recession, though he had the sense to keep
away from the monarchy.

Having hit the easy targets, Fitzpatrick moved on to more
positive things. Pat Riordan didn't attempt to follow what the
man was saying about the necessity for economic growth and
the means by which he would foster it. His moment was getting
near now. He fingered the smooth steel of the Armalite beneath
his anorak. It was still bright outside, but this big room had
only small windows in its sides and it was becoming quite
gloomy. Someone switched on lights over the stage area and
James Fitzpatrick made the obvious joke about bringing light
to our darkness; it elicited dutiful laughter. He was speaking
about the city now and the particular things that should be
done here. This was a logical progression, because everyone
knew his real aim was to become Lord Mayor of Manchester.
He was clever all right, thought Riordan: he'd been clever
long ago, when he'd been Seamus and dedicated to the Cause.

Thirteen minutes to eight. They'd synchronised watches
before he came in here. Time seemed to stand still as the
moment approached. Fitzpatrick was standing at the microphone, moving towards the climax of his argument and the
moment when he'd take questions from the audience, as he'd
promised to do at the outset. Patrick Riordan could hear all
sorts of tiny sounds now. He was pleased by that: it must be
a good thing that your senses became extra sharp as key
moments in your life approached.

He heard Cafferty start the car outside, exactly at ten to,
as they'd agreed. He glanced around him, swift and sharp as
a fox about to seize its chicken. There was no one behind
him and only one man level with him, yards away at the other
end of the row. He slid the Armalite from his anorak, rested
it on the back of the seat in front of him. No one in the hall
noticed the movement.

Fitzpatrick was making a point emphatically, waving his right arm in the air as he reached the climax of his peroration. Riordan was reminded of an old print of Gladstone speaking passionately about home rule for Ireland, which his mother had kept on the wall of their tenement home. He shot Fitzpatrick at that moment, watched his target whirl and scream with the blow of the impact. He fired twice more at the falling target before it hit the ground.

Then he was away, out of his seat, into the aisle, thrusting open the high wooden door and bursting into the sudden dazzle of the still bright evening outside. Cafferty flung the passenger door open as he saw him and he was into the car and away even as the first men appeared behind him on the single step of the former warehouse. 'Get your head down!' his driver yelled, and Riordan realised as the tyres screamed and the seat thrust against his back that Cafferty was wearing a crash helmet as some sort of protection against the bullets which would fly around his head if they didn't get clean away.

For the first time, Patrick Riordan considered the thought that he might not survive this.

They were away swiftly down the narrow little street, as Cafferty had planned. The road at the end of it was busy with traffic, so that they had to wait an agonising twenty seconds before they could swing left and be away. Twenty seconds which might prove crucial.

Patrick Riordan had planned his own movements meticulously and executed them as intended. What you could never plan or control were the movements of the enemy. The very things which had made James Fitzpatrick a target for the IRA avenger Riordan had also made him a candidate for the state security services. He didn't have a permanent bodyguard; resources didn't run to that. It was reckoned now that only the fanatical rump of provisional IRA zealots would have any grievance against a man who had supported them steadily until the Sunningdale Agreement had brought the settlement which most Irishmen found acceptable.

But fanatics existed. Indeed, the security services kept a note of the movements of Patrick Riordan, a declared avenger, who had never accepted the peace which most of his colleagues had welcomed. Riordan's former commander, Dominic McGuiness, might now represent official Ireland and be about to shake the hand of the British queen. His former Sinn Fein inspiration Gerry Adams might now be encouraging the Irish Parliament to cooperate with the English. But men like Riordan were still killing, which meant that men like James Fitzpatrick still needed a degree of protection. When he spoke at public meetings, the system dictated that there would be a security man sited discreetly in the hall to protect him.

Not a top man, perhaps: resources were inevitably spread thinly in this Olympic year. The man assigned to Fitzpatrick was young. He was certainly not incompetent, but neither was he experienced. He had chosen to sit at the table on the platform beside his charge, when he might have been better advised to move around and observe in the body of the hall. And because he was young, this would be the first time his services had ever been called upon. However much you told yourself that you must be perpetually alert, that sooner or later you would be needed, you were still shocked when terrorism suddenly blazed into ugly life and you were the sole force to deal with it.

Booth leapt over the fallen target. The rules were that you didn't stop to check on injuries, once your charge had been attacked. You went straight for the man with the gun and you shot to kill. The idea of downing a man by shooting at his legs was a ridiculous myth dreamed up by idealists. He was down the aisle between the rows of seats like a sprinter, pistol in hand, careless of his own safety as he had to be in the pursuit of an assassin.

His quarry's car was away already, reaching the end of the street as he wrenched open the door of the Mondeo. The grey VW was delayed mercifully by the main road traffic for a little while. He could hear its driver gunning his engine impatiently. The grey car disappeared as Booth moved after it. Then he had himself to wait for agonising seconds at the end of the cul-de-sac before he was able to swing into the line of traffic.

The VW was a CC GT and could probably outdistance even his two-litre Mondeo on the open road. That was irrelevant here, for there was too much traffic around for anyone to make

full use of an engine's potential. That was one of the complications for security. One at least of the men in the VW was a
desperate man with a lethal weapon. Unsuspecting citizens
were in danger if he was cornered in the wrong place. If he
should choose to shoot his way out and members of the public
were killed or injured, the man who had trapped him would
be subjected to the spotlight of an official enquiry.

Booth tried to explain the safety issues as rapidly as he could
to the Police Armed Response Unit he contacted as he drove.
He yelled details frantically into his microphone as he twisted
the wheel of the Mondeo to overtake startled city drivers. He
wasn't gaining much on his quarry; he could see the grey VW
passing cars in front of him as horns blared in protest. He was
trying not to use his own horn, in the probably futile hope
that the driver and passenger in the VW wouldn't realise that
he had spotted them and was on their trail.

The police came back to him. He was on the road to Oldham.
Provided his quarry kept to this major road, the Armed
Response Unit would head the VW off at a roundabout close
to the entry to the town. They were closing access to other
traffic at this moment. He was approximately 3.4 miles from
this point at present. They would let Booth's Mondeo through,
but he should be prepared to find the VW stationary when he
arrived at this point, with one and possibly two armed and
hostile men within it. He should leave it to the armed security
staff to make arrests; they were trained for situations like this
and wearing body armour.

Booth grinned, despite himself. They were teaching granny
to suck eggs, but he didn't mind that. He could look after
himself, but if these men were asserting their superiority in
what would be a highly publicised and highly dangerous arrest,
he didn't mind that. No doubt they'd spent long days preparing
for life-and-death situations, but found they only rarely got
the chance to be involved in one. Bit like him, really.

There were three cars between him and the VW now. One
of them obligingly turned left and deserted the drama. The
terrorist driver was good, he thought dispassionately, watching
him pass swiftly through a diminishing gap between parked
vehicles and an approaching bus without even touching his

brakes. He saw the white face of the gunman turned back towards him, looking for pursuers.

The cars in front of him were more cautious about the narrow gap left by the approaching bus. They slowed, almost stopped. Booth wasn't too frustrated by that, now that he knew that the VW was to be intercepted. Force of numbers would defeat the enemy, as it almost always did.

At that moment, the VW turned off the appointed route. It swung at the last possible minute and without use of its indicator on to a road which forked left, away towards Royton and the trans-Pennine M62. Booth had to fling the Mondeo from the outside lane where he'd been overtaking sharply across the traffic on his left, accelerating hard to avoid contact but provoking blaring horns from his rear.

He was immediately behind the VW, some forty yards back from it. Its driver and passenger knew now that they were being followed and knew that it was the Mondeo that bore their hunter. Booth radioed the change of route urgently to the Armed Response Unit, which was now waiting uselessly in the wrong place. He knew from the sound that an Armalite had been used in the assault upon James Fitzpatrick. Now his blood chilled as he saw the man in the passenger seat of the VW preparing to use it again, on him.

The end was swift and decisive, as it usually was in counter-terrorist operations. Booth was amazed by the way time seemed suddenly to be suspended and things to happen in exceptionally vivid slow motion. Death came like this, whether to you or to the enemy, he supposed. You joined security for the excitement, yet in the crisis it was never exciting. Whatever was happening just seemed inevitable.

The speeding VW suddenly screeched to an agonised halt, slewing half sideways across the road in front of Booth's Mondeo. He would have hit it had he not had his forty yards of leeway. Then the men were out of it, with the man from the passenger seat firing a quick burst from the Armalite at the Mondeo as Booth stood on the brake pedal. He saw the windscreen to his left shatter as he flung himself sideways and downwards. It was a surprise to find that he had not been hit.

As he half-scrambled and half-fell out of the car, trying to keep the cool metal of its body between him and the bullets from the Armalite, Booth realised what was happening. The men were leaving the stolen VW, deserting it in the middle of the road where it would cause traffic chaos and impede pursuit. They were transferring to a Ford Focus, which a third man was already driving out of the parking bay and on to the road ahead of the abandoned VW. Had it not been for Booth, they would have got clean away, leaving security and police services fruitlessly tracking down the stolen VW.

The man with the Armalite could have seen him off; the firepower odds were overwhelmingly in his favour. But he had downed his target in a hall three miles away; he was intent now upon escape. Patrick Riordan snatched a look at Booth, but decided he was not a percentage target as he crouched behind the wing of the Mondeo. Cafferty was already wrenching open the door of the Focus, yelling at him from ten yards away to be quick.

It was good that these things happened in slow motion, thought Booth, as he pressed himself hard against the metal shield of his car. Your brain worked coolly and well when events were slowed down like this. He would get one chance of hitting the man with the Armalite, he reckoned, before he was in the car and away. This was the man he wanted. The other one was just his driver and probably not a killer at all.

He was close enough to have a good chance of a hit, even with a pistol. He held it in both hands and rested it on the top of the Mondeo's wing. It felt firm and steady in his hands, firmer even than the weapons they held in the controlled environment of the shooting gallery, where they did their regular shooting exercises and examined the targets afterwards.

Riordan had almost reached the car when he was hit. He felt the enemy bullet in his body, didn't know whether it was one slug or two, whirled with the impact, heard himself screaming as he had never thought he would scream as he hit the ground, felt the subsidiary blow of the tarmac upon the side of his face. The Armalite clattered down beside him, tantalisingly beyond his failing reach. He raised one arm hope-lessly towards Cafferty, heard the car accelerate away from him and leave him to the enemy. It was the rule that they should get away. But he felt nevertheless deserted as he lay and waited for death.

It took Riordan a second or two to feel the severity of the pain. He surely couldn't stand this for long. In the same instant, he realised that his hunter was standing over him, kicking the Armalite even further away, pointing the pistol steadily at his stricken head, uttering words he could not hear and did not want to understand.

The ambulance was there within twelve minutes. The crumpled assassin was lifted gently and stowed carefully within its protecting womb, treated as tenderly as if he had been a pregnant woman. The paramedics fought to save the life of the man who had come to their city to kill.

Patrick Riordan was but dimly conscious of these things. The last noise he heard before he drifted out of consciousness was someone in the ambulance saying that he thought James Fitzpatrick was wounded, not dead. It was the most grievous blow of all.

EIGHTEEN

It was a flat in a block which contained thirty similar residences. This one was on the ground floor, scarcely twenty yards from the main entrance. Peach and Northcott inspected the red Audi in Brian Jacobs' allotted parking space as they moved the twenty yards from their police Focus to the entrance. They noted that it was as clean inside as it was gleaming outside, that it looked as if it had been recently valeted. That was the kind of detail CID men note automatically.

Brian Jacobs met them at the door of the flat before they had time to knock. He was in casual gear, which looked as if it had been as carefully chosen as the blue suit he had worn when he had met them at his place of work four days previously. The attractive but slightly untidy black hair had been cut and styled since Tuesday. His hands were as clean and well-groomed as if they had been professionally manicured.

He settled his visitors on the sofa opposite the big window and the bright morning light. There was a smell of coffee from the kitchen adjacent to this square, pleasant living area.

The man was more nervous in his home on Saturday morning than he had been in his office at work.

Peach wasn't going to say anything to put him at his ease. The DCI took his time, looked for a moment at the picture of Derwentwater with the fells of Catbells behind it, accepted the offer of coffee and biscuits. He sniffed the coffee, then sipped it appreciatively. He began his questioning obliquely, because he sensed that Jacobs wanted them to be direct and get this over with quickly. 'You haven't any children, Mr Jacobs?'

'I have one boy. He lives with my ex-wife. That's when he's at home. He's in his second year at Warwick University.'

Peach nodded. 'This place is far too neat and tidy to have kids around it, whatever their age might be.'

Brian Jacobs took a sudden gulp of his coffee. Too large and too impulsive a gulp: it almost scalded his tongue, causing him to gasp and down his cup hastily on to the low table between them. Peach looked at the liquid spilt into the saucer for a moment, as if it had great significance. 'Thank you for agreeing to see us this morning. We need to ask you some more questions.'

'I'm willing to help, though I can't think I'll be able to tell you anything which will push things forward.'

'Push things forward, yes. Well, let's see, shall we? DS Northcott?' Peach settled more comfortably and raised his black and expressive eyebrows towards the big black man, who was sitting uncomfortably beside him on the very edge of the sofa.

DS Northcott looked somehow even more threatening with the small notebook clasped in his huge hands. 'Could you clarify the nature of your relationship with Mrs Jean Parker for us, please?'

'That has nothing to do with the death of Dominic O'Connor.'

'Then why did you choose to conceal it when we spoke on Tuesday?'

'I didn't "choose to conceal it". It had nothing to do with

your case and it still has nothing to do with it. It is a private matter between Jean and me and I simply chose to let it remain so.'

Peach was suddenly animated by one of his eager smiles. 'A most unwise decision, as things have turned out. Concealment always excites suspicion, in cynical chaps like us.'

'It wasn't concealed. Jean told you all about it when you first spoke to her.'

'Correction. She told us nothing about your association with her. She merely gave us your name as a known enemy of Dominic O'Connor.'

'Which was clearly very frank of her.'

'Very frank indeed. So much so that we believe that it was what was agreed between the two of you beforehand, as evidence of that frankness. We believe that Mrs Parker gave us your name as an enemy of the murder victim to try to convince us of her good faith, whilst at the same time electing to conceal the fact that she had a close relationship with you. We have to ask ourselves why she chose to do that.'

'Because it was private. Because it was our own business and no one else's.'

'It makes you into a couple with both motive and opportunity for the murder of Dominic O'Connor. A man whom you hated and whom you now plan to replace as Financial Director at Morton Industries.'

'That situation is a fact of life. It's not something we contrived. Motive and opportunity don't mean that either of us chose to kill O'Connor. I'm even prepared to admit that I'm glad that he's dead and if there's the opportunity to obtain the position I should have had years ago I'll take it. That doesn't make me a murderer.'

'No. But the fact that you chose to conceal as much as you could of this makes you a strong suspect. Just as the fact that Mrs Parker concealed how close she was to you until yesterday and then only admitted it because she had no alternative also excites our interest. Concealment is never a good idea, even for the innocent, Mr Jacobs.' His tone implied that he would need much convincing before he accepted the innocence of this particular pair.

'Jean told me that she'd informed you all about us yesterday.'

Peach's smile this time comprehended the fact that he expected the pair to compare notes after each meeting with him. 'That was only when she realised that there was no alternative, Mr Jacobs. As the only one of our suspects who combines a declared hatred of the victim with a known history of violence, you are now almost our prime suspect, I'd say. Would you agree, DS Northcott?'

'Indeed I would, sir. Not our only suspect – we have to bear in mind that a woman could easily have killed Dominic O'Connor – but perhaps our prime suspect, as you say.'

'Jean didn't kill O'Connor.'

'And why would you seem so certain of that, sir? You're not confessing to the crime yourself, are you?'

'Of course I'm not! I'm just certain that it isn't in Jean's nature to steal in and kill anyone like that.'

Peach shook his head with one of his sadder smiles. 'Ah, if only you knew how often we've heard thoughts like that, Mr Jacobs. We never know what lurks in the hearts of even those we think we know quite intimately. I only hope that we don't have to listen to Mrs Parker voicing that notion about you. Does she know about your previous history of violence?'

'It was in 1989, for God's sake! It feels as if it was a different person in a different life.'

'I'll take that as a no, then.' Peach's voice hardened suddenly. 'Unfortunately for you, it was the *same* person in the *same* life. A person who attacked and almost killed someone with a knife. Have you come up with anyone who can support your story that you were nowhere near Dominic O'Connor's house last Friday night?'

'No. But the innocent sometimes don't have alibis.'

'True. And the guilty never have them.'

'I was here from around eight o'clock on Friday night. I didn't kill the bloody man, any more than Jean did.'

'You were unbalanced about him.'

Brian recognised that word. It had come from Jean. She had used it to him when she'd been exasperated by the extremes of his hatred of Dominic O'Connor. He felt a sense of betrayal that she should also have told these calm and relentless bastions of the law that he was 'unbalanced'. He said as calmly as he could, 'Dominic O'Connor had given me good cause to be unbalanced. I didn't kill him, though. Someone else did that for me.'

'You could have twisted that cable round his neck. You could have wound it tight and watched him die. You'd have enjoyed that.'

Peach was pushing hard, harder than his normal code allowed, searching for some sort of reaction, some flicker of the face which might reveal even for a split second that the man was guilty. He got nothing. Brian Jacobs said harshly, 'Your forensic people have examined my car. You've no doubt questioned people in the area around O'Connor's house to try to place me in that area on Friday night. You've come up with nothing. That's because there is nothing. I left the golf club at around half past seven as I told you and drove straight home, without going near the O'Connor house. I didn't kill the sod, and neither did my Jean.'

It wasn't politically correct, that 'my Jean'. You shouldn't claim ownership of a woman any more. But DCI Peach found he thought better of Brian Jacobs for it, as they drove back to the station. It wouldn't affect his judgement on whether the man was a murderer one iota.

There was an unexpected message back at Brunton police station. Would the man in charge of the Dominic O'Connor murder enquiry please ring the security service number in Manchester as soon as possible? Technically, that should have been Tommy Bloody Tucker, but the head of Brunton CID had held a media conference on the previous Saturday, and couldn't be expected to make a weekend appearance in the CID section for at least another year.

Peach rang the number immediately. A man with the rank of commander asked him loftily if he knew of a man called Patrick Riordan. 'I do indeed,' said Percy breezily. 'I had occasion to interview him on Thursday morning in connection with the murder in Brunton of Dominic O'Connor.'

'That's the man.' The voice softened as they became two professionals in pursuit of a common enemy. 'He committed a terrorist act in Manchester last night. His target had security cover – to whit, one man with a pistol acting as his bodyguard, who was at his side when he was shot. It's touch and go, but apparently the odds are that the target will survive. Rather better odds than are being offered on Patrick Riordan, whom our man chased and severely wounded before making an arrest. Riordan is currently in Manchester Royal Infirmary, with bullet wounds in lung, chest and shoulder. It's possible he won't recover or won't say anything, but apparently he's mentioned your man Dominic O'Connor in his ramblings.'

'Can we speak to him?'

'We've bullied the medics into allowing us to see him for five minutes or so. I thought it might be worth your while joining our man, in case Riordan gives you anything useful before he pops his clogs. Best thing that can happen to the murderous sod, in my view. Three o'clock at Manchester Royal, if you can make it. Ask for Jefferson at reception.'

Scene of Crime and Forensics had not produced a great deal from the examination of the room at the back of his house where Dominic O'Connor had been found dead. The few alien fibres found on his clothing were either from his wife's garments and thus hardly suspicious or from sources not identifiable. The two hairs which were neither his nor his wife's might be useful if they provided a match with someone eventually arrested for his murder, but were as yet anonymous. The probability was that they would prove to have no connection with this crime.

There was one tangible and perhaps significant find. DCI Peach dispatched his wife to interview the probable owner of it. He thought it would be interesting to have a woman's view on the person he had found to be the most enigmatic female involved in this multi-layered case. DS Lucy Peach took DC Brendan Murphy with her to interview Sarah O'Connor, the victim's sister-in-law and former mistress, who was also the widow of his murdered elder brother.

Lucy had not seen the huge modern mansion where the widow of the elder O'Connor brother lived. She was surprised by her emotions as they drove up the drive and parked in the ample space by the front door. She had been involved for months in the investigation into the recruitment and abduction of care-home girls. She had questioned wretched teenagers about prostitution, rape and sadomasochism. Arrests had now been made and the local people who had driven and financed these vicious things were arrested and awaiting trial. But Lucy could not rid her brain of the thought that the money for this place had come at least partly from that awful trade.

It was possible, even probable, that the woman she was here to see had known nothing about the sources of the income which supported her luxurious lifestyle. Lucy watched the elegant, dark-haired woman closely as she ushered them into the huge sitting room. She looked too intelligent to have known nothing and suspected nothing about the darker areas of her husband's business empire. Sarah O'Connor seemed to DS Peach like one of those women who took care not to know things which might embarrass her. She'd met a few such people in her years in CID and she didn't like the breed.

But that was nothing to do with why she was here today, she told herself firmly. DC Murphy could do the talking; she'd listen, observe, and report back to Percy in due course.

Sarah O'Connor crossed her elegant ankles and said to Murphy, 'I remember you, DC Murphy. You're the man with the Irish name who's never been to the emerald isle'

Only the English ever spoke of the emerald isle nowadays, Murphy thought waspishly. He repeated what he had said many times before, working hard not to sound irritated. 'I've lived all my life in Lancashire. My grandmother was Irish, but I never knew her. I've never even been to Ireland, north or south.'

'Nor had I, until I met Jim. I never quite felt at home there, when I visited with Jim. I don't expect I shall go there much, once he's been buried. There'll be a lot of his old friends and rugby mates coming here from Ireland for the funeral.' She looked round at the expensive furnishings and carpet, then out at the garden which stretched away below the long, low window. 'There's only me and my daughter here now and Clare's away at university most of the time. Neither of us enjoys rattling around in a huge place like this. I shall move quite soon to something smaller.'

She'd already said that to Percy and Clyde Northcott on Tuesday, Lucy noted; she'd read the notes on that meeting before coming here today. The woman was nervous, despite her calm exterior and the cold dark eyes above the confident smile. Brendan Murphy said, 'We're here in connection with the death of Dominic O'Connor, not that of James.'

'I guessed that. We all know how Jim died, don't we? But I've accounted for all my dealings with Dominic. I haven't anything else to tell you.'

Murphy didn't comment on that. 'Certain things were found at the scene of the crime. You are probably aware from your own experience that everything in the immediate vicinity of a suspicious death is examined very carefully. Anything which might have significance is taken to our forensic laboratories for detailed investigation.'

'Of course I am aware of that. But you will have found nothing which will connect me with the death of Dominic. I've admitted that we had an association, but it was long over at the time of his death.'

'You've also admitted to bitter resentment at the manner in which Dominic O'Connor ended your affair.'

Sarah glanced at Lucy. 'I was as resentful as any woman would be who's been ditched cruelly and unceremoniously in favour of a younger model. I then got over it and carried on with the rest of my life. I propose to continue doing that now.'

Murphy nodded and produced a polythene container which he held out a little awkwardly at arm's length for inspection by the woman in the simple dark green dress. 'Do you recognise this?'

Lisa lifted her hands automatically towards the object, then dropped them back heavily to her sides. It was a sapphire, set skilfully in gold. The very delicate gold chain which had carried it was broken, glittering like an accusation within the drab polythene.

There was panic suddenly on the face which had been so resolutely calm. 'That pendant's mine. Unless you've dug up one exactly the same to frame me.'

That suggestion sounded ridiculous even in her own ears and she wished she hadn't made it. Now at last DS Peach spoke to her. 'It's yours, Mrs O'Connor. It was found in the room where Dominic O'Connor died, by the scene of crime team investigating his death. Can you account for its presence there?'

'No. Perhaps it had been there for a long time.'

'Does that really seem likely to you?'

'No. I knew I'd lost it. Perhaps Dominic kept it.'

'That doesn't seem likely either, according to everything we've learned about him. The likeliest explanation is that you lost it last Friday night, when you were twisting a cable tight round that victim's neck.'

'I didn't do that. I was nowhere in the vicinity of that house on Friday night.' Sarah looked from one to the other of her questioners, searching for some sign that they believed her.

She found nothing to comfort her in their impassive faces.

The big hospital in Manchester was busy; on a Saturday afternoon, many families visited patients, so that there were many rather subdued children in the corridors.

Peach met the tall, grey-haired man from the security services in the reception area as he had been directed. He had expected Jefferson to be a younger and fitter man, but it seemed the terrorist incident was serious enough to involve top brass rather than field operators. His rank was a help when they came to the room where Patrick Riordan had been isolated. Jefferson told the sister who came out to meet them that access to her patient had already been authorised, that state security and perhaps other lives in the future might be involved. The rather grim-faced medic didn't go through the ritual of protest and the stuff about responsibility to patients which Percy usually met when he sought access to a villain.

The sister nodded acceptance and said merely, 'Mr Riordan is very ill. I must ask you to conclude your business in no more than ten minutes.'

Peach grinned at the fresh-faced constable who sat on a chair outside the door. As a young copper, he had himself endured hours of boredom as sentinel to villains in hospital, all of them less interesting and lower profile than Patrick Riordan. Once inside the quiet room, they worked their way carefully to the bedside through the machine feeding the drip in the arm, the oxygen canister and the heart monitor. The figure beneath them might have been a corpse, for all the movement it evinced.

The older man, who had seemed so much in control, was suddenly diffident here. The nearness of death in the slight figure beneath the blankets brought its own uncertainties, perhaps even a reluctant respect. Jefferson spoke softly, addressing the shape twice as 'Mr Riordan'. Receiving no reaction, he then glanced hopefully at DCI Peach.

Percy set his fingers upon the forearm which was, apart from the thin face, the only unbandaged flesh above the blankets. 'You listening, Riordan?'

For a moment, it seemed that he had not been heard. Then the shape stirred fractionally. The eyelids flickered open in slow motion, as if a great effort was being forced into this tiny, instinctive movement. The head turned a fraction, the brown eyes gazed for what seemed a long time into the face of the man whose hand was still upon the sinewy forearm. The bloodless lips moved, framed words, said unexpectedly, 'You're Peach.'

'I am. And you're in trouble.'

The faintest of smiles moved the narrow mouth for a moment. They could scarcely catch his words as he said, 'I shot the bastard. I shot that traitor, Seamus Fitzpatrick.'

Peach glanced at his companion and received a nod of assent from the older man. 'You didn't kill him, Pat. He's going to recover. You might have made Jim Fitzpatrick into a hero.'

A frown furrowed the forehead for a few seconds, then cleared, as if even the energy involved in that was too much for the stricken figure beneath the sheets. The eyes which had shut opened again, looked for a moment at the ceiling, then swivelled painfully towards Peach's face. 'I'm dying.'

Peach's fingers pressed a fraction harder on the cold skin of the forearm. 'I think you probably are, Pat, yes.'

'I did that other traitor, you know. I got Dominic O'Connor. He didn't live.'

'You're confessing to murder. Be careful here, Riordan.'

'I don't need to be careful. I'm a soldier, an avenging soldier. I carried out my orders. Those who matter will remember me.'

For a brief moment, the vision of glory which had driven his life energised the mortally wounded man and his voice rose above the whisper they had strained to hear. But the effort exhausted his dying brain and he drifted again into unconsciousness.

Peach spoke to him twice more, shifted his fingers on the wrist to feel the pulse which still moved faintly there, then nodded to the blue-clad figure who had appeared in the doorway of the quiet room. 'We've finished here, Sister.'

NINETEEN

Lucy Peach said to her husband, 'I didn't much like Sarah O'Connor. But for what it's worth, I didn't feel she was a murderer.'

Percy nodded. 'We got a confession this afternoon. Patrick Riordan said in Manchester Royal Infirmary that he killed Dominic O'Connor, because he was a traitor to the republican cause.'

'That lets her off the hook then.'

'And Brian Jacobs and Jean Parker. And Ros O'Connor and John Alderson. Unless the confession was the last fling of a dying fanatic.'

As if to reinforce that idea, the phone rang two minutes later. Patrick Riordan had died twenty minutes earlier, at eight twenty on that Saturday night. Neither Lucy nor Percy spoke for a little while; they were silenced by the finality of death, despite their familiarity with it. Then Lucy said, 'You'll get your weekends back – be able to play golf again. You've had a busy time with these two murders. I expect Tommy Tucker will want to call a news conference to brag about his efficiency.'

Percy, who was gazing towards the glory of the clear western sky as the long May day died slowly, gave only an abstracted smile, even at the mention of Tucker. He watched purple infringing on crimson for another minute before he said quietly, 'I don't believe Patrick Riordan killed Dominic O'Connor.'

On Sunday morning he made a phone call and then collected DS Northcott. They had a brief discussion of tactics in the car, but otherwise little was said. The climax of an important case made even these experienced men a little nervous. You couldn't afford to get things wrong now. If you did, lawyers would pounce gleefully upon your errors many months into the future.

The high detached house with its smooth red Accrington brick elevations had stood impressively on this high spot for well over a hundred years now. The metallic grey Ford Fiesta which the CID men recognised as belonging to John Alderson stood in front of the house. Northcott wondered as he parked beside it whether this tranquil, impressive residence had ever before witnessed either a homicide or the subsequent arrest of the murderer.

The first time they had come here, they had rung the bell repeatedly before moving to the rear of the house and discovering the body of Dominic O'Connor in his self-contained office. Now, on what would be their final visit, they heard the sound of movement in the house in response to Clyde's first pressing of the bell.

Ros O'Connor seemed neither dismayed nor surprised to see them here at half past nine on a Sunday morning. She smiled up at Northcott. 'I'd forgotten quite how tall you are. And handsome with it, too. But I expect the female officers make you well aware of that!'

Northcott gave her an embarrassed smile but no words. But she apparently didn't expect any. She said cheerfully, 'John's here. He's been here overnight. Well, we don't need to make a secret of our relationship any more, do we? I'm planning to see Father Brice this week to discuss the details of our marriage. We shan't do it for a few months, of course, and we shall have to explain that John's been divorced from his first wife. But I don't anticipate that being the difficulty it would once have been for Holy Mother Church!'

She had delivered all this by the time she had led them down the hall and into the high, square sitting room, where John Alderson rose to meet them. He looked as if he would like to tell Ros she was speaking too much, but he did not know how to do that in front of the two CID men.

Peach bided his time, waiting for the stream of words from this bright and brittle woman to cease before he spoke. She gave him his cue eventually. When they were all comfortably seated, she said breezily, 'You must be here about Dominic's death, I suppose. It's impressive to see them working like this at weekends, isn't it, John? Do you have some news for us?'

Peach watched her for a moment, like a man waiting for a roulette wheel to stop spinning, before he said, 'A man confessed to the murder of your husband last night. He was a member of the provisional IRA and he considered Mr O'Connor a traitor to the cause of Irish republicanism. Dominic was one of a list of targets Riordan was seeking to eliminate. On Friday night he shot and wounded another man on his list, James Fitzpatrick.'

'I don't know Mr Fitzpatrick.'

'There is no reason why you should. He is a prominent Labour politician in Manchester. That is where Patrick Riordan shot him twice on Friday night in an assassination attempt. Riordan was pursued by the security services and was severely wounded himself. I spoke to him in hospital yesterday afternoon. He declared his responsibility for the death of Mr O'Connor. Patrick Riordan died at eight twenty last night.'

Ros O'Connor's small, perfectly formed features looked as surprised and innocent as those of a kitten whose bed has suddenly disappeared. It was John Alderson who now spoke quickly, as if he feared what she might say if he waited for her to respond. 'Then that surely concludes your case. It will be a relief to all of us to have it settled.'

Ros looked at him as if she had for a moment forgotten his presence. Then she turned brightly back to Peach and said, 'Yes, that's right, isn't it? You must be very pleased about that. It's good of you to come round here so early on a Sunday morning to give us the news.'

'Except that it is hardly news at all, Mrs O'Connor. I don't believe that Patrick Riordan killed Dominic O'Connor. I believe that he knew he was dying and that he was claiming what his fanatic's mind considered the glory attached to this murder of a traitor to the republican cause.'

The silence which fell upon the room seemed profound, after the nervous torrent of Ros's words before it. It was Alderson who said eventually, 'Surely a confession is a confession? Unless you have strong reasons to think it false, you cannot simply choose to disregard it.'

'No. But I have those strong reasons, Mr Alderson. I think the person who tightened that cord so mercilessly around Dominic O'Connor's neck is in this room at the moment.'

'I didn't kill Dominic. I was in my own house, not here, on that Friday night.' Alderson glanced sideways at the untroubled face of the woman he planned to marry. 'And Ros wasn't here at that time either. She was with her sister in Settle. There is a whole family who can bear witness to that.'

'I accept that. But Mr O'Connor wasn't killed on Friday night.'

Ros leaned forward, looking like the naïve and excited child she still was in so many respects. She said almost coquettishly, 'This is intriguing, Chief Inspector Peach. Do tell us more!'

Peach looked at her with the first signs of distaste he had allowed himself. 'This death was carefully engineered and planned. Planned by you, Mrs O'Connor.'

'But that can't be so, Chief Inspector. I wasn't around at the time. I was forty miles away in Settle.'

'You were around all right. You twisted that cable hard into your husband's neck, some time around the middle of that Friday afternoon.'

Ros shuddered theatrically. 'You're being very cruel, talking like this, Mr Peach. I still had feelings for Dominic, even though I didn't love him any more. That's why I made him the snack meal he liked so much and left it with him when I went off to my sister's house.'

'You didn't leave it with him. You watched him eat those sandwiches and fruit and cake at lunchtime. Probably you ate with him.'

She laughed, a small, tinkling sound which was more eerie

because no one else in the room was even smiling. 'This is silly. Dominic died during the evening. Your post-mortem report told you that.'

'No. The body was not discovered until twenty-four hours after death and it had been subjected to temperatures ranging from not much above freezing to ninety degrees Fahrenheit. The estimated time of death was based on analysis of the stomach contents, which showed that the items we've just mentioned were consumed approximately two hours before death. We were foolish enough for some days to accept your assurance that the meal had been consumed at around six thirty. The reality is that it had been eaten five hours or more before that. Two hours after it had been consumed, you returned from the house to your husband's office, carrying the cable which you used to garrotte Dominic O'Connor.'

John Alderson began to protest, but Peach's eyes never left the kittenish face with its untroubled, innocent reaction to this gravest of accusations. Ros spoke evenly, with a strange control. 'He deserved it, you know. He treated me badly, Dominic did. He took so many other women to bed, when I was available to him. And now, when John and I have got together, he was in the way of what we wanted to do. I worked it out, you see. If I removed him it would be simple justice, and at the same time it would allow John and me to move forward.'

The detectives had what they wanted now. Peach's only aim was to keep her talking about this. He felt no need to caution her; he had no doubt that she would sign a written statement of her confession in due course. Murderers like this lived in a private world. It was a world where flattery was often a useful weapon. He said unemotionally, 'It was clever of you to think of giving yourself an alibi like this. I expect you knew the body was unlikely to be discovered quickly.'

She nodded eagerly, entranced now by the memory of her own ingenuity. 'I know about post-mortems and stomach contents. I read a lot of crime novels.' She looked straight into Peach's face, for the first time in many minutes. 'What put you on to me, Chief Inspector?'

The use of the cliché by this slight, bright-faced figure would have been comic in other circumstances. Peach said wearily, 'You overplayed your hand. Gilded the lily. Whatever other tired phrase you care to use, Mrs O'Connor. The sapphire pendant you left for us to find was too obvious a device.'

'That belonged to Sarah. She deserved to be involved in this. She'd slept with Dominic, when he was married to me. I found the pendant in his car and I kept it.' She leaned forward confidentially, anxious to convince them of her cleverness. 'I thought it might come in useful, sooner or later, you see. And it did.' She folded her arms and rocked herself gently on her seat, content with this display of her cunning. 'I put a letter from her to Dominic in there as well. She deserved to be implicated, don't you think?'

'But the pendant didn't ring true. You'd already told us that Dominic was careful not to leave around any traces of the liaisons he'd conducted. It didn't make sense that he'd have kept a sentimental memento of a dead affair. The person most likely to have kept that pendant and planted it at the scene of the murder was you.'

Ros considered the idea for a moment, her head a little on one side. Then she nodded her acceptance of it. 'It was me who broke the chain, you know. I enjoyed that. I put it in the drawer of Dominic's desk when I'd killed him, as though he'd kept it as a memento. It was one of the last things I did in the room, when I prepared it for discovery. I didn't know at the time who would find Dominic there. I never thought it would be a DCI and his detective sergeant. I wasn't sure when I heard whether that was a good thing or a bad thing.'

At a nod from his senior officer, Clyde Northcott stood up and set his hand gently on the shoulder of Ros O'Connor. They half-expected her to interrupt the words of arrest, to respond to the notion that it might prejudice her defence in court if she withheld information which she might wish to use there. But she said nothing, listening carefully with her head still tilted a little, as if she comprehended her role as the silent, central figure in this police ritual.

It was only when Northcott had finished delivering the familiar rigmarole that she looked suddenly at the horrified face of John Alderson. Perhaps she had for a time forgotten his presence here as she acted out her own central role in this drama. 'John had nothing to do with this. I wish to state that to you. He is not even an accessory after the fact.'

Peach wondered how much this strange, deadly, childlike woman understood of the law, how much she knew about the part played by an accessory after the fact. The lawyers would have to consider how much if anything Alderson had known about this crime and how far he had contrived to conceal it.

They took her out to the police car which Peach had instructed should follow them here and installed her carefully on the back seat of it. Ros O'Connor sat very upright beside the female officer in the rear of the car as they journeyed sedately back into Brunton. She turned once to check that her nemesis in the shape of Peach and Northcott was following in the car behind her. She looked sharply to her left for ten seconds as they passed the building where her husband had worked.

Otherwise, Ros O'Connor kept her head very still and gazed directly ahead, as if looking forward eagerly to the next interesting stage in her progress as an arrested murderer.